Co[illegible]

Ta[illegible]

A Funny H[illegible]y of Beer and Brewing

The story, all names, characters, and incidents portrayed in this production are fictitious. No identification with actual persons (living or deceased), places, buildings, and products is intended or should be inferred except where permission was granted.

Book Cover by John-Paul Rye

Illustrations by John-Paul Rye

First edition 2024

The moral of the author has been asserted.

A CIP catalogue record of this book is available from the British Library

ISBN 978-1-917642-32-3

Introduction: Raise a Glass to Brewing and Blunders

Brewing beer is one of humanity's oldest crafts, almost as old as storytelling itself. It's a tale of ingenuity, passion, and occasionally, outright hilarity. From ancient brewers who accidentally fermented wild grains to modern-day crafters pushing the limits of flavour (pickle beer, anyone?), the history of brewing is bubbling over with mishaps, mischief, and moments of brilliance.

This book is a tribute to the brewers who weren't afraid to get their hands sticky, their barrels frothy, and their reputations a little tarnished in the pursuit of the perfect pint. But it's also about something bigger: the connection between people and their brews. Beer has been the centrepiece of celebrations, the catalyst for debates, and the secret ingredient to countless ingenious (and absurd) moments throughout history.

So, grab your favourite ale, lager, stout, or whatever quenches your thirst, and settle in for a journey through time. This isn't just a history book, it's a pint-sized adventure filled with laughter, lessons, and the occasional spill.

Setting the Scene: A Taster of What's to Come

What can you expect from these pages? Think of this book as a pub crawl through history, with each chapter visiting a different era and its brewing quirks. Along the way, you'll meet characters like:

400 BC....... Democles the Daring

A Greek brewer who accidentally invented "festival ale" when a storm soaked his barley, leading to the wildest Dionysian festival in Athens' history.

350 BC....... Borgia the Bold

An Etruscan brewer who experimented with herbs, crafting a brew so intoxicating it convinced his warriors they could negotiate peace with the gods.

300 BC....... Claudius the Creative

A Roman brewer whose ale became famous for inspiring "better Latin," causing hilariously bad poetry among his patrons.

250 BC....... Heliodorus the Hoppy

An Alexandrian brewer who added spices to beer, creating a brew so bitter it was traded as medicine across the Mediterranean.

200 BC....... Nivitus the Noble

A Gaulish brewer whose ale was so prized, it was demanded as tribute by invading Roman generals.

150 BC....... Felix the Festive

A Carthaginian brewer whose "peace ale" turned war negotiations into merry banquets, albeit with a few ale-fueled brawls.

100 BC....... Lucius the Lavish

A Roman brewer whose decadent ales made him a favorite at feasts, until they overshadowed the emperor's own celebrations.

50 BC....... Gaius the Giddy

A brewer for Roman toga parties whose ales inspired wild adventures and questionable decisions among the Roman elite.

0 AD....... Aurelius the Adventurous

A brewer in Britannia who blended wild honey and berries into his ale, causing a festival to last an entire week.

50 AD....... Tiberius the Tasty

A brewer in Roman Britain who claimed his ales gave soldiers courage, though his brew was so strong, it more often led to naps.

100 AD....... Magnus the Mighty

A brewer on Hadrian's Wall who created a strong, warming ale that kept Roman guards cheerful in the biting cold.

150 AD....... Antonius the Altruist

A brewer who gifted his "peace ale" to rival tribes, inadvertently starting the first documented bar brawl.

200 AD....... Valerius the Victorious

A Roman-British brewer whose "divine ale" was thought to bring good harvests, and good excuses for feasts.

250 AD....... Helga the Hearty

A Saxon brewer whose ale became the star of her tribe's winter festivals, inspiring drinking games that became local tradition.

300 AD....... Eadric the Eccentric

An Anglo-Saxon brewer who experimented with hops, creating an ale so pungent it deterred raiders.

350 AD....... Tarl the Tall

A towering brewer who brewed ale in barrels so large, villagers used them as rafts during floods.

400 AD....... Branoc the Brave

A Celtic brewer who used ale barrels to block invading Saxons, and then celebrated with the "victory brew."

450 AD....... Aethelred the Ale-Maker

An Anglo-Saxon brewer whose recipe was so beloved, it became a form of currency in local markets.

500 AD……. Cynhelm the Clever

A brewer who tricked a grumpy earl with his "enchanted brew," earning his village protection from royal taxes.

550 AD……. Beorn the Bold

A brewer whose strong ale fortified his village during harsh winters, and turned snowball fights into legendary contests.

600 AD……. Hilda the Hoppy

A nun and brewer whose ale funded her abbey, making her a brewing pioneer and a saint among thirsty villagers.

650 AD……. Cynric the Cheerful

A brewer whose ale was so celebrated, it turned a Saxon king's war council into a singing contest.

700 AD……. Alfred the Alewright

An Anglo-Saxon brewer who claimed his ale was blessed by saints, only to have it accidentally blessed by a local goat, which became the village mascot.

750 AD……. Ethelbert the Enthusiast

A brewer who introduced a "seven-day ale" for weeklong feasts, which caused so much merriment that the village forgot to harvest their crops.

800 AD……. Guthrum the Generous

A Viking-era brewer who used his "mead-inspired ale" to lure enemies into a feast, where they drank so much, they forgot why they were fighting.

850 AD……. Hrothgar the Happy

A brewer who combined honey and barley to create a celebratory ale so sticky, half his village got their hands stuck to their mugs.

900 AD……. Ealdric the Alchemist

A Saxon brewer whose "magic ale" convinced invading Vikings to swap their weapons for mugs, turning battlefields into beer festivals.

950 AD....... Osric the Opportunist

A brewer who claimed his ale had mystical properties, earning him a seat at the lord's table, until they realized it just tasted really good.

1000 AD....... Beornwyn the Bold

A brewer who created an ale so strong, it became known as "Dragon's Breath" after it caused her village to hallucinate fire-breathing goats.

1050 AD....... Aldred the Alewright

A monk who brewed "Heaven's Pint," which was so popular that pilgrims came more for the ale than the sermons.

1100 AD....... Margery the Merry

A brewer who hid her ale from tax collectors by disguising her barrels as "holy relics," fooling even the bishop.

1150 AD....... Geoffrey the Jolly

A tavern keeper who challenged rival brewers to an "ale-off" and won with his secret ingredient, his wife's apple pie spices.

1200 AD....... Beatrice the Brave

A brewer who used her clever ale to distract knights feuding in her village, turning their jousting match into a singing competition.

1250 AD....... Harold the Hefty

A brewer whose massive barrels doubled as parade floats, accidentally launching the first-ever "Ale Festival."

1300 AD....... Agatha the Altruist

A brewer who turned her alehouse into a refuge during the plague, claiming her "Plaguebreaker Ale" could cure anything but bad singing.

1350 AD....... Margery the Mischievous

A brewer accused of witchcraft who turned her trial into a village feast by serving her infamous *Witch's Brew* to her accusers.

1400 AD....... Wilfred the Witty

A brewer who challenged the guild's strict rules by creating a purple ale that baffled inspectors and became a town favorite.

1450 AD....... Tobias the Tinkerer

A brewer who powered a steam engine with his "experimental stout," saving the town fair and sparking local legends.

1500 AD....... Edith the Ingenious

A brewer whose "Hearth Ale" was so warming that it convinced the villagers to hold winter feasts outside, sparking a snowball war.

1550 AD....... Margery the Mischievous

A brewer who crafted a truth-telling ale to expose spies in her village, accidentally inspiring England's first spy novel.

1600 AD....... Gideon the Gutsy

A brewer who convinced Puritans to drink his "Pious Pint" by claiming it was brewed with the Ten Commandments in mind.

1650 AD....... Tobias the Trickster

A brewer who used barrels of ale to smuggle forbidden goods, but turned it into a joke when the inspectors got drunk on the evidence.

1700 AD....... Samuel the Sociable

A brewer who created the first "Happy Hour" by giving factory workers light ale breaks, boosting productivity and sparking workplace cheers.

1750 AD....... Agatha the Ambitious

A brewer who convinced smugglers her ale barrels were cursed, scaring them off and saving her brewery's precious stock.

1800 AD....... Harold the Handy

A brewer who invented *Steam Stout*, an ale so strong it literally powered a failing carnival ride, delighting the crowd.

1850 AD....... Tobias the Tinkerer

A brewer whose experimental stout accidentally powered a town's broken steam carousel, making him an instant local legend.

1900 AD.......   Edith the Enterprising

A brewer who crafted a "worker's pint" so energizing that it inspired an impromptu cricket match during factory breaks.

1950 AD.......   Edith the Intrepid

A Cold War brewer who used her "truth-telling ale" to unmask suspicious strangers in her village, turning paranoia into laughter.

2000 AD.......   Dave the Digital Brewer

A tech-loving brewer whose AI-powered beer recipes caused viral chaos with glitter-filled ales that confused, and delighted, the internet.

2024 AD.......   Rob from The Hidden Tap

A daring brewer whose futuristic ales, crafted in collaboration with AI, nearly broke a craft beer festival's ticketing system with their popularity.

Each chapter dives into the challenges, triumphs, and laughable mistakes of these brewers and their times. You'll learn how beer evolved with technology, culture, and the quirks of human nature, all while chuckling at the absurdity of it all.

This book isn't just about brewing techniques or tasting notes; it's about the joy of creation, the courage to experiment, and the unshakable truth that wherever there's beer, there's bound to be a story.

So, whether you're a beer aficionado, a history buff, or just someone who appreciates a good laugh, welcome to the frothy, funny world of brewing history. Cheers!

400 BC - 350 BC: The Dawn of Brewing

- **Techniques**: Brewing begins with simple techniques involving basic grain soaking, heating, and fermentation. Early Britons soak barley or wheat in water to create a mash. The mash ferments naturally with wild yeasts from the air.
- **Method**:
    1. Grains are soaked in water until they germinate.
    2. The grains are dried over fires, creating malt.
    3. The malt is mashed with water in clay pots or animal-skin pouches.
    4. The resulting liquid ferments naturally over days.
- **SPV (Strength, Preservation, and Variability)**: Low alcohol content (around 2-3%), with little preservation. The brews spoil quickly.
- **Recipes**: Early brews use barley and wheat, with flavouring from herbs like meadowsweet, mugwort, and heather. Honey may be added for sweetness.
- **Social Aspect**: Beer is central to Celtic tribal gatherings, consumed in feasts and ceremonies. Brewing is predominantly a household task performed by women.

Barmides the Brewer: The Accidental Innovator

In the ancient city of Athens, circa 400 BC, science as we know it was just beginning to take shape. Philosophers debated the nature of existence, architects built marvels like the Parthenon, and one man, Barmides the Brewer, was unknowingly conducting his own form of experimentation.

Barmides wasn't your typical brewer. While others followed recipes handed down through generations, Barmides saw his brewing process as a blank canvas, ready for a splash of creativity. Unfortunately, he wasn't exactly meticulous. Measurements? Optional. Ingredients? Whatever looked interesting. Yet somehow, his beer always turned out delicious, if a little unpredictable.

The Experiment That Changed History

One day, with the Festival of Dionysus approaching, Barmides decided to create a new brew. "Why stick to barley alone?" he mused. "What if I add honey? Or figs? Or this peculiar herb the apothecary called *epichlorus*? What's the worst that could happen?"

Barmides didn't know it, but he was performing an early form of what we now call *scientific experimentation.* He observed his ingredients, hypothesized they would improve the flavor, and tested his theory by brewing a batch.

When the fermentation was complete, he poured himself a mug. The result? A brew unlike anything Athens had ever tasted. Sweet, spicy, and oddly refreshing. But what Barmides hadn't expected was the side effect. A few sips in, he found himself laughing uncontrollably at his own reflection in the copper brewing pot. "By Zeus, I'm hilarious!" he declared, though his cat (whom he believed was Socrates reincarnated) seemed unimpressed.

Chaos at the Festival

At the festival, Barmides' experimental beer became the star attraction. Patrons lined up to try it, and soon the effects were evident. Stoic philosophers burst into laughter, generals recited terrible poetry, and playwrights proclaimed it the "nectar of the gods."

But there was more. A shy sculptor, emboldened by the brew, began sketching curved designs that would later inspire generations of architects. An aspiring politician, usually dull and serious, delivered a ridiculous speech that inadvertently became the foundation of Athenian comedy. Chaos reigned, but so did creativity.

The Science of Serendipity

Though the elders of Athens considered banning Barmides' brew, cooler heads prevailed. They realized that this "Laughing Lager" had unlocked something unexpected: it encouraged innovation. People began seeing the world differently, thinking outside the box (or amphora). They even regulated its sale, marking one of the earliest known attempts at civic policy-making.

Barmides retired shortly after, content to let his invention take on a life of its own. But his story lives on as a reminder that some of the greatest scientific discoveries come from curiosity, bold experimentation, and a willingness to embrace the unexpected.

STEM Lesson

Barmides' story is a humorous example of *serendipity in science*. Throughout history, many discoveries have been made by accident, from penicillin to X-rays. What matters is how we respond to these "happy accidents." Barmides could have abandoned his brew after its surprising effects, but instead, he shared it with the world, sparking creativity and innovation.

Next time you're trying something new, remember Barmides: don't fear mistakes, they might just lead to your greatest invention.

350 BC - 300 BC: Early Methods and Tribal Traditions

- **Techniques**: Hot stones are added to grain-water mixtures to heat mashes. Fermentation occurs naturally.
- **Method**:
    1. Grain is malted by spreading it to germinate.
    2. Mash is made in wooden vessels using hot stones to heat the liquid.
    3. Wild yeasts ferment the liquid over 3-5 days.
- **SPV**: Alcohol remains low, around 2-3%, and brews spoil quickly.
- **Recipes**: Barley mash flavoured with foraged herbs, such as bog myrtle and heather.
- **Social Aspect**: Brewing is communal, performed as part of shared feasts. Women are key to the process, and beer is a staple in diets.

Euthanos the Brewer: The Genius Behind the "Bottomless Amphora"

In 350 BC, in the Macedonian city of Pella, a brewer named Euthanos was well-known for two things: his booming laugh and his knack for over-engineering everything. While most brewers focused on perfecting the taste of their ales, Euthanos was obsessed with efficiency. "Why make a single amphora of beer," he often declared, "when you could make an amphora that fills itself?"

Euthanos' brewery was more of a workshop filled with odd contraptions than a traditional brewing space. Pulley systems, water wheels, and clay pipes crisscrossed the room. His neighbors joked that he might be a better inventor than a brewer, though they appreciated the free beer samples.

The Problem to Solve

One day, Euthanos faced a dilemma. The Festival of Hephaestus was just days away, and his regular customers insisted he provide ale for the celebrations. "Fine," he thought, "but I refuse to waste my time refilling amphorae. I'll invent a system that pours beer automatically!"

And so began Euthanos' most ambitious project yet. He called it the *Bottomless Amphora*. The idea was simple (at least to him): a large clay vessel would continuously refill itself from an underground reservoir via a series of levers and siphons. "A self-refilling beer jug will make me famous!" he proclaimed.

The Festival Debut

On the day of the festival, Euthanos unveiled his invention with great fanfare. The amphora stood in the center of the plaza, decorated with vines and garlands. A crowd gathered as Euthanos tapped the first mug. To everyone's amazement, beer flowed freely from the amphora's spout, and didn't stop. The crowd cheered, and Euthanos basked in the glory of his engineering brilliance.

But then, the problems began.

When Science Goes Too Far

The amphora, it seemed, *really was bottomless*. No matter how much beer was poured, the reservoir underneath kept supplying more. At first, the crowd was thrilled. "Drink up!" Euthanos shouted. "There's plenty for everyone!"

But soon, the beer overflowed. It spilled onto the plaza, soaking tunics and sandals alike. Children turned it into a makeshift slip-and-slide, while elders shouted about the disrespect to Hephaestus. A visiting philosopher tried to calculate the flow rate but ended up drenched instead.

Euthanos frantically tried to shut off the system, but his levers jammed. "It's not a *problem*," he insisted, as beer continued to flood the streets, "it's an *abundance of innovation!*"

The Aftermath

By the end of the day, the entire city smelled of ale, and the festival-goers were in high spirits, if a little soggy. Euthanos eventually managed to cut off the beer supply (by digging up the reservoir), but his invention became the talk of Macedonia.

While the *Bottomless Amphora* was retired, Euthanos' story lived on as a cautionary tale about overcomplicating simple tasks. As one wag put it, "Sometimes, all you need is a regular jug and a steady hand."

STEM Lesson

Euthanos' misadventure highlights the importance of *testing* your inventions under real-world conditions. Many great inventors, from Archimedes to Edison, faced setbacks when their designs didn't work as intended. However, they learned from these mistakes, and often improved their ideas.

The key takeaway? Innovation isn't just about grand ideas; it's about practical solutions. And maybe, just maybe, it's okay to refill your amphora the old-fashioned way.

300 BC - 250 BC: Expansion of Grain Use

- **Techniques**: More experimentation occurs with grain ratios. Barley remains dominant, but oats are occasionally included.
- **Method**:
    1. Grains are malted and mashed in wooden tubs.
    2. Heat is applied using hot stones, producing a thick, porridge-like wort.
    3. Fermentation occurs over days, guided by wild yeasts.
- **SPV**: Slight increases in strength as fermentation times are adjusted, around 3-4%.
- **Recipes**: Mixed grain brews (barley with oats) flavoured with herbs.
- **Social Aspect**: Brewing remains domestic, tied to family consumption and celebrations.

Demetrion the Brewer: The Father of Foam Science

Setting the Scene

In 300 BC, in the bustling Greek city of Corinth, a brewer named Demetrion was famous for his bubbly personality, and his even bubblier beer. While other brewers focused on rich flavors or perfecting fermentation, Demetrion was obsessed with one thing: foam. "The foam," he declared to anyone who would listen, "is the crown of the drink! A beer without foam is like a chariot without wheels!"

Demetrion's obsession wasn't purely aesthetic. He believed the foam held secrets of the universe. "If Archimedes can study water displacement in his bath," he often said, "then I shall study beer foam in my cup!"

The Foam Problem

One day, while preparing a batch of beer for the Festival of Poseidon, Demetrion ran into a problem. His latest brew, made with a new combination of grains, refused to foam. No matter how he poured it, the top remained flat. To Demetrion, this was a disaster of epic proportions.

"This won't do!" he cried. "How can I serve a foamless beer to the people of Corinth? They'll think I've lost my touch!" Determined to fix the issue, Demetrion turned his brewery into a laboratory, complete with amphorae bubbling over fires, funnels made from hollow reeds, and even a goat-powered stirring machine.

A Questionable Solution

After days of experimenting, Demetrion had a breakthrough, or so he thought. He discovered that adding *fizzy salts* (a mysterious mineral he'd acquired from a traveling merchant) to the beer created an abundance of foam. Pleased with his discovery, he brewed an enormous batch of his "Foam-Enhanced Ale" and prepared to unveil it at the festival.

The Festival Fiasco

On the day of the festival, Demetrion's beer stall was packed. Patrons were eager to try his famous brew, now advertised as having "the tallest, fluffiest foam in all of Greece!"

At first, the beer was a hit. Every mug poured was topped with a towering head of foam, and the crowd cheered Demetrion's ingenuity. But as the day went on, strange things started happening. The foam, it turned out, *never stopped growing*. Mugs overflowed, tables were buried, and soon, entire amphorae were erupting like frothy volcanoes. Children squealed with delight, chasing waves of foam, while adults scrambled to keep their sandals dry. A visiting philosopher attempted to calculate the rate of foam expansion but was swept away by a tidal wave of bubbles.

Demetrion, meanwhile, tried to reassure the crowd. "This is not a disaster!" he shouted, knee-deep in foam. "It's a *new experience* in beer enjoyment!"

The Aftermath

By nightfall, the festival grounds were a sea of foam. The citizens of Corinth dubbed the event "The Great Foam Flood," and Demetrion became both a local legend and a source of endless jokes.

"Demetrion," one merchant quipped, "should have been a sculptor, for he's clearly better at making mountains than making beer."

Despite the fiasco, Demetrion took it in stride. "I may have overdone it," he admitted, "but I've proven that beer foam is worth studying!" He spent the rest of his life refining his foam-making techniques and eventually became known as the first true beer scientist.

STEM Lesson

Demetrion's story is a playful reminder of the importance of *balance* in experimentation. While innovation often involves pushing boundaries, it's equally important to consider practicality. His fizzy salts were a precursor to modern carbonation techniques, showing how even mishaps can lead to valuable discoveries.

Next time you pour a fizzy drink, think of Demetrion, and be glad your foam doesn't take over the room!

250 BC - 200 BC: Brewing as a Community Activity

- **Techniques**: Brewing techniques are refined to improve consistency. Mash heating becomes more systematic.
- **Method**:
  1. Malted grains are crushed and soaked in water.
  2. Hot stones heat the mash to extract sugars.
  3. Wort is strained and left to ferment naturally in large wooden tubs.
- **SPV**: Alcohol content stabilises at 3-4%, but spoilage remains common.
- **Recipes**: Barley mash with added herbs like mugwort, yarrow, and heather.
- **Social Aspect**: Brewing becomes a shared task, with larger batches for feasts and tribal gatherings.

Philostratos the Brewer: The Man Who Invented the "Portable Party"

Setting the Scene

In 250 BC, in the vibrant Egyptian city of Alexandria, a brewer named Philostratos was renowned for his adventurous spirit and eccentric ideas. Alexandria, the intellectual hub of the ancient world, was home to the Great Library and a melting pot of scholars, philosophers, and inventors. Philostratos considered himself their equal, not with books or theories, but with beer.

"My brewery is a temple of creativity!" he proclaimed. "And beer is the nectar of innovation!"

Philostratos had one goal: to make beer accessible to everyone, everywhere. "Why should a man have to sit in a tavern to enjoy a good brew?" he mused. "What if beer could travel *with* you?"

The Great Invention

One day, after watching workers transport amphorae on carts, Philostratos had a revelation. "Why not create *mini amphorae*?" he declared. "Small enough to carry, yet sturdy enough to hold beer!"

He got to work crafting clay vessels the size of a large water jug. To make them more convenient, he added a looped handle and a reed spout, so drinkers could sip directly from the container. Philostratos called his creation the *Amphorita,* which he confidently described as "the future of beer."

His friends were skeptical. "Who needs portable beer?" one asked. "What's next, a traveling symposium?"

"Mark my words," Philostratos retorted, "soon everyone will carry an Amphorita to festivals, markets, even on chariot rides!"

The Market Test

Philostratos decided to debut his invention at the annual Festival of Serapis. He set up a booth where patrons could purchase freshly filled Amphoritae. Business was slow at first. People were intrigued but unsure about drinking beer from a clay jug.

Then, a local bard, inspired by the novelty, began singing a tune about the joys of "beer on the go." The crowd quickly caught on. Soon, festival-goers were strolling through the streets, Amphoritae in hand, singing, laughing, and occasionally spilling their drinks.

Philostratos beamed with pride. "I've revolutionized beer!" he declared.

The Problem with Innovation

However, problems arose as the night wore on. The Amphoritae were surprisingly heavy when filled, and clumsy revelers kept dropping them. The streets echoed with the sound of breaking clay, and beer flowed freely, onto the cobblestones instead of into mouths.

To make matters worse, one overzealous philosopher insisted on testing the durability of his Amphorita by hurling it against a wall. The result? A shower of beer, shards of clay, and an injured pride.

"Perhaps the world wasn't ready for the Amphorita," Philostratos muttered, as his customers staggered away, sticky and empty-handed.

The Aftermath

Despite the setbacks, Philostratos refused to give up. "Every great invention has its challenges!" he insisted. Over time, he improved the design, using lighter materials and adding a lid to prevent spills.

While the Amphorita never became as popular as Philostratos hoped, his idea of portable beer containers laid the groundwork for future innovations. Historians might debate whether he truly invented the first "beer bottle," but in Alexandria, he became a legend, half genius, half cautionary tale.

STEM Lesson

Philostratos' story highlights the importance of *trial and error* in innovation. His idea of portable beer was ahead of its time, but the execution needed refinement. Many inventions, from the wheel to the smartphone, began as flawed prototypes.

The lesson? Don't be afraid to fail. Every mistake is a step toward improvement, and sometimes, a really funny story.

200 BC - 150 BC: Growing Importance of Beer

- **Techniques**: Introduction of wooden staves to build better fermentation vessels.
- **Method**:
    1. Grains are malted and mashed in larger wooden vessels.
    2. Wort is heated and strained.
    3. Fermentation occurs naturally with slight experimentation in timings (5-7 days).
- **SPV**: Alcohol strength reaches 4-5%, making beer a more substantial dietary component.
- **Recipes**: Barley mash with honey and herbs for added sweetness and flavour.
- **Social Aspect**: Beer becomes essential for survival, offering calories and safe

Cato the Brewer: The Man Who Tried to Brew with Logic

Setting the Scene

In 200 BC, in the Roman Republic, brewing beer was far less popular than making wine. Romans considered beer a "barbarian's drink," but one man, Cato the Brewer, was determined to change that. Cato wasn't a typical brewer, he was a philosopher who believed everything could be perfected through logic and reason.

"Wine is for poets," he declared, "but beer is for thinkers! With careful planning and calculation, I shall create the perfect brew."

Cato's brewery wasn't just a workshop, it was a laboratory. He kept wax tablets filled with detailed observations, diagrams of fermentation processes, and even an abacus for calculating barley-to-water ratios.

The Logical Brew

One day, Cato decided to create a beer so perfect it would rival Rome's finest wines. He called it *Cerevisia Optimus* (The Supreme Beer).

Step one: Ingredients. Cato insisted that every grain of barley must be identical in size and weight. He spent hours measuring each kernel with a tiny set of scales, discarding anything that didn't meet his exact standards.
Step two: Temperature control. Believing precision was key, Cato constructed a clay thermometer by marking temperature changes on a rod submerged in water.
Step three: Timing. Cato developed a "brew clock," powered by dripping water, to ensure each step of the process was perfectly timed.
After weeks of preparation, he finally brewed his masterpiece. The result? A beer so bitter, even the local legionaries wouldn't drink it. "It tastes like philosophy," one soldier joked. "Complicated and dry."

The Festival Fiasco

Not one to give up, Cato decided to showcase his beer at the Festival of Saturnalia. He set up a stall with a large banner reading, *"Cerevisia Optimus: Brewed with Logic!"*
Curious Romans gathered, intrigued by the promise of a "scientific beer." However, when they tasted it, their faces twisted in confusion. "Why is it so... precise?" one farmer asked. "It's like drinking a scroll!"
Cato tried to explain the intricacies of his process, but the crowd grew restless. To make matters worse, his brew clock malfunctioned and began spewing water everywhere. Children cheered, thinking it was part of the entertainment, while Cato frantically tried to save his notes from being drenched.

The Aftermath

By the end of the festival, Cato had sold only one mug of beer, to a philosopher who bought it out of pity. Dejected but undeterred, Cato returned to his brewery. "Perhaps," he admitted, "beer needs more than logic. Perhaps it needs... flavor."
Over time, Cato loosened his strict methods, experimenting with honey, herbs, and even figs to create a more enjoyable brew. While his beer never replaced wine in Roman society, it gained a small but devoted following among scholars who appreciated both its taste and the thought behind it.

STEM Lesson

Cato's story shows that while precision and planning are essential in science, creativity and adaptability are just as important. Many of history's greatest inventions, from vaccines to space exploration, required both careful calculations and bold leaps of imagination.
The lesson? Don't get so caught up in logic that you forget the human element. Science, like brewing, is both an art and a craft.

150 BC - 100 BC: Development of Brewing Techniques

- **Techniques**: Early sieving methods appear, improving clarity of wort.
- **Method**:
    1. Malted grains are heated in larger vessels, often shared within communities.
    2. Early sieves made from woven fibres or reeds are used to clarify wort.
    3. Fermentation occurs for 5-7 days.
- **SPV**: Consistent alcohol levels (4-5%), but spoilage remains an issue.
- **Recipes**: Barley remains primary, with variations in herbs for flavour.
- **Social Aspect**: Brewing solidifies as a communal task tied to rituals and feasting.

Marcellus the Brewer: The Man Who Invented "Mood Beer"

Setting the Scene

In 150 BC, in a small Roman town near Carthage, there lived a brewer named Marcellus. Marcellus wasn't an ordinary brewer; he had a flair for drama and a fascination with the rising popularity of Greek philosophy. He was convinced that beer could be more than just a drink, it could be an experience.

"Why should wine have all the poetry?" he asked. "Beer can evoke emotions too! With the right ingredients, I'll craft a brew to match every mood!"

His friends thought he was mad. "Beer is beer, Marcellus," they said. "It's meant to quench thirst, not start philosophical debates!" But Marcellus was undeterred.

The Experiment

Marcellus set out to create what he called *Cerevisia Sententia* (Mood Beer). To match each feeling, he experimented with unusual ingredients:

- For joy: Honey and sweet herbs.
- For anger: Spices like pepper and mustard seed.
- For love: Figs and rose petals.
- For deep thought: Bitter herbs and a pinch of salt.

He brewed tirelessly, jotting down his results on wax tablets. After weeks of tinkering, he prepared four distinct batches, ready to unveil his emotional beers to the town.

The Great Reveal

At the festival of Saturnalia, Marcellus set up a booth with signs advertising his creations: *"Drink Joy!" "Sip Love!" "Taste Anger!" "Think Deep!"*

Curious townsfolk gathered to try his concoctions. At first, the results were promising. The honeyed "Joy" brew had people laughing and singing, while the rosy "Love" brew inspired more than a few blushes among the crowd.

But trouble began when a gladiator tried the "Anger" brew. He declared it "too mild" and demanded Marcellus add more spices. Obligingly, Marcellus dumped an entire pouch of peppercorns into the mix. The next sip sent the gladiator into a coughing fit so violent that his helmet flew off.

Meanwhile, the "Deep Thought" brew worked *too well.* Philosophers drank it and began debating whether beer or wine was the true drink of the gods. The argument grew so heated that one scholar stood on a barrel and proclaimed, "If beer makes us think, does it not surpass wine, which merely makes us dance?"

The Inevitable Chaos

As the night wore on, the festival turned into a comedy of errors. The "Joy" drinkers danced wildly through the streets, crashing into market stalls. The "Anger" drinkers engaged in a pepper-fueled shouting match with the philosophers. And the "Love" drinkers? Let's just say the town square saw a lot of impromptu serenades, most of them off-key.

Marcellus, delighted by the chaos, raised his own mug of "Deep Thought" and declared, "This is exactly what I envisioned! Beer for every emotion!"

The Aftermath

Though Marcellus' Mood Beer experiment was short-lived (the town council banned "Anger" beer after the peppercorn incident), his idea lived on. Locals remembered him fondly as the brewer who dared to mix beer with philosophy.

Years later, a traveling Roman poet would immortalize Marcellus in a short verse:

"To Marcellus, who brewed by the heart,
And gave beer a noble, emotional start."

STEM Lesson

Marcellus' story reminds us of the importance of experimentation, and the risks of going too far. His Mood Beers were an early attempt at using science (and a little artistry) to create something unique, even if the results didn't always go as planned.

The lesson? Innovation often involves taking risks, making mistakes, and laughing at the results. Who knows, your next wild idea might just change the world (or at least make it more fun)!

Antipater the Brewer: The Man Who Fermented Time

Setting the Scene

In 150 BC, in the ancient city of Pergamon, there lived a brewer named Antipater. Pergamon was a hub of learning and culture, home to one of the greatest libraries of the ancient world. Antipater was not just a brewer; he fancied himself an amateur scholar, always eager to blend his love for beer with the latest intellectual trends.

"Why should philosophy be confined to scrolls?" he mused. "Surely, enlightenment can be sipped from a mug!"

The Quest for Preservation

One day, Antipater became obsessed with a problem that had been plaguing brewers for centuries: how to keep beer fresh for longer periods. "If we can preserve knowledge in libraries," he thought, "why can't we preserve beer just as well?"

He heard tales of Egyptian brewers using natural preservatives and Roman winemakers storing their vintages for years. Determined to outdo them all, Antipater set out to create a beer that could stand the test of time.

The Great Experiment

Drawing inspiration from the scholars around him, Antipater devised an elaborate plan. He theorized that if he could slow down the aging process of beer, he could keep it fresh indefinitely. His solution? Build a giant hourglass-like contraption that would regulate the flow of time around his beer barrels.

He called it the "Chrono-Fermentor 3000" (even though no one knew what "3000" stood for). The device was an impressive assembly of gears, sands, and levers, all centered around his prized barrels. Townsfolk gathered to watch as he activated the machine.

"Behold!" Antipater announced. "I shall manipulate time itself to preserve the perfect brew!"

When Time Stood... Still?

At first, nothing seemed to happen. The sands flowed, the gears turned, and Antipater waited eagerly. After several hours, he decided to taste the beer. To his delight, it was as fresh as when he had first brewed it. "Success!" he shouted.

However, his celebration was premature. As days went by, strange things occurred around the brewery. Roosters crowed at midnight, shadows stretched in odd directions, and the sundials nearby spun erratically. The townspeople grew concerned.

"Your machine is confusing the sun!" an old woman cried. "Our bread won't rise properly!" complained the baker.

Antipater realized that his Chrono-Fermentor might be slightly overcomplicating things. In his attempt to slow down time for his beer, he had inadvertently created temporal chaos in Pergamon.

The Humbling Conclusion

Seeing the distress he had caused, Antipater quickly dismantled his contraption. He apologized to the townspeople, who, despite the inconvenience, couldn't stay mad at the well-meaning brewer.

In the end, Antipater returned to traditional methods. He discovered that by storing his beer in sealed clay jars and keeping them in cool caves, he could preserve the freshness without disrupting the space-time continuum.

The whole affair became a local legend, and Antipater earned the affectionate nickname "The Time-Turner Brewer." His story was told for generations as a humorous reminder that sometimes the simplest solutions are the best.

STEM Lesson

Antipater's misadventure highlights the timeless principle of Occam's Razor: the simplest solution is often the correct one. While his ambition and creativity were commendable, his overly complex approach led to unintended consequences.

In science and engineering, it's important to consider practicality and potential side effects when solving a problem. Antipater eventually found that proper storage techniques were sufficient to preserve his beer, a solution still used in various forms today.

100 BC - 50 BC: Roman Influence

- **Techniques**: Introduction of Roman pottery for brewing and storage.
- **Method**:
    1. Roman ceramic vessels are used for mashing and fermenting.
    2. Grains are malted with greater consistency, ensuring better sugar extraction.
    3. Natural fermentation continues, with clearer brews.
- **SPV**: Improved preservation and slight strength increases (4-6%).
- **Recipes**: Barley mash flavoured with local herbs.
- **Social Aspect**: Brewing begins to face competition from Roman wine.

Lucius Fermentus: The Brewer Who Tried to Please the Gods

Setting the Scene

In 100 BC, in the heart of Rome, Lucius Fermentus was the go-to brewer for anyone looking for a good time. His beers were the talk of the town, and his tavern was always packed with soldiers, philosophers, and merchants. But Lucius wasn't content with his fame. "I've conquered the palates of men," he declared one day, "but what about the gods?"

Inspired by the temples dotting the Roman Forum, Lucius set out to brew the ultimate beer, a divine drink so extraordinary that even Jupiter himself would grant it his thunderous approval.

The Divine Brew

To craft his masterpiece, Lucius decided to incorporate ingredients he believed would appeal to the gods:

- Honey for sweetness, to honour Venus, goddess of love.
- Grapes for Bacchus, the god of wine (and, Lucius hoped, beer too).
- Herbs for Mars, the god of war, to give the brew a "strong kick."
- And a pinch of ash from a sacred temple fire, to symbolise Jupiter's mighty lightning.

Lucius named his creation *Ambrosia Fermenta* and planned to offer it during a public feast in the Forum. "The gods will *feel* this beer," he proclaimed, "and the people will cheer my name!"

The Feast of Saturnalia

On the day of the feast, a massive crowd gathered to witness Lucius' offering to the gods. Priests performed rituals, musicians played festive tunes, and Lucius stood proudly beside a massive amphora of *Ambrosia Fermenta*.

The first mugs were poured for the priests, who sipped cautiously. At first, they nodded approvingly. "Interesting," one said. "Quite... unique." But soon, their faces turned red, and one began sneezing uncontrollably, perhaps from the ash?

The crowd, oblivious to the priests' discomfort, eagerly lined up for their share. Lucius poured mugs for the people, and the reactions were... mixed.

One soldier shouted, "It tastes like honeyed lightning!"
A merchant exclaimed, "I think it's fighting my stomach!"
Meanwhile, a philosopher declared, "This beer has transcended taste and become a metaphor for chaos!"

The Ominous Sign

As more people drank, the chaos grew. Some began singing hymns to Jupiter, while others started an impromptu wrestling match in honour of Mars. Then, just as Lucius raised his own mug to toast the gods, a sudden clap of thunder echoed across the Forum.

"Jupiter approves!" someone shouted, as the crowd cheered.

But Lucius wasn't so sure. The thunder was followed by a torrential downpour that soaked the crowd and flooded the amphora of *Ambrosia Fermenta,* diluting the beer beyond recognition. The festival-goers, now drenched, took it as a sign to disperse, though many were still singing praises to Lucius' brew as they wandered off.

The Aftermath

Though the feast didn't go as planned, Lucius' reputation soared. "Even Jupiter tasted my beer!" he boasted, conveniently ignoring the fact that the storm had likely been a coincidence.

Ambrosia Fermenta became a local legend, though no one could quite agree on whether it was divine or disastrous. Lucius, ever the showman, leaned into the ambiguity. "What is perfection, if not the pursuit of the impossible?" he'd say, pouring another mug for a curious patron.

STEM Lesson

Lucius' story highlights an important lesson about *ambition in science and innovation*. His bold experiment reminds us that not every big idea works perfectly, but even failures can lead to unexpected success, or at least a good story.

When you try something new, don't be afraid of the storm. Sometimes, the real achievement is in daring to brew something extraordinary.

50 BC - 0 AD: The Celtic-Roman Brewing Fusion

- **Techniques**: Adoption of Roman-style kilns for grain drying improves malt quality.
- **Method**:
    1. Malted barley is dried in primitive kilns.
    2. Brewing in ceramic amphorae improves fermentation consistency.
- **SPV**: Alcohol levels stabilise at 5-6%.
- **Recipes**: Barley brews with honey and herbs like rosemary, yarrow, and meadowsweet.
- **Social Aspect**: Beer remains a commoner's drink, while elites prefer wine.

Bryn the Brewer: The Celtic Genius Who Invented "Druid Brew"

Setting the Scene

In 50 BC, long before the Romans conquered Britain, the Celtic tribes ruled the land. Among them lived Bryn the Brewer, a man whose love for beer was rivalled only by his love for storytelling. Bryn was the tribal brewer, tasked with creating the ale served at feasts, ceremonies, and the occasional brawl.

But Bryn was no ordinary brewer. He believed that his beer could do more than quench thirst, it could bring people closer to the spirits of the earth and sky. "A true brew," he proclaimed, "should make you feel like you've touched the soul of the forest!"

The Brew That Would Unite the Tribes

One day, during a meeting of the local druids, Bryn overheard a heated discussion. The druids were trying to unite the tribes for a great festival but couldn't agree on anything, not the location, the sacrifices, or even the menu.

Bryn saw an opportunity. "What if," he announced, "I brew a beer so magical, so enchanting, that it brings everyone together in harmony?"

The druids laughed. "Bryn, your last 'magical brew' turned half the village green for a week!" one said. But Bryn was undeterred.

The Experiment
Bryn set to work crafting what he called *Druid Brew*. He foraged ingredients from the sacred groves and meadows:

- Wild honey, to capture the sweetness of life.
- Heather flowers, for the spirit of the moors.
- Berries from the sacred yew tree, because... why not?
- And a touch of mistletoe, the druids' favourite magical plant.

He brewed the concoction under the light of a full moon, chanting ancient songs (or at least humming them, he wasn't great with lyrics). After days of fermenting in a hollowed-out oak log, *Druid Brew* was ready.

The Festival
At the festival, Bryn unveiled his creation in a grand ceremony. The tribes gathered around as he poured the first mugs of *Druid Brew*, golden and fragrant. "Drink deeply," he said, "and feel the magic of the land!"

The first sips were met with awe. The beer was sweet, floral, and strangely invigorating. "It's like drinking the summer breeze!" one warrior declared. Another shouted, "I can taste the forest!" Even the druids, notorious for being hard to impress, nodded approvingly.

But then things got... odd.

One elder began reciting poetry to a tree, insisting it was his long-lost brother. A group of warriors decided to re-enact a battle, but with interpretive dance. The druids began a chant so loud it scared off a flock of birds, which the villagers took as a divine sign.

The Aftermath
By nightfall, the festival had turned into a chaotic yet joyful spectacle. Tribes that had once been rivals danced together around the fire. Arguments were forgotten, and everyone sang songs (mostly out of tune).

Bryn, watching the scene unfold, beamed with pride. "My brew didn't just unite the tribes, it made history!"

The druids, however, were less enthusiastic the next morning when they realized the mistletoe had caused some... unintended side effects. "Perhaps," one said, nursing a headache, "next time we should skip the 'magical' part."

Despite the chaos, *Druid Brew* became a legend, and Bryn was celebrated as the brewer who brought the tribes together, if only for one wild night.

STEM Lesson

Bryn's story reminds us that experimentation is key to innovation, but so is understanding your ingredients! His wild creativity led to an unforgettable brew, but it also highlights the importance of testing and knowing the properties of what you're working with.

The lesson? Embrace your bold ideas, but don't be afraid to refine them. Even a chaotic result can lead to something extraordinary, or at least a really good party.

0 AD - 50 AD: Brewing in Roman Britain

- **Techniques**: Roman influence begins to shape brewing techniques. While ale remains a staple, brewing adopts more structured methods, including the use of ceramic vessels for greater durability and consistency. Some rudimentary boiling methods are introduced, inspired by Roman wine production techniques.

- **Where Brewing Was Done**:
  Brewing shifts slightly with Roman urbanisation. While traditional Celtic brewing continues in rural homes, Romanised towns introduce shared brewing facilities. These may be attached to villas or communal kitchens. Rural tribes still use roundhouses, though some adopt Roman-style ovens for malting grains.

- **How It Would Have Looked**:
  In rural areas, brewing scenes remain rustic, centred around fire pits. In urban areas, larger ceramic amphorae stand in orderly rows, storing ale and other fermented beverages. Brewing in urban settlements takes on a semi-commercial aspect, as ale is exchanged at markets.

- **Involvement of Villagers**:
  Villagers assist in gathering local ingredients, including herbs and honey. Roman military camps also foster brewing, as soldiers prefer local ales over imported wines. Women retain their role as primary brewers, though men in towns begin adopting brewing as a trade.

- **Equipment Used**:

  - **Ceramic Amphorae**: Durable, elongated pots used for storage and fermentation.

  - **Roman Kilns**: Used for controlled drying of grains, leading to improved malt consistency.

  - **Wooden Mallets**: Crushed malt grains more efficiently.

  - **Bronze or Copper Cauldrons**: Occasionally used for mashing in larger-scale operations.

- **Recipes (Detailed)**:

  - **Ingredients**:

    - 4 kg of malted barley
    - Water from springs or rivers
    - Additives like meadowsweet, rosemary, and yarrow
    - Honey for sweetness (optional)

  - **Method**:

1. **Malting**: Barley is spread on woven mats and germinated for 3-4 days. Roman kilns dry it evenly over low heat for 2 days.
2. **Crushing**: Crushed with mallets or by hand using mortars.
3. **Mashing**: Malt is soaked in warm water (50-60°C) in ceramic or wooden vessels. Mash is stirred for 2 hours.
4. **Boiling (Optional)**: Some brewers experiment with heating the wort to sterilise it, but this is rare.
5. **Fermentation**: Wort is poured into amphorae and left uncovered for natural fermentation (5-7 days). Herbs are added on day 2.
6. **Drinking**: Ale is consumed fresh, served from amphorae or wooden barrels.

- **SPV (Strength, Preservation, and Variability)**:
  - **Strength**: Alcohol content rises to 3-4%.
  - **Preservation**: Improved through amphora storage, but ale still spoils within a week.
  - **Variability**: Slightly reduced due to better grain drying and ceramic vessels.
- **Social Aspect**:
  Brewing continues as a communal activity in villages but gains prominence in Roman towns as a traded commodity. It serves as a common drink for soldiers and workers. Feasts in Roman villas often feature ale alongside wine, showing its growing importance.

Aelfric the Brewer: The Man Who Brewed "Time-Travel Ale"

Setting the Scene

In 0 BC, in a small Celtic village on the misty British Isles, a brewer named Aelfric was known for his peculiar ideas and even more peculiar ales. While others brewed beer for feasts and rituals, Aelfric dreamed of something greater. "What if," he mused one evening, "beer could show us visions of the past, or even the future?"

His friends laughed. "Aelfric, just stick to making beer that doesn't make people hiccup for hours!" But Aelfric couldn't be stopped. Inspired by the druids' mysterious rituals and his own wild imagination, he decided to create an ale that would bend time itself.

The Time-Bending Brew

Aelfric gathered ingredients he believed held mystical powers:

- Juniper berries, for clarity of vision.
- Elderflowers, because they were said to ward off evil spirits.
- Fern spores, which he swore were connected to the mysteries of the forest.
- And a splash of water from the sacred spring near the standing stones, just in case.

He brewed the ale under the stars during the winter solstice, convinced that the alignment of the heavens would infuse it with magical properties. After days of careful fermentation, Aelfric proudly unveiled his creation: *Chrono Ale*.

"It's not just beer," he declared to the villagers. "It's a journey through time!"

The Festival of First Sips

At the village feast, the locals were both skeptical and curious. Aelfric poured mugs of the golden brew, and one by one, people began to drink. At first, nothing seemed unusual. The ale was delicious, sweet and herbal with a strange, warming aftertaste.

But then, the "time travel" began.

One elderly woman shouted, "I see my wedding day! Oh, look at young me, such a beauty!" A warrior proclaimed, "I'm in the middle of a great battle! Victory is ours!" Even the village bard stood up and declared, "I've seen the future, I'll write a song so great that it'll echo through the ages!"

Aelfric was thrilled. "It works!" he exclaimed, though he noticed that everyone's "visions" were remarkably self-flattering.

Unintended Consequences

As the night wore on, the visions grew stranger. One man insisted he'd traveled so far into the future that he'd seen flying carts and talking stones. A farmer claimed he'd visited the past and convinced a mammoth to let him ride it.

Then the village chief stood up, eyes wide, and proclaimed, "The gods have spoken to me! They say this ale is... cursed!" This caused a brief panic, until the chief admitted he'd drunk too much and was seeing double.

The Aftermath

The next morning, the villagers woke up with sore heads and vague memories of their "travels through time." While some dismissed the ale as mere fantasy, others swore they'd truly glimpsed the past and future.

As for Aelfric, he became a legend in the village. "Aelfric the Time Brewer," they called him, though his later attempts to recreate *Chrono Ale* never quite worked the same way.

Still, his experiment left a lasting legacy: the idea that beer isn't just a drink, it's an experience.

STEM Lesson

Aelfric's story reminds us of the power of curiosity and experimentation. While his "time-travel ale" might have been more imagination than science, it demonstrates how new ideas, no matter how strange, can inspire creativity and bring people together.

The lesson? Think big, dream bigger, and don't be afraid to pour a little magic into your experiments. Who knows what you might discover?

50 AD - 100 AD: Brewing During Roman Expansion

- **Techniques**: Brewing becomes more standardised with the influence of Roman engineering. Larger fermentation vessels and storage solutions, including underground cellars, are introduced. Boiling the wort becomes more common, inspired by Roman hygiene practices.
- **Where Brewing Was Done**: Brewing begins to move into specialised facilities. Villas feature dedicated brewing rooms, and legionary camps have communal brewing areas to supply soldiers. Rural homes and communal spaces still serve as primary brewing hubs for local communities.
- **How It Would Have Looked**: Large-scale brewing areas in Roman villas include rows of amphorae and organised drying spaces for malt. Military brewing sites resemble small industrial setups, with multiple cauldrons and brewing vats. In rural villages, brewing remains a smoky, home-based process.
- **Involvement of Villagers**: Roman occupation integrates locals into production systems. Villagers work alongside Romans in brewing, often adopting new tools and techniques. Soldiers demand consistent supplies, boosting ale production.
- **Equipment Used**:
  - **Fermentation Vats**: Larger ceramic or wooden vats for brewing.
  - **Cauldrons**: Copper or bronze cauldrons for mashing and boiling.
  - **Kilns**: Improved Roman kilns produce more consistent malt.
  - **Storage Amphorae**: Ceramic pots used for long-term storage.
- **Recipes (Detailed)**:
  - **Ingredients**:
    - 5 kg of malted barley
    - Fresh water (stream-fed)
    - Herbs such as rosemary, meadowsweet, or sage for flavour
    - Optional: Honey for sweetness

- **Method**:

    1. **Malting**: Barley grains are spread on woven mats to germinate. Turn grains daily and dry in Roman kilns for 2-3 days at low heat.

    2. **Crushing**: Grains are coarsely crushed using wooden mallets or stone.

    3. **Mashing**: Add crushed malt to a large cauldron. Pour water (60-70°C) and stir for 1-2 hours to extract sugars.

    4. **Boiling**: Transfer the wort to a cauldron and boil for up to 1 hour, adding herbs halfway through.

    5. **Fermentation**: Pour the wort into fermentation vats or amphorae. Cover loosely and allow to ferment for 5-7 days.

    6. **Storage**: Transfer the beer to amphorae or wooden barrels for short-term storage.

    7. **Drinking**: Ale is consumed fresh, usually within 1-2 weeks.

- **SPV (Strength, Preservation, and Variability)**:
    - **Strength**: Stabilises at 3-4% alcohol by volume.
    - **Preservation**: Improved through boiling and amphora storage.
    - **Variability**: Moderately reduced due to standardisation of kilns and brewing vessels.
- **Social Aspect**: Beer evolves into both a local staple and a traded commodity. Roman soldiers consume ale as part of their rations, and communal brewing becomes an economic activity. Ale is still served at feasts, but it also gains prominence in Roman marketplaces as a drink for workers and soldiers alike.

Cassius the Brewer: The Man Who Tried to Impress the Romans

Setting the Scene

In 50 AD, Britain was under Roman occupation, and life in the village of Brittania Minor (a name that sounded more important than it was) had taken a strange turn. The locals were adjusting to Roman roads, Roman baths, and, most distressingly, Roman wine.

For Cassius, the village brewer, this was a crisis. "Wine!" he exclaimed. "It's sour grape juice! How can anyone prefer that to a good, hearty ale?" Determined to prove that British beer was superior, Cassius decided to brew something so impressive, even the Romans would raise their goblets to him.

The Grand Plan

Cassius set out to create a beer he called *Brittanica Maxima,* a brew that would showcase the strength and character of Britain. He decided it needed:

- Barley from the richest fields.
- Wild honey, for sweetness.
- Nettles, for a "kick."
- And a touch of bog myrtle, a local herb he thought would make it "exotic."

Cassius believed presentation was key, so he carved a large amphora in the Roman style and engraved it with heroic scenes of Celtic warriors defeating Roman soldiers. "If the beer doesn't win them over," he muttered, "the amphora surely will."

The Roman Banquet

Cassius' big moment came when the local Roman governor hosted a banquet to celebrate the completion of a new aqueduct. Cassius arrived with his amphora of *Brittanica Maxima* and announced, "This is the finest drink in all of Britain! Better than wine!"

The Romans, intrigued by his confidence (and slightly amused by the amphora's carvings), agreed to try it. Cassius poured the beer into fine Roman goblets, and the banquet hall fell silent as the first sips were taken.

The Reactions

At first, the Romans were pleasantly surprised. "Not bad," one murmured. "It's... earthy," said another. Cassius beamed with pride. But then, the nettles made their presence known.

One senator began coughing. "What is this... spiciness?" he gasped. Another scratched his throat and muttered, "It's like drinking a hedge!"

The governor, always diplomatic, tried to smooth things over. "It's certainly... unique," he said, though his face betrayed a different story.

The real trouble began when one legionary, eager to impress, gulped down his entire goblet. The bog myrtle, unbeknownst to Cassius, had mild hallucinogenic properties. The soldier stood up, pointed to the amphora's carvings, and shouted, "The Celts are attacking!" Chaos erupted as half the banquet ran outside to prepare for battle.

The Aftermath

By morning, the banquet was the talk of the province. The Romans, despite the fiasco, couldn't stop laughing about "the barbarian beer that started a phantom war." Cassius, though initially mortified, embraced the fame.

He rebranded *Brittanica Maxima* as "The Warrior's Brew," claiming it was so powerful it could inspire visions of glory. It became a hit with local Britons and even a few adventurous Roman soldiers.

The Legacy

Cassius never quite won over the Roman elites, but his story endured as a tale of British ingenuity and stubbornness. His amphora, though ridiculous to the Romans, became a symbol of defiance, proudly displayed in the village tavern for years to come.

STEM Lesson

Cassius' story is a fun example of how cultural exchange and experimentation can lead to unexpected outcomes. While his beer may not have been a Roman favourite, his creativity and boldness made an impact.

The lesson? Don't be afraid to think big and take risks, even if your "nettles and bog myrtle" idea doesn't go quite as planned. Sometimes, the attempt is just as important as the result, and a good laugh never hurts.

100 AD - 150 AD: Refining Brewing Practices

- **Techniques**: Brewing becomes more refined as the Romans introduce improved tools and processes. Techniques for consistent malting, mashing, and fermentation evolve, with a focus on creating stable and predictable beer.
- **Where Brewing Was Done**: Brewing spreads further into Roman villas, larger towns, and settlements. Villas and estates often have dedicated malting and brewing spaces, while towns see early proto-breweries supplying local populations. Legionary camps continue to prioritise brewing to meet soldiers' needs.
- **How It Would Have Looked**: Brewing areas in Roman villas feature permanent kilns, larger cauldrons, and amphora storage rooms. Town breweries include multiple fermentation vats, work tables for crushing and mashing, and tools for straining wort. Legionary camps create portable setups with smaller vats and cauldrons for mobile brewing.
- **Involvement of Villagers**: Villagers supply grains, herbs, and honey to larger brewing operations. Skilled brewers, often slaves or workers in Roman households, manage brewing processes. Brewing shifts from a domestic activity to a more structured trade.
- **Equipment Used**:
    - **Permanent Kilns**: More advanced designs for drying malt consistently.
    - **Larger Amphorae**: Designed for both fermentation and storage.
    - **Iron Tools**: Introduced for crushing grains and stirring mashes.
    - **Wooden Barrels**: Begin to appear for local beer transport and short-term storage.
- **Recipes (Detailed)**:
    - **Ingredients**:
        - 6 kg of malted barley or a barley-wheat mix
        - Water sourced from springs or aqueducts
        - Herbs such as coriander, rosemary, or fennel for flavour
        - Honey or grape must for added sweetness

- **Method**:

  1. **Malting**: Barley is spread in controlled spaces, turned daily, and dried in kilns over 2-3 days.
  2. **Crushing**: Grains are crushed using iron or stone tools.
  3. **Mashing**: Mix crushed malt with water (60-70°C) in cauldrons, stirring regularly for 2 hours.
  4. **Straining**: Strain wort using fine woven sieves to remove husks.
  5. **Fermentation**: Transfer wort into large amphorae and ferment naturally for 5-7 days. Herbs are added on day 3.
  6. **Storage**: Store beer in amphorae or barrels in cool, shaded areas.

- **SPV (Strength, Preservation, and Variability)**:
  - **Strength**: Steady at 4-5% alcohol by volume.
  - **Preservation**: Improved with cooler storage methods and the use of herbs.
  - **Variability**: Reduced as brewing practices become standardised.
- **Social Aspect**: Brewing becomes a structured trade, with skilled labourers producing ale for estates, towns, and markets. Ale remains a key drink for soldiers and workers, while wealthier Romans prefer wine. Communal feasts still feature beer, which is seen as both a staple and a symbol of community.

Tiber the Brewer: The Man Who Brewed the First "Luxury Ale"

Setting the Scene

In 100 AD, Roman Britain was thriving, or so the Romans liked to think. Towns were growing, roads stretched across the land, and Roman wine flowed freely at every banquet. But in the small town of Aquae Barleia (modern-day Barley-on-Thames), one man was determined to prove that beer was still the drink of choice for the discerning Briton: Tiber the Brewer.

Tiber was no ordinary brewer. Having grown up in a Romanized village, he considered himself both a Celt and a connoisseur of Roman luxury. "Why settle for ordinary beer?" he declared. "I shall create a brew so refined, it will rival the finest Roman wines!"

The Luxury Brew

Tiber decided that his beer needed to be as extravagant as a Roman banquet. He gathered ingredients fit for an emperor:

- Barley malt soaked in honey, for sweetness.
- Wild herbs from the nearby forest, for a touch of mystery.
- Crushed oyster shells, which he'd heard Romans used to "elevate" their drinks.
- And a handful of gold flakes, because nothing said "luxury" like drinking metal.

Tiber's masterpiece, *Aurum Ale* (Golden Ale), was brewed in a massive clay pot decorated with Celtic spirals and Roman laurel leaves. "This," he proclaimed, "will be the drink of emperors!"

The Roman Governor's Banquet

Eager to impress, Tiber brought his *Aurum Ale* to the local Roman governor's banquet. The governor, a pompous man named Lucius Plinius, was known for his love of fine wine and his disdain for "barbarian" traditions.

"My good Lucius," Tiber said with a grin, "this ale is unlike anything you've tasted. A true fusion of Celtic spirit and Roman sophistication!"

Plinius, curious but skeptical, agreed to try it. The banquet hall fell silent as the first goblets of *Aurum Ale* were poured. The golden flakes shimmered in the candlelight, drawing gasps of admiration.

The Reactions

At first, the guests sipped cautiously. The honey sweetness delighted them, and the herbal notes added intrigue. "It's... not bad," Plinius admitted, though his tone suggested he was reluctant to compliment anything not made of grapes.

But then came the crunch.

One senator chewed thoughtfully, then froze. "What... is this texture?" he asked, alarmed. Another guest spat out what appeared to be a chunk of oyster shell.

"It's the taste of the sea!" Tiber explained proudly. "A symbol of Britannia's strength!"

The governor raised an eyebrow. "And the gold?"

"For health and wealth, of course!" Tiber replied.

Moments later, a particularly enthusiastic legionary downed his goblet and declared, "I AM INVINCIBLE!" before attempting to arm-wrestle a statue.

The Chaos

The banquet descended into chaos. The oyster-shell crunching became a game of "guess the ingredient," while the gold flakes left some guests with glittering beards and hands. One philosopher suggested the drink might grant immortality, sparking an impromptu debate that nearly ended in a food fight.

Meanwhile, Plinius, overwhelmed by the absurdity of it all, muttered, "Barbarians truly have no limits." But secretly, he ordered another goblet.

The Aftermath

The next morning, Tiber was hailed as both a genius and a lunatic. While some guests swore never to touch beer again, others demanded more of his "luxury ale."

Tiber's fame spread across the province, and though his oyster-and-gold recipe never caught on widely, his boldness inspired future brewers to experiment with new flavors and ideas.

STEM Lesson

Tiber's story is a fun example of how experimentation and creativity can lead to unexpected results. While his *Aurum Ale* was far from perfect, it pushed the boundaries of what beer could be, and sparked curiosity and conversation.

The lesson? Don't be afraid to mix tradition with innovation. Even if your ideas don't turn out as planned, they might just make history, or at least make people laugh.

150 AD - 200 AD: Expansion and Organisation

- **Techniques**: Brewing operations expand significantly, driven by demand from Roman soldiers and growing towns. Improved organisation and trade networks ensure a consistent supply of ingredients. Brewing techniques begin to involve batch standardisation for larger quantities.
- **Where Brewing Was Done**: Dedicated brewing sites, such as proto-breweries, appear in larger towns and near military camps. Rural households continue brewing for local consumption, while larger estates manage centralised brewing facilities.
- **How It Would Have Looked**: Roman proto-breweries feature rows of kilns for malting, large mashing vessels, and interconnected amphorae for fermentation and storage. Military camps include mobile setups for brewing on campaigns. Rural homes still use smaller, less organised setups with basic tools.
- **Involvement of Villagers**: Brewing becomes more professionalised, with villagers employed by estates or proto-breweries to produce ale in bulk. Women in rural households continue traditional brewing, while men in towns join brewing trades to meet urban and military demand.
- **Equipment Used**:
    - **Batch Kilns**: Larger kilns capable of processing higher quantities of malt.
    - **Interconnected Fermentation Amphorae**: To standardise batch production.
    - **Bronze Mixing Tools**: For stirring and maintaining consistency during mashing.
- **Recipes (Detailed)**:
    - **Ingredients**:
        - 8 kg of malted barley
        - Water from aqueducts or wells
        - Flavouring herbs: fennel, bay leaves, and rosemary
        - Optional: Honey or dried fruits

- **Method**:

    1. **Malting**: Barley is processed in larger kilns for consistency. Turn grains regularly to avoid burning.
    2. **Crushing**: Use iron or bronze tools for efficient crushing.
    3. **Mashing**: Combine crushed malt with water at 60-70°C, stirring continuously in larger cauldrons for 2-3 hours.
    4. **Boiling**: Introduce boiling as a standard step for sterilisation and flavour infusion.
    5. **Fermentation**: Ferment wort in interconnected amphorae, ensuring consistent temperature and yeast distribution.
    6. **Storage**: Transfer to barrels or larger amphorae for extended storage.

- **SPV (Strength, Preservation, and Variability)**:
    - **Strength**: Strength increases slightly, averaging 5% alcohol by volume.
    - **Preservation**: Significant improvement with boiling and controlled fermentation.
    - **Variability**: Reduced further due to standardised practices.
- **Social Aspect**: Brewing transforms into an organised industry, particularly in urban centres. Ale is distributed through markets, with townspeople and soldiers as primary consumers. Communal brewing declines in urban settings but remains vital in rural communities. Beer solidifies its role as a staple beverage across social classes.

Gwynn the Brewer: The Man Who Invented the "Mighty Ale of Britannia"

Setting the Scene

By 150 AD, Roman Britain was a melting pot of Roman sophistication and Celtic tradition. In the thriving town of Lindum (modern-day Lincoln), Gwynn the Brewer was a local legend. Known for his oversized personality and even larger beer mugs, Gwynn had one motto: "If you can drink it, I can brew it!"

Gwynn prided himself on his bold, experimental ales, which often earned him the dubious nickname "Gwynn the Gutsy." But despite the occasional misstep (his nettle ale was still talked about, though not in a good way), Gwynn was determined to make a name for himself.

The Emperor's Visit

One fateful day, word spread that a Roman envoy, representing Emperor Antoninus Pius himself, would visit Lindum. The town leaders scrambled to prepare a grand feast to impress their esteemed guests. Gwynn, never one to miss an opportunity for glory, volunteered to brew the centerpiece drink: *The Mighty Ale of Britannia*.

"Britain is more than Roman roads and baths!" Gwynn proclaimed. "We need an ale that shows our true strength, and maybe knocks a Roman or two off their fancy sandals."

The Brew

Gwynn set out to craft the most powerful and memorable beer in history. For this, he needed special ingredients:

- Barley malt soaked in river water "blessed" by a passing druid.
- Local honey, because Gwynn claimed it added "British courage."
- A generous helping of wild juniper berries, to give it "a punch like a legionary's fist."
- And a dash of fermented horseradish for "a warrior's kick."

The ale was brewed in an enormous cauldron, stirred by a team of villagers armed with oars, and left to ferment in an underground cellar, which Gwynn dramatically called "the Cave of Power."

The Feast

On the big day, the Roman envoy arrived in full splendor, draped in silk togas and flanked by legionaries. The feast began with roasted boar, fresh bread, and delicate Roman wine. But when Gwynn appeared, carrying a massive wooden keg on his shoulders, all eyes turned to him.

"Behold!" Gwynn roared. "The Mighty Ale of Britannia! Strong enough for warriors, bold enough for emperors!"

The Romans, intrigued by the spectacle, agreed to try the ale. Gwynn poured the first mugs, and the frothy, golden liquid shimmered in the firelight. "To Britannia!" he toasted.

The Reactions

The first sips were met with a mix of awe and confusion. The honey sweetness charmed the crowd, but the horseradish heat hit moments later, leaving some guests gasping.

"This... this is unlike anything I've tasted!" the envoy stammered, his eyes watering. A Roman senator coughed and declared, "It feels like a battle in my mouth!"

The legionaries, however, loved it. "A drink for true warriors!" one shouted, raising his mug high. Encouraged, the crowd drank more, and more, and soon the feast turned into chaos.

The Chaos

Fueled by Gwynn's ale, the normally stoic Romans began to let loose. Legionaries challenged villagers to wrestling matches, the senator composed an impromptu poem about Britannia's "fiery spirit," and the envoy, now thoroughly drunk, declared that Gwynn's ale "could conquer Gaul!"

Gwynn, basking in the glory, decided to give a demonstration of the ale's strength by attempting to lift his giant cauldron. It did not go well. The cauldron tipped over, spilling ale everywhere and soaking the guests. Rather than be offended, the crowd cheered, calling it a "blessing of Britannia."

The Aftermath

The next morning, the Romans left Lindum with sore heads but fond memories. The envoy even took a keg of Gwynn's ale back to Rome, where it was said to have caused a minor stir in the Senate.

As for Gwynn, his reputation as the boldest brewer in Britain was cemented. Though his "Mighty Ale" was never replicated exactly (likely for the best), his story became a local legend, passed down through generations.

STEM Lesson

Gwynn's story shows the importance of creativity and experimentation in problem-solving. While his methods were unconventional, he captured the essence of his culture and used local resources to create something truly unique.

The lesson? Be fearless in your ideas, but remember that innovation often comes with unexpected (and sometimes hilarious) consequences. And always have a backup plan if your cauldron tips over.

200 AD - 250 AD: Brewing Advancements in Roman Britain

- **Techniques**: Brewing continues to advance under Roman influence. Standardised batch brewing becomes common, with improvements in fermentation control and grain malting processes. The use of boiling to stabilise the wort is widely adopted, enhancing beer quality and longevity.
- **Where Brewing Was Done**: Brewing facilities are established near Roman towns, military camps, and larger estates. Dedicated malting and fermentation spaces are common in villas, featuring permanent kilns, large fermentation vats, and organised storage areas. Smaller-scale brewing persists in rural households, primarily for local consumption.
- **How It Would Have Looked**: Brewing in Roman settlements is well-organised. Villas have spacious brewing rooms with large amphorae lined along walls, kilns for malting grains, and copper cauldrons for mashing. Military camps feature portable brewing setups to supply soldiers. In rural areas, brewing remains less formal, with simple tools and clay pots used near hearths or outdoor spaces.
- **Involvement of Villagers**: Villagers work alongside Roman brewers, supplying grains, herbs, and honey. In rural settings, women continue to brew for household consumption, while men often engage in larger brewing operations managed by estates or proto-breweries. Brewing becomes both a household task and an emerging trade.
- **Equipment Used**:
    1. **Permanent Kilns**: Used to dry grains consistently for improved malting.
    2. **Fermentation Amphorae**: Ceramic vessels used for controlled fermentation.
    3. **Copper or Bronze Cauldrons**: Employed for mashing and boiling the wort.
    4. **Wooden Barrels**: Begin to replace amphorae for easier transport and storage.
- **Recipes (Detailed)**:
    - **Ingredients**:

        - 7 kg of malted barley (or a mix of barley and wheat)
        - Clean water from wells or aqueducts
        - Herbs such as coriander, fennel, and rosemary
        - Optional: Honey or dried figs for sweetness
    - **Method**:
        1. **Malting**: Spread grains in drying kilns for 2-3 days, turning regularly for even drying.
        2. **Crushing**: Coarsely crush dried malt with stone or iron tools.
        3. **Mashing**: Add crushed malt to a copper cauldron with water (60-70°C). Stir for 1-2 hours to extract sugars.
        4. **Boiling**: Boil the wort for 1 hour, adding herbs during the final 20 minutes.
        5. **Fermentation**: Transfer the wort to fermentation amphorae or barrels. Allow to ferment for 5-7 days, covered with cloth to keep out contaminants.
        6. **Storage**: Store the beer in wooden barrels in cool, shaded areas for up to a month.

- **SPV (Strength, Preservation, and Variability)**:
    - **Strength**: Alcohol content stabilises around 4-5%.
    - **Preservation**: Improved through boiling, controlled fermentation, and barrel storage.
    - **Variability**: Further reduced due to standardisation of brewing techniques and equipment.
- **Social Aspect**: Brewing becomes increasingly professionalised. Roman estates produce beer for local markets, military supply, and urban consumption. Ale continues to be a staple drink for soldiers and workers, while rural communities maintain household brewing traditions. Beer strengthens its role as both a daily necessity and a social beverage during communal gatherings.

Eadric the Brewer: The Man Who Brewed "Imperial Strength" Ale

Setting the Scene

In 200 AD, Roman Britain was thriving with towns, forts, and Roman baths, but deep in the countryside, the Celtic traditions still flourished. In a small village near modern-day York, Eadric the Brewer was known for his hearty ales and even heartier sense of humour.

Eadric took great pride in his craft, boasting that his brews could invigorate a farmer, impress a druid, and even make a Roman forget about wine. "My beer is the true *spiritus* of Britannia!" he often declared, much to the amusement of his neighbors.

The Roman Challenge

One day, a group of Roman soldiers stationed at the nearby fort came to Eadric's tavern. They were unimpressed by the rustic decor and the earthy mugs of ale.

"This is nothing compared to Roman wine," one soldier scoffed, swirling his drink dramatically.

Eadric, not one to take an insult lightly, leaned over the bar and grinned. "Oh, you think Roman wine is better, do you? I'll brew something so strong, even the emperor himself would be impressed!"

The soldiers laughed. "We'll believe it when we taste it," one said. "Make it *imperial strength*, and maybe we'll call it decent."

Eadric accepted the challenge with gusto. "You lot sit tight. You're about to taste history!"

The Imperial Strength Brew

Determined to outdo himself, Eadric gathered his most potent ingredients:

- Extra-malted barley for maximum strength.
- Heather honey, to sweeten the deal.
- A handful of mysterious herbs gifted by the local druid, which Eadric accepted without asking too many questions.
- And just for show, a dash of crushed blackberries to give it a regal, purple hue.

Eadric brewed the concoction in his largest cauldron, stirring it with a sturdy oar he borrowed from the village fisherman. He muttered incantations he'd overheard from druids (though he didn't know what they meant) and declared, "This brew will conquer empires!"

The Taste Test

A week later, Eadric unveiled his *Imperial Strength Ale* to the Roman soldiers. The drink was dark, thick, and fragrant, with a foam so sturdy it could support a coin.

The soldiers laughed as they took their first sips, but their laughter quickly turned to wide-eyed amazement.

"It's... it's magnificent!" one soldier exclaimed.
"It feels like a chariot hit me!" shouted another, thumping his chest.

Buoyed by their approval, Eadric poured himself a mug and took a swig. "By the gods!" he spluttered, coughing. "This stuff could wake the dead!"

The Chaos

As the soldiers drank more of the *Imperial Strength Ale*, the effects became... noticeable. One soldier climbed onto a table and began shouting in Latin about his love for Britannia. Another challenged the village blacksmith to a wrestling match (which he promptly lost).

The commander of the fort, who had come to investigate the commotion, took one sip and declared, "This is not ale, it's a weapon!"

Meanwhile, Eadric's neighbors joined the fun, turning the tavern into a lively (if slightly chaotic) celebration. Even the druid, drawn by the noise, showed up and declared the ale "a spiritual experience."

The Aftermath

The next morning, the Romans stumbled back to their fort, groaning about the "Celtic curse" in their heads but praising Eadric's brewing skills. The commander, impressed by the strength of the brew, ordered barrels of *Imperial Strength Ale* to be delivered to the fort regularly.

Eadric's fame spread, and his ale became the talk of the region. Some claimed it was so strong it could "fell a legion," while others swore it was blessed by the gods. Eadric, ever the showman, leaned into the myth, calling himself "Brewer to the Emperor" (though he never left Yorkshire).

STEM Lesson

Eadric's story is a fun reminder of the role experimentation plays in innovation. His willingness to push boundaries (and his occasional luck) resulted in something truly memorable, even if it was a little unorthodox.

The lesson? Bold ideas and a touch of creativity can lead to success, but be prepared for unexpected outcomes. And always remember: measure your ingredients carefully, especially if the local druid is involved!

250 AD - 300 AD: Brewing During Roman Decline

- **Techniques**: Brewing techniques remain consistent, but resource constraints and political instability in late Roman Britain begin to impact production. Larger estates continue to use advanced Roman brewing methods, while smaller operations revert to simpler practices.
- **Where Brewing Was Done**: Brewing persists in Roman villas and military camps, although the scale decreases in some regions due to declining Roman authority. Rural households and smaller settlements continue to brew for personal and local use, relying on traditional tools and methods.
- **How It Would Have Looked**: Roman brewing setups, though still present, begin to show signs of reduced maintenance. Kilns and fermentation vessels in larger estates remain functional but are less frequently upgraded. Rural homes rely on clay pots and wooden troughs for smaller-scale brewing near hearths or outdoor spaces.
- **Involvement of Villagers**: Villagers increasingly take on brewing responsibilities as Roman oversight diminishes. Women maintain their role as household brewers, while local craftsmen create or repair brewing equipment. In some areas, small-scale trade networks form around beer production.
- **Equipment Used**:
  1. **Kilns**: For malting grains, though often older and less efficient.
  2. **Wooden Fermentation Troughs**: Gradually replace amphorae in rural areas.
  3. **Clay Pots**: Commonly used for boiling and fermenting in smaller setups.
  4. **Wooden Barrels**: Widely adopted for storage and transport.
- **Recipes (Detailed)**:
  - **Ingredients**:
    - 6 kg of malted barley or wheat
    - Fresh water from wells or streams
    - Herbs such as mugwort, yarrow, and bay leaves

        - Optional: Honey or dried fruits for flavour

    - **Method**:

        1. **Malting**: Spread grains thinly in drying areas or kilns, turning frequently to avoid mould.
        2. **Crushing**: Use stone or wooden tools to coarsely crush malted grains.
        3. **Mashing**: Combine malt with water (55-65°C) in clay pots or wooden vessels. Stir thoroughly for 1-2 hours.
        4. **Boiling**: Boil the wort for 30-60 minutes, adding herbs during the last 15 minutes.
        5. **Fermentation**: Transfer the wort to wooden troughs or barrels. Ferment for 5-6 days in a cool area.
        6. **Storage**: Store the finished beer in barrels or clay jars for up to 2 weeks.

- **SPV (Strength, Preservation, and Variability)**:
    - **Strength**: Maintained at around 4-5% alcohol.
    - **Preservation**: Moderately effective, though some beers spoil without proper storage.
    - **Variability**: Increases slightly in rural areas due to less consistent equipment and methods.
- **Social Aspect**: Beer remains a crucial part of daily life for hydration and nutrition, especially as Roman influence wanes. Villagers gather for local feasts, where beer serves as a communal beverage. While urban brewing declines, rural households adapt to sustain traditional beer-making practices, fostering local community bonds.

Cadan the Brewer: The Man Who Tried to Brew "Eternal Ale"

Setting the Scene

In 250 AD, Roman Britain was at its peak. Roads crisscrossed the land, villas dotted the countryside, and the legions kept the peace. But deep in the western hills of Britannia, life remained delightfully chaotic. In a small village near modern-day Wales, Cadan the Brewer was renowned for his eccentric ales and even more eccentric ideas.

Cadan wasn't just a brewer, he fancied himself a philosopher and inventor. "Why settle for ordinary ale," he often mused, "when you can brew something extraordinary? Something... eternal?"

His friends, used to his wild schemes, usually just nodded and let him get on with it.

The Quest for Eternal Ale

One day, inspired by tales of Roman gods and Celtic legends, Cadan decided to brew a beer that would grant the drinker eternal vitality. "If the Romans can have their fancy wine and their immortal emperors," he declared, "we Britons deserve an ale that defies time itself!"

He set out to create what he called *Cerevisia Aeternum,* Eternal Ale. To achieve his ambitious goal, he gathered ingredients he believed would capture the essence of immortality:

- Barley grown in the shadow of ancient standing stones.
- Honey from hives said to be blessed by druids.
- Herbs from the sacred grove, collected under a full moon.
- And water from a Roman aqueduct (because, as Cadan said, "Even the Romans know a thing or two about engineering.")

The Brewing Process

Cadan's brewing process was as elaborate as his vision. He chanted Celtic blessings while stirring the mash, burned rosemary to "purify the brew," and insisted the fermentation vessel be placed at the highest point in the village to "absorb the power of the heavens."

When curious villagers asked what he was doing, Cadan replied, "I'm creating the drink of the ages! It'll make you feel as strong as a Roman, as wise as a druid, and as happy as a farmer with a bumper harvest."

The Grand Unveiling

Weeks later, Cadan unveiled his *Cerevisia Aeternum* at the village festival. The ale was a deep golden colour, with a fragrant aroma that hinted at honey and herbs. Villagers gathered around as he poured the first mugs.

"To eternity!" Cadan toasted, raising his own mug high.

The first sips were met with mixed reactions.

"It's... very herbal," one villager said, grimacing slightly.
"Tastes like a meadow," another muttered.
But the Romans stationed nearby, intrigued by the spectacle, declared it "exotic" and ordered a full amphora to be sent to their fort.

The Unexpected Side Effects

As the festival continued, strange things began to happen. The villagers, convinced by Cadan's claims of vitality, started racing each other around the field. One elderly farmer, after his third mug, declared he could lift a boulder and almost succeeded, until the boulder rolled onto his foot.

The Romans, meanwhile, began debating whether the ale truly granted eternal life or just made you feel like it did. One legionary, after downing an entire goblet, attempted to wrestle a sheep, claiming, "I am invincible!" (The sheep won.)

As the night wore on, the "eternal" energy wore off, leaving everyone with sore heads and tales of exaggerated heroics.

The Aftermath

The next morning, as villagers nursed their hangovers, Cadan was unrepentant. "Perhaps eternity is a bit more... intense than we expected," he said, stroking his chin. "But you can't deny it worked, for a while!"

Though *Cerevisia Aeternum* didn't make anyone immortal, it became a village favourite for festivals and celebrations. The Romans continued to order it, dubbing it *"Ale of the Gods"* (though they kept a bucket of water nearby for first-time drinkers).

As for Cadan, he became a local legend, known as the brewer who dreamed big and brewed even bigger.

STEM Lesson

Cadan's story is a playful example of the importance of experimentation and bold ideas. While his brew didn't achieve immortality, it brought joy, laughter, and a sense of community, valuable outcomes in their own right.

The lesson? Science, like brewing, is as much about the journey as the result. Even if your big idea doesn't work as planned, it might lead to something equally remarkable, or at least unforgettable.

300 AD - 350 AD: Transitioning Brewing Practices

- **Techniques**: Brewing techniques begin to blend Roman methods with local innovations as Roman influence continues to wane. Boiling remains a crucial step, but fermentation becomes more varied due to the increased use of wild yeasts. Kiln-dried malts continue to improve consistency in brewing.
- **Where Brewing Was Done**: Brewing is primarily carried out in rural households and small settlements. Larger estate breweries still operate but are fewer in number. Communal brewing spaces begin to emerge in some villages, fostering shared resources and knowledge.
- **How It Would Have Looked**: Brewing areas in rural homes are simple yet effective. Clay pots and wooden troughs are placed near hearths, while drying racks or kilns for malted grains are positioned in outdoor or semi-covered areas. Communal brewing spaces feature larger cauldrons and fermentation vessels for shared use, reflecting a cooperative approach.
- **Involvement of Villagers**: Brewing becomes increasingly collaborative. Women oversee household brewing, while men often participate in communal brewing efforts. Village gatherings for brewing sessions also serve as social events, strengthening community ties. Knowledge of brewing techniques is passed down orally.
- **Equipment Used**:
    1. **Clay and Wooden Vessels**: For mashing, fermenting, and boiling.
    2. **Stone or Brick Kilns**: Used for drying malted grains.
    3. **Wooden Sieves**: Employed to strain wort and remove husks.
    4. **Barrels and Amphorae**: For fermentation and short-term storage.
- **Recipes (Detailed)**:
    - **Ingredients**:
        - 5 kg of malted barley or mixed grains
        - Fresh water from wells or streams

        - Herbs such as mugwort, heather, and bay leaves
        - Optional: Honey or dried berries for additional flavour
    - **Method**:
        1. **Malting**: Dry grains in kilns or open-air drying racks, turning frequently for uniform drying.
        2. **Crushing**: Use wooden or stone tools to crush the malt coarsely.
        3. **Mashing**: Combine malt with warm water (50-60°C) in clay or wooden vessels. Stir and let steep for 1-2 hours.
        4. **Boiling**: Heat the wort in clay pots or cauldrons for 45-60 minutes. Add herbs during the last 15 minutes of boiling.
        5. **Fermentation**: Pour the wort into barrels or amphorae and cover loosely. Allow to ferment for 4-6 days.
        6. **Storage**: Store the beer in cool, shaded areas. Consume within 2-3 weeks.
- **SPV (Strength, Preservation, and Variability)**:
    - **Strength**: Consistently around 4-5% alcohol.
    - **Preservation**: Slightly improved with better barrel storage but still limited.
    - **Variability**: Moderate, influenced by the use of wild yeasts and local herbs.
- **Social Aspect**: Brewing is deeply ingrained in daily life, serving as both sustenance and a social activity. Communal brewing sessions create opportunities for storytelling, music, and the exchange of techniques. Beer is a central feature of village gatherings, celebrations, and rituals, continuing its role as a unifying element in communities.

Lugus the Brewer: The Man Who Invented "Fort Ale"

Setting the Scene

By 300 AD, Roman Britain was a patchwork of bustling towns, imposing forts, and resilient Celtic traditions. In a small village near Hadrian's Wall, Lugus the Brewer was renowned for his creativity, his booming laugh, and his questionable decisions.

Lugus prided himself on his ability to brew ale for any occasion, but his latest challenge came from an unlikely source: the Roman garrison stationed nearby.

The Roman Demand

One evening, a group of legionaries stomped into Lugus' tavern after a long patrol along the wall. "Your ale is fine," said the centurion, "but we need something stronger. Something that can warm us on the coldest nights and put hair on the smoothest Roman chest!"

Lugus, never one to back down from a challenge, grinned. "Stronger, eh? You lot want an ale that can stand up to the northern winds? Give me a week, and I'll brew you something that'll make you forget you're stationed in Britannia!"

The Romans laughed. "We'll see, Briton. But if it's weak, we're taking our coin to the wine merchant."

The Creation of "Fort Ale"

Determined to impress, Lugus set to work. He decided his ale needed to be not only strong but also bold enough to reflect the ruggedness of the Roman soldiers and the wild beauty of Britannia. His recipe included:

- Double-malted barley for an extra kick.
- Heather honey to remind the Romans of Britannia's natural bounty.
- A handful of dried nettles, because "a little bite never hurt anyone."
- And a touch of fermented juniper berries for a sharp, woodsy finish.

To infuse it with strength and character, Lugus fermented the ale in a barrel he had fortified with iron bands salvaged from an old Roman cart. "If the barrel can handle the weight of Roman stone," he reasoned, "it can handle my brew!"

The Grand Reveal

On the promised day, Lugus proudly unveiled his creation: *Fort Ale*. The Roman soldiers crowded into the tavern, eager to try the brew that Lugus claimed could "fortify both body and spirit."

The first mugs were poured, and the soldiers raised them high. "To Lugus and his Fort Ale!"

The initial reactions were promising. "It's rich!" one soldier exclaimed.
"Strong as Mars himself!" said another, thumping his chest.
But as they drank more, the ale's true character revealed itself. The nettles added a surprising heat, the juniper made it unusually sharp, and the extra malt made it deceptively potent. Before long, the soldiers began to feel invincible, or at least, very bold.

The Chaos

Fueled by the ale, one legionary decided to challenge a Celtic warrior to a wrestling match. The warrior, equally emboldened by the brew, accepted. The resulting tussle overturned tables, sent mugs flying, and became the highlight of the night.
Meanwhile, the centurion, clearly impressed, declared, "This ale is a weapon of morale! We must requisition it for the entire fort!"
Lugus, delighted, toasted the centurion, only to realize moments later that the soldiers were now chanting, "To the wall!" They stormed out of the tavern and climbed onto Hadrian's Wall, waving their mugs and shouting, "The Picts won't dare cross tonight!"

The Aftermath

The next morning, the fort commander was less amused. The soldiers, nursing monumental hangovers, were ordered to scrub every inch of the wall as punishment. Lugus, however, was hailed as a hero among the legionaries.
Fort Ale became the drink of choice for the garrison, and Lugus' fame spread throughout the northern frontier. The Romans even offered him a small stipend to keep the soldiers supplied, on the condition that they only drink it *after* patrol duty.

The Legacy

Lugus' *Fort Ale* became a legend, remembered as the brew that could bring Romans and Britons together, if only for a night of chaos.

STEM Lesson

Lugus' story highlights the value of experimentation and creativity in solving problems. His ability to adapt traditional brewing techniques to meet the demands of his Roman customers is a testament to ingenuity and resourcefulness.
The lesson? Don't shy away from challenges or bold ideas. Sometimes, the best results come from taking risks, though it's wise to test your creations before letting a Roman legion drink it all at once!

350 AD - 400 AD: Brewing in a Time of Change

- **Techniques**: Brewing continues to adapt as Roman Britain approaches its end. Techniques such as boiling and malting remain central, but local innovation increasingly replaces Roman methods. The use of wild yeasts and regional herbs for flavouring becomes more pronounced.
- **Where Brewing Was Done**: Brewing occurs mainly in rural households, small villages, and communal spaces. Roman-style villas with dedicated brewing areas become rare, while localised brewing practices in homes and shared village facilities flourish.
- **How It Would Have Looked**: Brewing setups are simple, with clay pots, wooden barrels, and troughs arranged near hearths or in outdoor areas. Communal brewing spaces include larger cauldrons and shared storage vessels. The atmosphere is one of practicality and cooperation, reflecting the shift toward local traditions.
- **Involvement of Villagers**: Brewing is an essential community activity. Women manage household brewing, while men often assist in larger-scale communal efforts. Villagers collaborate during harvests to gather grains and herbs, ensuring a steady supply of ingredients for brewing.
- **Equipment Used**:
    1. **Clay Pots and Wooden Vessels**: For boiling and fermenting wort.
    2. **Kilns and Drying Racks**: For malting barley and other grains.
    3. **Wooden Sieves**: To strain the wort before fermentation.
    4. **Barrels and Amphorae**: Used for fermentation and short-term storage.
- **Recipes (Detailed)**:
    - **Ingredients**:
        - 6 kg of malted barley or mixed grains
        - Fresh water from wells or rivers
        - Regional herbs such as mugwort, heather, and meadowsweet
        - Optional: Honey or dried apples for sweetness

- **Method**:

    1. **Malting**: Spread grains thinly on drying racks or in kilns. Turn regularly until fully dried.

    2. **Crushing**: Use wooden tools or stones to crush the malt coarsely.

    3. **Mashing**: Combine crushed malt with warm water (50-60°C) in clay pots or wooden troughs. Stir thoroughly and let steep for 1-2 hours.

    4. **Boiling**: Heat the wort in clay or metal cauldrons for 45 minutes to 1 hour, adding herbs during the final 20 minutes.

    5. **Fermentation**: Pour the cooled wort into barrels or amphorae. Cover loosely and ferment for 4-6 days.

    6. **Storage**: Store in barrels or clay jars in cool spaces. Consume within 2-3 weeks for optimal freshness.

- **SPV (Strength, Preservation, and Variability)**:

    - **Strength**: Remains steady at 4-5% alcohol by volume.

    - **Preservation**: Limited by the absence of advanced storage methods; beer must be consumed quickly.

    - **Variability**: High, influenced by local ingredients and brewing conditions.

- **Social Aspect**: Brewing plays a vital role in community life. Beer serves as both sustenance and a social lubricant during gatherings and celebrations. Communal brewing days bring villagers together, fostering collaboration and the sharing of knowledge. As Roman influence fades, brewing becomes a symbol of local resilience and tradition.

Eofric the Brewer: The Man Who Brewed "Barbarian Ale"

Setting the Scene

By 350 AD, Roman Britain was a strange mix of Roman luxury and the rugged traditions of its native people. In the bustling market town of Corinium (modern-day Cirencester), a brewer named Eofric was known for his ability to turn almost anything into ale. "If it grows or ferments," he would say, "it belongs in a barrel!"

Eofric's ales were famous across the region, but he dreamed of something more. "The Romans think their wine is so refined," he muttered one day, "but I'll brew an ale so bold it'll make even the fiercest barbarian weep with joy!"

The Barbarian Threat

One day, word came that a group of Pictish traders, wild-looking men with blue-painted faces and fiery tempers, were visiting the town. The townsfolk were wary. "What if they cause trouble?" whispered one merchant.

Eofric, however, saw an opportunity. "Trouble? Nonsense!" he declared. "I'll brew an ale so mighty it'll turn those barbarians into friends!"

The townsfolk laughed nervously, but Eofric got to work.

The Creation of "Barbarian Ale"

Determined to impress (and perhaps outdrink) the Picts, Eofric decided his ale needed to be as wild and untamed as the traders themselves. He gathered:

- Barley malt, because even barbarians appreciate a good foundation.
- Smoked peat from the nearby marshes, for a flavour as rugged as the northern hills.
- A pinch of bog myrtle, because it sounded exotic.
- And a generous helping of wild honey, to "sweeten the savagery."

Eofric brewed the ale in a giant clay pot decorated with Roman and Celtic motifs, calling it *Cervisia Ferox*, Barbarian Ale. To add an extra flair, he painted his face blue before the unveiling. "If they're going to drink like Picts," he reasoned, "I might as well look the part."

The Encounter

When the Pictish traders arrived, they were greeted by Eofric, who offered them mugs of *Barbarian Ale*. The traders eyed the drink suspiciously, but after a bit of persuasion (and some exaggerated toasts), they took their first sips.

Their reaction was immediate. "Strong!" one bellowed, pounding the table. "It's like drinking fire!" Another wiped tears from his eyes and declared, "This is no Roman wine, it's a drink for warriors!"

Eofric beamed with pride. The townsfolk, emboldened by the traders' enthusiasm, began drinking as well.

The Chaos

As the night wore on, the ale lived up to its name. The Picts and townsfolk, now thoroughly drunk, decided to prove their strength by engaging in a series of increasingly ridiculous challenges:

- A contest to see who could drink the fastest (won by a Pict, though he promptly fell asleep in the barrel).
- A wrestling match between a Roman legionary and a Pict, which ended when both tripped over a chicken.
- And a collaborative attempt to build a "better Hadrian's Wall" out of empty barrels, which collapsed almost immediately.

Eofric, watching the chaos unfold, declared it a resounding success. "If ale can bring Romans, Britons, and Picts together," he said, "then it truly is the drink of the gods!"

The Aftermath

The next morning, the town square was littered with empty mugs, toppled barrels, and one very confused goat (no one could remember where it came from). The Picts, nursing their hangovers, thanked Eofric for his hospitality and declared him an honorary barbarian.

Eofric's *Barbarian Ale* became a local legend, celebrated for its ability to unite even the most unlikely of drinking companions. Traders from across the region began visiting Corinium just to try it, though Eofric wisely advised, "Only drink it if you've nothing important to do the next day."

STEM Lesson

Eofric's story highlights the importance of adaptability and innovation in science and craft. By understanding his audience and experimenting with local ingredients, he created something that transcended cultural boundaries, if only for one wild night.

The lesson? Creativity and boldness can bridge divides, spark laughter, and bring people together. Just be prepared for the occasional goat-related mystery.

400 AD - 450 AD: Brewing in Post-Roman Britain

- **Techniques**: With the Roman Empire's withdrawal from Britain, brewing techniques rely heavily on local traditions. Boiling, malting, and fermentation continue to be central, but the absence of Roman infrastructure leads to a resurgence of simpler, regionally varied methods. Herbal flavouring grows in prominence.

- **Where Brewing Was Done**: Brewing predominantly takes place in rural homes and small villages. Communal brewing spaces are more common in regions with strong community ties. Wealthier households may have slightly more advanced setups, but these are exceptions rather than the norm.

- **How It Would Have Looked**: Brewing scenes are practical and rustic. Hearths serve as the main brewing areas, with clay pots and wooden barrels arranged nearby. Outdoor drying racks for malting grains are a common sight, as are large communal cauldrons in village spaces. Brewing areas are often shared by multiple families in smaller settlements.

- **Involvement of Villagers**: Brewing is a collective effort, with women overseeing household brewing and men assisting during larger-scale community projects. Villagers collaborate to gather grains and herbs, often foraging for wild flavourings. Brewing knowledge is passed down orally and adapted to suit local conditions.

- **Equipment Used**:

    1. **Clay and Wooden Vessels**: For mashing, boiling, and fermenting.

    2. **Drying Racks and Simple Kilns**: Used for malting grains.

    3. **Wooden Sieves**: To strain the wort before fermentation.

    4. **Barrels and Jars**: For short-term storage and transportation.

- **Recipes (Detailed)**:

    - **Ingredients**:

        - 5 kg of malted barley, oats, or wheat

        - Fresh water from streams or wells

        - Herbs such as yarrow, mugwort, and heather
        - Optional: Honey or wild berries for sweetness
    - **Method**:
        1. **Malting**: Spread grains on racks or in simple kilns to dry. Turn frequently for even drying.
        2. **Crushing**: Use stones or wooden mallets to crush malted grains coarsely.
        3. **Mashing**: Mix crushed malt with warm water (50-60°C) in clay or wooden containers. Stir and let sit for 1-2 hours.
        4. **Boiling**: Heat the wort in large cauldrons for 45 minutes to 1 hour. Add herbs during the last 20 minutes.
        5. **Fermentation**: Pour the wort into barrels or jars. Cover loosely and allow to ferment for 4-7 days.
        6. **Storage**: Store the finished beer in cool, shaded areas. Consume within 2 weeks.

- **SPV (Strength, Preservation, and Variability)**:
    - **Strength**: Consistently around 4-5% alcohol.
    - **Preservation**: Limited by the absence of advanced storage; beer must be consumed quickly.
    - **Variability**: High, reflecting local ingredients and varying brewing practices.
- **Social Aspect**: Beer remains an essential part of daily life, providing nutrition and a safe alternative to drinking water. Communal brewing sessions strengthen social bonds and ensure a reliable supply for celebrations and rituals. As Britain adjusts to the post-Roman era, brewing becomes a vital link to community identity and resilience.

Osric the Brewer: The Man Who Tried to Brew "The Last Roman Ale"

Setting the Scene

By 400 AD, Roman Britain was on the brink of change. The Roman Empire was pulling its legions back to the mainland, and the Britons were left to fend for themselves. In a small village near Londinium, a brewer named Osric found himself grappling with a brewing crisis.

Osric, a man of great enthusiasm but questionable foresight, had built his reputation on crafting ales inspired by Roman luxury. "If the Romans leave," he lamented, "who will drink my Imperial Nectar Ale? Who will appreciate my amphora-shaped mugs? We can't let civilization fall into chaos, or worse, wine!"

Determined to preserve what he saw as the last bastion of Roman culture, Osric announced, "I shall brew the greatest ale in history, a drink so magnificent, it will make the Romans *stay*!"

The Brew to Save Britannia

Osric set out to create his masterpiece, which he called *Cerevisia Ultima Romana*, The Last Roman Ale. He wanted the brew to reflect both the strength of the Roman legions and the wild spirit of Britannia. His ingredients included:

- Barley malt soaked in mead, for sweetness and strength.
- A handful of crushed fennel seeds, which he believed were "very Roman."
- Wild heather flowers, to give it a "touch of the British soul."
- And a splash of seawater for "the taste of conquest."

Osric brewed the ale in a massive clay amphora, which he decorated with carvings of Roman gods, Celtic knots, and, inexplicably, a chicken (because, as he said, "everyone loves chickens").

The Roman Farewell Banquet

When word spread that the local Roman garrison was holding a farewell feast, Osric seized the opportunity. He arrived at the banquet carrying his enormous amphora of *Cerevisia Ultima Romana*, wearing a laurel wreath for added effect.

"Friends!" he proclaimed, "Before you depart for Rome, taste this ale, a drink so powerful, so inspiring, you'll forget why you wanted to leave!"

The soldiers, bemused but intrigued, agreed to try it.

The First Sips

The first mugs were poured, and the soldiers raised them high. "To Britannia!" they toasted.

The initial sips were met with murmurs of approval. "Sweet, yet bold," one centurion said.
"It's got a kick," another added, wincing slightly at the fennel.

But then, the seawater made itself known. "What is that... brininess?" a soldier asked, looking puzzled.
"It's the taste of Rome's naval power!" Osric exclaimed, though his confidence wavered as he noticed a few soldiers discreetly pouring their mugs into a nearby potted plant.

The Chaos

Despite its odd flavor, the ale quickly took effect. One legionary declared he could feel the strength of Mars coursing through him and began arm-wrestling anyone within reach. Another, inspired by the heather, started reciting improvised poetry about Britannia's rolling hills.

The real trouble began when the amphora's carvings were misinterpreted. A slightly inebriated centurion pointed to the chicken and exclaimed, "Osric has foretold an omen! The Chicken of Britannia will rise and reclaim the empire!" This sparked a heated (and entirely nonsensical) debate about whether the chicken symbolized courage or breakfast.

Meanwhile, Osric beamed, oblivious to the chaos. "They love it!" he said to himself, pouring another round.

The Aftermath

By the end of the night, the banquet hall was a mess of spilled ale, overturned chairs, and one very confused rooster (no one could explain where it had come from). The Romans, thoroughly entertained, decided they wouldn't forget Britannia, or Osric's ale, anytime soon.

The next morning, as the soldiers prepared to leave, the centurion approached Osric. "Your ale was... unforgettable," he said diplomatically. "We'll tell tales of it in Rome."

Osric took this as the highest praise. Though the Romans still departed, *Cerevisia Ultima Romana* became a local legend, known as the ale that could "make a Roman laugh, cry, and wrestle a table, all in one night."

The Legacy

Osric's brewery flourished long after the Romans left, and his amphora, complete with its mysterious chicken carving, was displayed proudly in the village square.

STEM Lesson

Osric's story reminds us of the importance of experimentation and the value of learning from unexpected results. While his ale didn't save the Roman occupation, it brought joy, laughter, and unity to a community facing change.

The lesson? Bold ideas can lead to memorable outcomes, even if they don't go as planned. And always double-check your ingredient list, because a little seawater goes a long way.

450 AD - 500 AD: Brewing in Early Anglo-Saxon Britain

- **Techniques**: Brewing evolves as Anglo-Saxon culture integrates with existing traditions. Malting, mashing, and fermenting remain fundamental, but brewing becomes more diverse, influenced by regional ingredients and methods. Wild yeasts are predominantly used, and herbal additives continue to flavour beer.

- **Where Brewing Was Done**: Brewing is centred in rural households, with village-level brewing spaces becoming more established in some areas. Halls of local leaders (or "chiefs") often have dedicated brewing facilities to provide ale for feasts and gatherings.

- **How It Would Have Looked**: Brewing takes place in simple settings, either inside homes or in outdoor communal areas. Wooden barrels and clay pots are common, while drying racks for malted grains are visible near hearths or in shared village spaces. In wealthier households, larger cauldrons and more sophisticated storage vessels are used.

- **Involvement of Villagers**: Brewing is a shared responsibility, with women managing domestic brewing and men assisting with grain processing and communal projects. Local leaders ensure an ample supply of ale for their halls, often enlisting villagers to assist with large-scale production.

- **Equipment Used**:

    1. **Clay Pots and Wooden Troughs**: For boiling and fermenting.
    2. **Drying Racks and Simple Kilns**: For preparing malted grains.
    3. **Wooden Sieves**: To strain the wort before fermentation.
    4. **Barrels and Jars**: For storage and transport.

- **Recipes (Detailed)**:

    - **Ingredients**:

        - 6 kg of malted barley, rye, or wheat
        - Fresh water from wells or streams
        - Herbs such as mugwort, heather, and bog myrtle
        - Optional: Honey or fruit for sweetness

- **Method**:

    1. **Malting**: Spread grains on drying racks or simple kilns, turning frequently to avoid mould.
    2. **Crushing**: Use wooden or stone tools to crush malted grains into a coarse consistency.
    3. **Mashing**: Combine crushed malt with warm water (50-60°C) in clay or wooden vessels. Stir thoroughly and let steep for 1-2 hours.
    4. **Boiling**: Boil the wort in large cauldrons for 45 minutes to 1 hour, adding herbs during the final 15-20 minutes.
    5. **Fermentation**: Pour the cooled wort into barrels or clay jars. Cover loosely and ferment for 4-6 days in a cool area.
    6. **Storage**: Store the ale in barrels or jars, consuming within 2-3 weeks.

- **SPV (Strength, Preservation, and Variability)**:
    - **Strength**: Maintained around 4-5% alcohol.
    - **Preservation**: Limited; ale must be consumed quickly due to lack of advanced storage.
    - **Variability**: High, reflecting differences in local ingredients and brewing methods.
- **Social Aspect**: Beer is a central feature of Anglo-Saxon feasts and daily life. Chiefs and leaders host communal gatherings where ale flows freely, reinforcing social hierarchies and bonds. Household brewing ensures that families have a reliable source of sustenance, while communal brewing efforts strengthen village cohesion and shared traditions.

Wulfstan the Brewer: The Ale That Scared the Saxons

Setting the Scene

By 450 AD, Roman Britain was a distant memory, and the land was in turmoil. The Saxons, Angles, and Jutes were arriving in waves, and the Britons were struggling to defend their homes. In a small village in the hills of what is now Wales, Wulfstan the Brewer decided he had a role to play in defending his people, not with swords or spears, but with his wits and his beer.

Wulfstan was known for his bold experiments in brewing. "Why fight when you can drink?" he often said, though most villagers thought his ales were strong enough to double as weapons.

The Saxon Threat

One fateful day, news reached the village that a Saxon raiding party was nearby. The villagers panicked, but Wulfstan had an idea. "If we can't outfight them," he declared, "we'll outbrew them!"

The villagers stared at him, confused. "You want to fight the Saxons with beer?" asked the blacksmith.

"Not just beer," Wulfstan replied with a grin. "I'll brew an ale so terrifying, they'll think it's cursed!"

The Brewing of "Wulfstan's Wyrm-Ale"

Wulfstan gathered the strangest and strongest ingredients he could find to create a brew he called *Wyrm-Ale* (Dragon Ale):

- Barley roasted until it was as dark as a stormy sky.
- Wild honey mixed with nettles, for an otherworldly kick.
- Fermented yew berries, which the local druid assured him were "mystical" (but also a little dangerous).
- And a handful of wild mushrooms, because Wulfstan liked the idea of "adding a little madness."

The ale was brewed in an enormous cauldron over a roaring fire, with Wulfstan chanting nonsense that sounded vaguely magical. As it boiled, the brew emitted an ominous, greenish steam that even the bravest villagers refused to approach.

The Plan

Wulfstan's plan was simple: when the Saxons arrived, he would offer them his *Wyrm-Ale* as a gesture of peace. "They'll drink it, they'll see the 'magic,' and they'll run screaming back to their ships," he explained.

The villagers weren't entirely convinced. "What if they like it?" someone asked.

"They won't," Wulfstan replied confidently.

The Saxon Arrival

When the Saxons reached the village, Wulfstan stepped forward with his cauldron of *Wyrm-Ale,* flanked by villagers holding torches for dramatic effect.

"Welcome, mighty warriors!" he called. "Before you raid, let us offer you a drink of our finest ale!"

The Saxons, taken aback by the odd greeting, hesitated. "What's the catch?" their leader demanded.

"No catch," Wulfstan said, pouring a mug. "Just a little taste of Britannia."

The leader took the mug and sniffed it. The dark, foamy liquid hissed slightly, thanks to the mushrooms. He grimaced but, not wanting to seem cowardly, took a big gulp.

The Reactions

The first sip hit the Saxon leader like a thunderclap. "What is this sorcery?!" he bellowed, clutching his throat. His warriors, curious but cautious, tried it too. The nettles stung, the mushrooms swirled their senses, and the yew berries left a bitter, biting aftertaste.

One Saxon began laughing uncontrollably. Another claimed he saw a dragon in the clouds. The leader, eyes wide, shouted, "They've cursed us with their devil's brew!"

The raiders dropped their weapons and ran for their ships, tripping over each other in their haste. The villagers watched in stunned silence as the invaders fled, leaving behind their loot and their dignity.

The Aftermath

Wulfstan became a hero overnight. The villagers celebrated with what was left of the *Wyrm-Ale,* though most decided one mug was more than enough. The cauldron was placed in the village square as a symbol of their victory, and Wulfstan proudly declared, "Who needs swords when you have ale?"

Over time, *Wulfstan's Wyrm-Ale* became a legend, known as the brew that scared away the Saxons. Though no one dared to recreate the recipe, it was said that just a whiff of its fumes could keep invaders at bay.

STEM Lesson

Wulfstan's story is a reminder of the power of creativity and unconventional thinking in problem-solving. While his methods were unorthodox, they demonstrated how a bold idea can turn the tide in a challenging situation.

The lesson? Sometimes the best solutions are the ones no one expects, just make sure you know what's in your brew before you drink it yourself!

500 AD - 550 AD: Brewing in Early Medieval Britain

- **Techniques**: Brewing techniques become more defined during the early medieval period. Malting, mashing, and fermenting are firmly established, but the variability of wild yeast and regional herbs still creates diverse outcomes. Local ingredients dominate brewing, and boiling is consistently used to stabilise the wort.
- **Where Brewing Was Done**: Brewing remains a household and communal activity. Most brewing occurs in small rural homes, but larger village halls and manorial estates also produce ale for feasts and communal consumption. Brewing spaces are often outdoors or in designated sections of homes.
- **How It Would Have Looked**: Rural homes have simple brewing setups with clay pots and wooden barrels near hearths. Outdoor spaces are used for drying and malting grains, with simple kilns or racks visible in larger settlements. Communal brewing setups in village halls include larger cauldrons and fermentation vessels to produce ale in bulk for gatherings.
- **Involvement of Villagers**: Brewing remains a collaborative effort. Women are the primary brewers, managing household production, while men assist in larger-scale village or estate brewing. Villagers contribute grains, honey, and foraged herbs, fostering a sense of shared responsibility.
- **Equipment Used**:
    1. **Clay and Wooden Vessels**: Used for mashing, boiling, and fermenting.
    2. **Simple Kilns or Drying Racks**: For malting grains.
    3. **Wooden Sieves**: To strain wort before fermentation.
    4. **Barrels and Amphorae**: For fermentation and storage.
- **Recipes (Detailed)**:
    - **Ingredients**:
        - 6 kg of malted barley, oats, or wheat
        - Fresh water from wells or streams

        - Herbs such as yarrow, mugwort, and meadowsweet
        - Optional: Honey or dried fruits for flavour

    - **Method**:

        1. **Malting**: Dry grains on racks or in simple kilns for 2-3 days, turning frequently.
        2. **Crushing**: Coarsely crush malted grains using wooden mallets or stones.
        3. **Mashing**: Combine crushed malt with warm water (50-60°C) in clay pots or wooden troughs. Stir and let steep for 1-2 hours.
        4. **Boiling**: Boil the wort in cauldrons for 45-60 minutes. Add herbs during the last 15-20 minutes.
        5. **Fermentation**: Pour the wort into barrels or amphorae. Cover loosely and allow to ferment for 4-6 days.
        6. **Storage**: Store the ale in cool, shaded areas. Consume within 2-3 weeks.

- **SPV (Strength, Preservation, and Variability)**:
    - **Strength**: Alcohol content stabilises around 4-5%.
    - **Preservation**: Moderate, as boiling and fermentation improve longevity slightly.
    - **Variability**: High, due to wild yeast and regional ingredient differences.

- **Social Aspect**: Ale remains essential to daily life and communal gatherings. Village feasts and celebrations are centred around freshly brewed beer, reinforcing community bonds. In manorial estates, ale serves as a staple for workers and a key element of hospitality for guests. Brewing knowledge is passed through generations, solidifying its role as a cultural cornerstone.

Cedric the Brewer: The Man Who Brewed "Kingmaker Ale"

Setting the Scene

By 500 AD, Britain was a patchwork of warring kingdoms, each vying for control of the land. Saxons, Britons, and other tribes clashed regularly, but amidst the chaos, life went on. In a small village near the kingdom of Powys, Cedric the Brewer was known for his uncanny ability to create ales that could settle disputes, or start them, depending on how much people drank.

Cedric had a dream: to brew an ale so extraordinary that it would unite the warring kings, or at least get them too drunk to fight.

The King's Council

One day, Cedric heard that several kings from neighboring regions were gathering for a rare council meeting to discuss a truce. The idea of so many rulers in one place gave Cedric a bold idea. "If I can brew an ale worthy of kings, they'll name me their royal brewer! I'll go down in history!"

Ignoring the skeptical looks of his neighbors, Cedric set to work.

The Brew to Rule Them All

Cedric decided his ale needed to reflect the grandeur of kingship. His recipe included:

- Barley malt soaked in the water of a sacred spring, rumored to grant wisdom.

- Heather honey, to symbolize peace and sweetness.

- A splash of mead, because he believed a little alcohol in the alcohol never hurt.

- And a dash of ground acorns for "earthy strength", though Cedric wasn't entirely sure what that would do.

He brewed the ale in a massive oak barrel decorated with carvings of crowns, swords, and (for no particular reason) a smiling sheep. "This is it!" Cedric proclaimed. "The ale to end all battles!"

The Presentation

On the day of the council, Cedric arrived at the kings' gathering with his barrel of what he dubbed *Kingmaker Ale*. He approached the tent nervously, dragging the barrel behind him on a wobbly cart.

"Great kings!" he called. "Before you make your decisions, I offer you this ale, brewed with wisdom, peace, and strength. Drink it, and may it inspire a lasting truce!"

The kings, curious and slightly bored from hours of arguing, agreed to try it.

The Reactions

The first sips were met with thoughtful silence.

"This is... unusual," said one king, stroking his beard.

"I taste honey," said another, nodding approvingly.

"And... what is this bitterness?" asked a third.

"Acorns," Cedric replied proudly. "For strength!"

The kings exchanged glances, unsure whether to be impressed or concerned. But as they drank more, the ale's strength became apparent. Soon, they were laughing, toasting, and calling each other "brother." Cedric beamed. "My ale is working!" he whispered.

The Chaos

The merriment escalated quickly. One king decided to declare himself the "Ale King" and tried to wear the barrel as a crown. Another began composing a song about the glory of acorns, though he forgot the words halfway through.

The real trouble began when two kings, emboldened by the ale, declared a contest to see who could drink the most. The resulting spectacle involved overturned mugs, roaring cheers, and one unfortunate squire who was soaked in ale when the barrel tipped over.

As the night wore on, the kings abandoned their council entirely and started a wrestling match to decide who would get the last mug.

The Aftermath

The next morning, the kings woke up with sore heads and no memory of what they'd agreed upon, if anything. However, they all agreed on one thing: Cedric's *Kingmaker Ale* was unforgettable.

"Perhaps," one king said, rubbing his temples, "we should meet like this more often."

Another nodded. "But with less wrestling."

Cedric returned to his village a hero. Though the kings didn't name him royal brewer, they did order barrels of *Kingmaker Ale* for future gatherings. Cedric proudly declared himself "Brewer to the Bickering Kings" and carved a small crown into the next barrel for good measure.

The Legacy

Kingmaker Ale became a local legend, known as the brew that could turn arguments into laughter (and occasionally into wrestling matches). Cedric's barrel, complete with its smiling sheep carving, was kept in the village square as a reminder that even the smallest brewer can influence great events, albeit in unexpected ways.

STEM Lesson

Cedric's story is a lighthearted reminder of the power of experimentation and the unexpected ways science and creativity can bring people together. His ale didn't solve every problem, but it fostered camaraderie and left a lasting impression.

The lesson? Science and creativity often serve as bridges between people, even in the most divided times. And while your ideas might not always go as planned, they can still make a memorable impact.

550 AD - 600 AD: Brewing in the Late Early Medieval Period

- **Techniques**: Brewing techniques during this period evolve slightly, with more attention paid to consistent malting and fermentation. Local ingredients still dominate, and the use of herbal flavourings like mugwort and meadowsweet remains prevalent. Brewing remains a hands-on, practical process.

- **Where Brewing Was Done**: Brewing is primarily conducted in rural households and small villages. Communal brewing spaces in villages and manorial estates continue to play a significant role in producing larger quantities of ale for gatherings and feasts.

- **How It Would Have Looked**: Rural brewing setups include clay pots and wooden barrels positioned near hearths. Outdoor areas are used for drying and malting grains, with simple kilns or sun-drying methods common. Communal brewing sites have larger cauldrons and fermentation vessels to produce ale in bulk, fostering a cooperative environment.

- **Involvement of Villagers**: Brewing is a collaborative effort involving both men and women. Women manage household brewing, ensuring a steady supply of ale for daily consumption. Men assist with grain preparation and larger brewing projects for village or estate gatherings.

- **Equipment Used**:

    1. **Clay Pots and Wooden Barrels**: For mashing, boiling, and fermenting.
    2. **Simple Kilns and Drying Racks**: For malting grains.
    3. **Wooden Sieves**: To strain wort before fermentation.
    4. **Large Cauldrons**: For boiling wort in communal brewing spaces.

- **Recipes (Detailed)**:

    - **Ingredients**:

        - 7 kg of malted barley or mixed grains
        - Fresh water from wells or streams
        - Herbs such as heather, mugwort, and yarrow

        - Optional: Honey or dried fruit for sweetness

    - **Method**:

        1. **Malting**: Spread grains on drying racks or in kilns for 2-3 days, turning frequently to ensure even drying.

        2. **Crushing**: Coarsely crush dried malted grains using wooden mallets or stones.

        3. **Mashing**: Combine the crushed malt with warm water (55-65°C) in clay or wooden vessels. Stir thoroughly and steep for 1-2 hours.

        4. **Boiling**: Boil the wort in cauldrons for 45-60 minutes. Add herbs during the final 15-20 minutes of boiling.

        5. **Fermentation**: Transfer the wort to barrels or amphorae. Cover loosely and ferment for 4-6 days in a cool, shaded area.

        6. **Storage**: Store the ale in barrels or clay jars. Consume within 2-3 weeks for optimal freshness.

- **SPV (Strength, Preservation, and Variability)**:

    - **Strength**: Maintains a consistent alcohol content of 4-5%.

    - **Preservation**: Moderate, with boiled wort improving shelf life slightly.

    - **Variability**: High, due to the use of wild yeasts and regional ingredient differences.

- **Social Aspect**: Ale remains a staple beverage, central to both daily life and communal events. Village gatherings, celebrations, and feasts prominently feature freshly brewed ale. Brewing is not only a practical necessity but also a cultural tradition, with knowledge passed down through generations. On manorial estates, ale continues to be a key provision for workers and a symbol of hospitality.

Aethelwulf the Brewer: The Ale That "Tamed the Dragon"

Setting the Scene

In 550 AD, Britain was a land of legend and turmoil, where Saxons, Britons, and Picts fought for dominance, and tales of dragons and magic filled the air. In the small Saxon village of Meadhaven, Aethelwulf the Brewer was known for his booming laugh, his wild ideas, and his ale, which was said to be "as strong as a warrior and as unpredictable as a storm."

Aethelwulf loved the old tales of dragons, knights, and heroes, and he believed his ale could live up to those legends. "Why tell tales about slaying dragons," he often said, "when you could drink an ale that *feels* like taming one?"

The Dragon Problem

One day, a rumor spread through Meadhaven that a dragon had been sighted in the nearby hills. Farmers claimed to hear strange roars, and several sheep had gone missing. The villagers panicked, but Aethelwulf saw an opportunity.

"I'll brew an ale so mighty," he declared, "it will give us the courage to face the beast, or at least forget about it for a while!"

The Brewing of "Dragon's Breath Ale"

Determined to create an ale worthy of its name, Aethelwulf gathered ingredients that he believed would "capture the essence of a dragon":

- Smoked barley malt, to mimic the fiery breath of a dragon.
- Honey and wild berries, for sweetness and allure, because, as Aethelwulf reasoned, even dragons must like sweets.
- Spicy herbs, to "put a flame in the belly."
- And a pinch of powdered charcoal, to give it a dark, mysterious color.

The brewing process was dramatic, with Aethelwulf stirring the pot while chanting (nonsensical) spells and occasionally blowing on the fire to make it roar. The cauldron bubbled ominously, and the resulting brew was a deep crimson with a smoky aroma.

The Great Dragon Hunt

When the villagers gathered to discuss how to deal with the dragon, Aethelwulf unveiled his *Dragon's Breath Ale*. "Drink this," he proclaimed, "and you'll feel as bold as Beowulf himself!"

Skeptical but desperate, the villagers tried the ale. The first sips were met with wide eyes and gasps.

"It burns!" one farmer exclaimed.
"Like dragon fire!" another added, clutching his chest.

But soon, the warmth spread, and the villagers began to feel braver, or at least louder. "Let's find this dragon!" they shouted, brandishing pitchforks and torches. Aethelwulf, delighted by the chaos, grabbed his own mug and led the charge.

The Encounter

The "dragon" turned out to be a rather large and grumpy boar that had taken a liking to the sheep fields. Fueled by *Dragon's Breath Ale,* the villagers mistook its snorts and stomping for draconic ferocity.

"Stand firm!" Aethelwulf shouted, though he was hiding behind a haystack.

The boar, unimpressed by the villagers' shouts, charged at the nearest torch, causing the group to scatter. One farmer tripped, spilling ale on the boar's snout. The boar paused, sniffed the ground, and then began happily lapping up the spilled ale.

The villagers stared in disbelief as the "dragon" grew wobbly and eventually lay down, snoring loudly.

The Aftermath

The villagers returned to Meadhaven as heroes, dragging the snoring boar behind them. "We tamed the dragon!" they cheered, though no one mentioned the ale-soaked accident.

Aethelwulf was hailed as the savior of the village, and *Dragon's Breath Ale* became a local legend. The boar, affectionately named "Draco," became the village mascot, often seen lounging near Aethelwulf's brewery, hoping for a taste of his latest creations.

The Legacy

Dragon's Breath Ale became Meadhaven's most famous export, known for its smoky flavor and fiery kick. Travelers from far and wide came to try the legendary brew, though Aethelwulf always warned them, "Drink too much, and you might start hunting dragons yourself!"

STEM Lesson

Aethelwulf's story is a fun reminder of how creativity and resourcefulness can solve problems, even if the solution isn't what you expected. His experiment with bold flavors and unconventional ingredients created something unique and memorable, turning a moment of fear into a tale of triumph.

The lesson? Innovation often involves taking risks and thinking outside the barrel. Even if your "dragon" turns out to be a boar, you can still create something legendary.

600 AD - 650 AD: Brewing in the Early Middle Ages

- **Techniques**: Brewing begins to show signs of greater standardisation, influenced by cultural exchanges with European neighbours. The core techniques of malting, mashing, boiling, and fermenting remain consistent, with a stronger emphasis on refining these processes. Local ingredients such as wild herbs continue to play a key role.
- **Where Brewing Was Done**: Brewing is conducted in households, village brewing spaces, and on larger estates. Monasteries, which start to gain prominence in some areas, begin experimenting with brewing, laying the groundwork for more structured and larger-scale operations in the future.
- **How It Would Have Looked**: In rural settings, brewing is centred around hearths with clay pots and wooden barrels. Outdoor drying racks and kilns are used for malting grains. Communal brewing areas feature larger cauldrons and fermentation vessels. Monastic brewing spaces, though still developing, incorporate early structured designs with dedicated brewing rooms and larger storage areas.
- **Involvement of Villagers**: Women remain the primary brewers in households, producing ale for daily consumption. Men contribute to larger communal brewing efforts, particularly during festivals or when brewing for estates or monastic communities. Villagers often come together to pool resources and share brewing knowledge.
- **Equipment Used**:
    1. **Clay and Wooden Vessels**: Used for mashing, boiling, and fermenting.
    2. **Drying Racks and Kilns**: For preparing malted grains.
    3. **Wooden Sieves**: To strain wort before fermentation.
    4. **Barrels and Amphorae**: For fermentation and storage.
- **Recipes (Detailed)**:
    - **Ingredients**:
        - 6 kg of malted barley, oats, or wheat
        - Fresh water from wells or streams

        - Herbs such as mugwort, yarrow, and heather
        - Optional: Honey or dried fruits for sweetness
    - **Method**:
        1. **Malting**: Spread grains on drying racks or in kilns for 2-3 days, turning frequently to ensure even drying.
        2. **Crushing**: Coarsely crush dried malted grains using wooden mallets or stones.
        3. **Mashing**: Combine the crushed malt with warm water (55-65°C) in clay or wooden vessels. Stir thoroughly and steep for 1-2 hours.
        4. **Boiling**: Boil the wort in cauldrons for 45-60 minutes. Add herbs during the final 15-20 minutes of boiling.
        5. **Fermentation**: Transfer the wort to barrels or amphorae. Cover loosely and ferment for 4-6 days in a cool, shaded area.
        6. **Storage**: Store the ale in barrels or clay jars. Consume within 2-3 weeks for optimal freshness.

- **SPV (Strength, Preservation, and Variability)**:
    - **Strength**: Consistently around 4-5% alcohol by volume.
    - **Preservation**: Moderate, with boiled wort improving shelf life slightly.
    - **Variability**: High, due to wild yeast and regional ingredient differences.
- **Social Aspect**: Ale is deeply woven into daily life, serving as both sustenance and a social unifier. Villages often hold brewing days where multiple families participate, fostering collaboration and community bonds. Monasteries begin to experiment with brewing for both self-sufficiency and hospitality, marking the early stages of monastic brewing traditions. Ale remains a vital part of feasts, rituals, and communal gatherings, reinforcing its cultural significance.

Cuthbert the Brewer: The Ale That "Saved the Monastery"

Setting the Scene

By 600 AD, Christianity was spreading across Britain, and monasteries were becoming centers of learning, farming, and brewing. In a small monastery near Lindisfarne, Brother Cuthbert was renowned not for his piety or his scholarly work but for his exceptional ale.

"Brewing is my prayer," Cuthbert often said, though his fellow monks suspected he enjoyed the results a bit too much. Still, his ale was famous, and visiting bishops claimed it had "the flavor of divine inspiration."

The Viking Problem

One fateful morning, news reached the monastery that a band of Viking raiders had landed nearby. The monks panicked. "What can we do?" they cried. "We're farmers and scribes, not warriors!"

But Cuthbert had an idea. "We don't need swords to fight Vikings," he declared. "We need ale!"

The abbot raised an eyebrow. "Brother Cuthbert, this is no time for one of your experiments."

"Hear me out," Cuthbert replied. "If we can't outfight them, we'll outdrink them!"

The Brewing of "Valhalla Ale"

Cuthbert set to work crafting a brew that he hoped would astonish the Vikings, or at least keep them too distracted to raid. He called it *Valhalla Ale*, claiming it was inspired by the legendary feasts of Odin. His ingredients included:

- Barley malt soaked in honey for a sweet, warming taste.
- Juniper berries, which he thought would remind the Vikings of their homeland.
- A pinch of wild mint, "for a heavenly aroma."
- And a hefty dose of wild yeast, because "the stronger, the better."

He brewed the ale in the monastery's largest cauldron, praying over it as it bubbled and occasionally sampling it "for quality control."

The Viking Feast

When the Vikings arrived at the monastery, they were greeted not with resistance but with Cuthbert standing in the courtyard, holding a mug of ale and a loaf of bread.

"Welcome, mighty warriors!" he said, bowing slightly. "Before you pillage, taste the finest ale in all of Northumbria."

The Vikings, initially confused, accepted the mugs. The first sips were met with silence. Then, the leader grinned. "This is... incredible!" he roared.
The other Vikings nodded enthusiastically, gulping down the ale. "Bring more!" they demanded. Cuthbert, grinning, obliged.

The Chaos

As the Vikings drank more of the *Valhalla Ale*, their plans to raid the monastery dissolved into chaos. One warrior started singing Norse ballads, though no one could understand the words. Another challenged a monk to an arm-wrestling match, only to lose spectacularly when he burst into laughter mid-contest.
The Viking leader, now thoroughly drunk, declared, "This ale is proof the gods favor this place! We cannot raid a holy brewery!"
Encouraged, Cuthbert offered a toast. "To Valhalla Ale, may it bring peace to all who drink it!"

The Aftermath

By morning, the Vikings had passed out across the monastery grounds. When they awoke, groaning and clutching their heads, the abbot offered them bread, water, and a stern lecture about moderation.
The Vikings, sheepish but impressed, decided to spare the monastery. In fact, they struck a deal: they would protect the monks in exchange for regular shipments of *Valhalla Ale*.

The Legacy

Brother Cuthbert became a legend, known as the brewer who defeated the Vikings with ale. *Valhalla Ale* became the monastery's most famous export, and Cuthbert proudly declared, "Beer truly is the drink of peace!"
Though the abbot insisted on tighter controls for future brewing experiments, he admitted that Cuthbert's creativity had saved the day.

STEM Lesson

Cuthbert's story highlights the importance of creativity and adaptability in problem-solving. By thinking outside the barrel (and inside the cauldron), he turned a potentially dangerous situation into an opportunity for connection and peace.
The lesson? Science and creativity can be powerful tools for solving unexpected challenges. And sometimes, the right formula can bring even the fiercest opponents together.

650 AD - 700 AD: Brewing in the Developing Early Middle Ages

- **Techniques**: Brewing becomes increasingly influenced by the expanding monastic traditions. Techniques such as improved malting and fermentation gain traction. Herbs like mugwort and yarrow are staples for flavouring, though hops are still unknown in Britain. The boiling of wort ensures better preservation and stability.
- **Where Brewing Was Done**: Brewing is carried out in households, villages, and monasteries. Monasteries gain prominence as centres for brewing innovation and production, while households maintain traditional methods for local and domestic use.
- **How It Would Have Looked**: Brewing in households and villages features clay pots, wooden barrels, and drying racks. Monasteries establish more organised brewing spaces, with larger cauldrons and dedicated fermentation rooms. Outdoor kilns are common for drying malted grains.
- **Involvement of Villagers**: Women continue to oversee household brewing, producing ale for daily consumption. Monastic brewing involves monks who experiment with techniques and ingredients. Villagers contribute grains, honey, and herbs to communal brewing efforts.
- **Equipment Used**:
    1. **Clay and Wooden Vessels**: For mashing and fermenting.
    2. **Kilns and Racks**: For malting grains.
    3. **Wooden Sieves**: To strain wort before fermentation.
    4. **Barrels and Amphorae**: For fermentation and storage.
- **Recipes (Detailed)**:
    - **Ingredients**:
        - 6 kg of malted barley or oats
        - Water from wells or streams
        - Herbs such as yarrow, mugwort, and heather
        - Optional: Honey or fruit for sweetness

- **Method**:
    1. **Malting**: Dry grains on racks or in kilns for 2-3 days, turning frequently.
    2. **Crushing**: Coarsely crush malted grains using wooden mallets.
    3. **Mashing**: Mix malt with warm water (55-65°C) in wooden troughs. Let steep for 1-2 hours.
    4. **Boiling**: Boil the wort for 45-60 minutes. Add herbs in the final 15 minutes.
    5. **Fermentation**: Transfer the wort to barrels or amphorae. Cover and ferment for 4-6 days.
    6. **Storage**: Store the ale in barrels for up to 2 weeks.

- **SPV (Strength, Preservation, and Variability)**:
  - **Strength**: 4-5% alcohol.
  - **Preservation**: Moderate; boiling improves shelf life.
  - **Variability**: High, due to regional ingredients and wild yeast.
- **Social Aspect**: Ale is central to daily life, rituals, and feasts. Monasteries increasingly influence brewing culture, introducing structure and innovation. Villages rely on communal brewing to ensure a consistent supply of ale.

Edwy the Brewer: The Ale That "Tamed the Bard"

Setting the Scene

By 650 AD, Britain was a patchwork of small kingdoms, bustling monasteries, and lively villages. Storytellers, or bards, were central to village life, entertaining crowds with tales of heroes, gods, and the occasional exaggeration about their own bravery. In the kingdom of Mercia, in a small village by the river, Edwy the Brewer was renowned for his ale, and for being the only person who could handle the local bard, Leofric the Loud.

Leofric was a gifted storyteller, but he had one problem: after a few mugs of ale, his stories became *too* creative. "Once," Edwy sighed, "he told a tale about fighting an army of talking goats. The village believed him and refused to eat goat cheese for a month."

The Bard's Demand

One summer evening, Leofric announced that he was composing the "greatest tale Mercia has ever heard," but he needed inspiration. "Edwy!" he bellowed in the tavern. "Brew me an ale so magnificent it will spark my genius!"

The crowd cheered, but Edwy hesitated. "Leofric," he said cautiously, "your 'genius' tends to get out of hand after three mugs."

"Nonsense!" Leofric replied. "This will be my magnum opus! You wouldn't deny Mercia its greatest story, would you?"

Reluctantly, Edwy agreed. "Fine," he said, "but if I brew this, you must promise to tell the truth, just for one night."

Leofric laughed. "The truth? Easy! I'll make it sound even better than the truth!"

The Brewing of "Bard's Brew"

Edwy decided to craft a brew that was as bold and unpredictable as Leofric himself. His recipe included:

- Barley malt soaked in river water for a smooth, earthy base.
- Honey, for sweetness, to represent the bard's charm.
- Ginger root, for a fiery kick, to match his temper.
- A pinch of wild hops, "to keep him grounded", or so Edwy hoped.

The brewing process was dramatic. Edwy stirred the pot with a large wooden spoon, muttering, "May this tame the loudest of bards." He let the ale ferment longer than usual, ensuring it packed a punch worthy of Leofric's tales.

The Grand Unveiling

At the next village feast, Edwy presented his creation: *Bard's Brew*. The ale was a deep amber color, with a fragrant aroma of honey and spice. The villagers gathered around as Edwy poured the first mug for Leofric.

"Drink this," Edwy said, "and let it inspire your greatest, and most truthful, tale yet."

Leofric raised his mug, took a long sip, and paused. The crowd held its breath.

"This," he declared, "is the drink of gods!"

The Tale Gets Wild

As the night wore on, *Bard's Brew* worked its magic. Leofric began telling his tale: the story of a brave bard (himself, of course) who rescued a princess from a three-headed dragon. The villagers cheered as he described the dragon's fiery breath and his daring swordfight.

But by the second mug, the dragon had grown six heads, and the princess was now riding a unicorn. By the third mug, the dragon had been replaced by a "terrifying army of giant mushrooms," and Leofric claimed he had defeated them using only a lute and his wits.

Edwy groaned. "So much for the truth," he muttered.

The "Truthful" Twist

After his fourth mug, Leofric stood up and slurred, "But the real hero... is Edwy!" The crowd gasped as the bard pointed dramatically at the brewer.

"He brews ale so fine," Leofric continued, "it could tame a dragon, or a bard! And that, my friends, is the truth!"

The villagers erupted in laughter and applause. Even Edwy couldn't help but smile.

The Aftermath

The next morning, Leofric woke up with a pounding headache and only a vague memory of his performance. "Did I really call you a hero?" he asked Edwy.

"You did," Edwy replied, handing him a mug of water. "And for once, the truth didn't need any embellishment."

Bard's Brew became a village favorite, and Leofric's tale of the dragon (and the mushrooms) was retold for generations. Edwy, ever practical, began advertising his ale with the slogan: "Inspiration in a mug, drink responsibly!"

The Legacy
Bard's Brew became a symbol of community and creativity, reminding the villagers that even the wildest stories need a good ale to fuel them.

STEM Lesson
Edwy's story shows how experimentation and creativity can lead to unexpected successes. His thoughtful combination of ingredients reflected not only his brewing skills but also his understanding of his audience, namely, one very loud bard.

The lesson? Innovation is as much about understanding people as it is about perfecting your craft. And sometimes, the right brew can turn chaos into legend.

700 AD - 750 AD: Brewing in the Expanding Monastic Era

- **Techniques**: Monasteries refine brewing techniques, with improved malting processes and better control over fermentation. Household brewing evolves slowly, with traditional methods still dominant.
- **Where Brewing Was Done**: Brewing takes place in monasteries, villages, and rural homes. Monasteries develop early brewing manuals, standardising techniques.
- **How It Would Have Looked**: Monastic breweries are increasingly sophisticated, with structured layouts and larger storage capacities. Village brewing remains more rustic, with outdoor setups and shared tools.
- **Involvement of Villagers**: Monks lead brewing innovation, while women continue to manage household brewing. Villagers contribute resources and labour to support monastic brewing efforts.
- **Equipment Used**:
    1. **Larger Cauldrons**: For increased brewing capacity.
    2. **Wooden Vessels**: For fermentation and mashing.
    3. **Kilns**: For drying grains.
- **Recipes and SPV**: Recipes remain similar, with 4-5% alcohol content. Preservation and variability improve slightly due to monastic standardisation.
- **Social Aspect**: Monastic ale gains a reputation for quality, becoming a staple for pilgrims and travellers. Village brewing sustains local communities, with ale remaining central to daily life and celebrations.

Beornwulf the Brewer: The Ale That "Calmed the Witan"

Setting the Scene

By 700 AD, Anglo-Saxon Britain was a land of kingdoms and councils. The *Witan*, a gathering of wise men and nobles, advised kings on matters of law, land, and alliances. In a small village within the Kingdom of Wessex, Beornwulf the Brewer was a man of modest ambition but legendary skill with ale.

Beornwulf's ales were so renowned that they were often sent to the royal court for feasts. But his fame came with a unique challenge: when a local noble asked him to brew an ale for the upcoming Witan meeting, Beornwulf found himself with a task that could make, or break, his reputation.

The Witan's Challenge

The Witan was infamous for its bickering. "They argue over everything," the noble told Beornwulf. "Taxes, borders, sheep grazing... even whose beard is the longest. If you can brew something to keep them from fighting, I'll make sure you're rewarded handsomely."

Beornwulf scratched his head. "You want me to brew peace into a mug?"

"Exactly," said the noble. "And it better work, or they might argue about whether to exile the brewer!"

The Brewing of "Peacekeeper Ale"

Determined to rise to the challenge, Beornwulf decided to create a brew that was so smooth, so calming, it would leave even the most argumentative lord speechless. His recipe included:

- Barley malt soaked in chamomile tea, for relaxation.
- Honey, to sweeten even the sourest temper.
- Hops, which he had heard had a "soothing" effect (though no one really knew why).
- And a touch of mint, to "freshen the mind."

The brewing process was an event in itself. Beornwulf chanted old rhymes as he stirred the pot, claiming it added "harmony." He also enlisted the local baker to keep curious villagers away, muttering, "This isn't just ale, it's diplomacy in a barrel!"

The Witan Meeting

When the day of the Witan meeting arrived, Beornwulf delivered his ale to the council hall, where the nobles were already shouting about land boundaries.

"Before we begin," said the noble who had hired Beornwulf, "let us toast with this fine brew." The mugs of *Peacekeeper Ale* were distributed, and the room quieted as the lords took their first sips.

The Reactions

The initial silence was deafening. Beornwulf watched nervously as the lords tasted his creation. Finally, one elder nodded. "This is... pleasant," he said, stroking his beard.

Another lord, known for his fiery temper, leaned back in his chair and sighed. "It's... calming. Almost makes me forget how much I hate the ealdorman from Mercia."

The others chuckled, and for the first time in years, the Witan meeting began without a shouting match.

The Unintended Side Effects

However, as the meeting progressed, the ale's calming effects became a little *too* effective. One lord fell asleep mid-discussion, his snores echoing through the hall. Another stared dreamily out the window, murmuring about how beautiful the sheep fields looked in the sunlight.

When the scribe tried to record the decisions, he found that none of the lords could agree on what they'd actually decided, mostly because they didn't care anymore.

The Aftermath

Despite the hiccups, the noble who had hired Beornwulf declared the meeting a success. "No arguments broke out, and no one threw a sheep at anyone else this time," he said. "That's progress!"

Beornwulf's *Peacekeeper Ale* became the talk of the kingdom. While some questioned its usefulness for decision-making, it was soon requested at every feast and festival. "If it can calm the Witan," people said, "it can handle anything."

The Legacy

Beornwulf's ale became a symbol of diplomacy and good humor. His motto, "Better to sip than shout," was etched above the village tavern, and travelers came from far and wide to sample the brew.

STEM Lesson

Beornwulf's story highlights the importance of using science and creativity to solve real-world problems. By combining local ingredients with a thoughtful purpose, he created something that brought people together, even if it worked a little too well.

The lesson? Innovation doesn't always go as planned, but a creative approach can lead to unexpected successes, or at least a good laugh.

750 AD - 800 AD: Brewing at the Dawn of Hops

- **Techniques**: Brewing in Britain remains focused on herb-flavoured ales, with consistent malting, mashing, boiling, and fermentation techniques. Continental Europe begins experimenting with hops during this period, but their use has not yet reached British brewers. Boiling continues to be critical for stabilising wort and improving preservation.

- **Where Brewing Was Done**: Brewing is conducted in rural homes, village communal spaces, and increasingly in monasteries. Monasteries continue to refine brewing techniques, gaining renown for their ales. Household brewing remains vital for daily sustenance.

- **How It Would Have Looked**: Household brewing setups include clay pots, wooden barrels, and drying racks placed near hearths. Communal brewing areas in villages feature large cauldrons and fermentation vessels, often shared among families. Monastic breweries exhibit more organised layouts, with dedicated brewing spaces and early attempts at standardisation.

- **Involvement of Villagers**: Women oversee household brewing, while monks drive innovations in monastic brewing. Villagers collaborate to gather ingredients and share brewing resources, particularly for communal and celebratory brews.

- **Equipment Used**:

    1. **Clay and Wooden Vessels**: For mashing and fermenting.

    2. **Kilns and Drying Racks**: For malting grains.

    3. **Wooden Sieves**: To strain wort before fermentation.

    4. **Large Cauldrons**: For boiling wort in communal or monastic setups.

- **Recipes (Detailed)**:

    - **Ingredients**:

        - 6 kg of malted barley or mixed grains

        - Water from wells or streams

        - Herbs such as mugwort, heather, and yarrow

        - Optional: Honey or dried fruit for sweetness

- **Method**:

    1. **Malting**: Spread grains on drying racks or in kilns for 2-3 days, turning frequently for even drying.
    2. **Crushing**: Coarsely crush dried malt using wooden mallets or stones.
    3. **Mashing**: Mix the crushed malt with warm water (55-65°C) in wooden or clay vessels. Stir and steep for 1-2 hours.
    4. **Boiling**: Boil the wort in cauldrons for 45-60 minutes, adding herbs during the final 15-20 minutes.
    5. **Fermentation**: Transfer the wort to barrels or amphorae. Cover loosely and allow to ferment for 4-6 days.
    6. **Storage**: Store the ale in barrels or jars in cool areas. Consume within 2-3 weeks.

- **SPV (Strength, Preservation, and Variability)**:
    - **Strength**: Consistent at 4-5% alcohol by volume.
    - **Preservation**: Moderate; boiling improves shelf life but storage limitations remain.
    - **Variability**: High, due to the use of wild yeasts and local herbs.
- **Social Aspect**: Ale continues to play a central role in daily life and communal events. Monasteries expand their influence by producing high-quality ales, which are consumed by travellers, pilgrims, and local communities. Villages rely on communal brewing to supply ale for festivals and celebrations, reinforcing its cultural importance. While hops remain unknown in Britain, continental experimentation sets the stage for future innovations.

Aldred the Brewer: The Ale That "Stopped a Siege"

Setting the Scene

By 750 AD, Britain was a patchwork of kingdoms often at war, with forts and villages serving as battlegrounds. In the fortified village of Alesbury (aptly named for its love of beer), Aldred the Brewer was a local celebrity. His ales were famous for their rich flavor and, more importantly, their ability to lift spirits during hard times.

One fateful day, Aldred's brewing skills would be put to the ultimate test when Alesbury found itself under siege.

The Siege Begins

A neighboring warlord, jealous of Alesbury's prosperity (and possibly its beer), surrounded the village with his warriors, demanding their surrender. The villagers, terrified, gathered inside the fort's wooden walls, trying to figure out how to survive.

"What can we do?" they asked. "We're farmers, not fighters!"

Aldred, stroking his beard, declared, "What we need is a plan, and a pint. I'll brew an ale so powerful, it'll turn our enemies into allies!"

The villagers stared at him, bewildered. "How will ale stop an army?"

"Trust me," Aldred replied with a wink. "Nobody fights on an empty stomach, or with a full mug."

The Brewing of "Siege Ale"

Aldred set to work creating his masterpiece, *Siege Ale*. He gathered ingredients that he believed would make the brew both irresistible and disarming:

- Barley malt for a strong base, because "you need strength to end a siege."
- Honey and wild herbs, to give it a sweet and fragrant allure.
- Ginger root, for a fiery kick to spark conversation.
- And a handful of "special herbs" from the village healer, which Aldred claimed would "encourage a good nap."

The brewing process was an event in itself. Villagers gathered to watch as Aldred stirred the bubbling pot, humming a cheery tune and occasionally taking a sip for "quality control." By the time the ale was ready, the entire village was buzzing with anticipation.

The Plan

Under the cover of darkness, Aldred and a small group of villagers carried several barrels of *Siege Ale* to the edge of the enemy camp. They left the barrels in plain sight, along with a note written in Aldred's finest script:

"Brave warriors,
Alesbury surrenders not in fear, but in good faith. Enjoy this ale, brewed to honor your strength. May it bring peace to our lands.
, Aldred the Brewer"

The Enemy's Response

The warlord, intrigued by the gesture and the sweet aroma wafting from the barrels, ordered his warriors to drink. The first sips were met with grins and hearty laughter.

"This is incredible!" one warrior exclaimed.
"Better than anything we've had in our camp!" another shouted.

Soon, the entire camp was drinking and toasting to their "victory." The warlord, impressed, declared Aldred a genius and announced a feast.

The "Peace Talks"

By morning, the enemy camp was a scene of chaos, but the good kind. The warriors, still buzzing from the ale, began singing songs about friendship and trading battle stories that no one quite remembered correctly.

When Aldred arrived at the camp to "negotiate," he found the warlord in high spirits.

"You've won us over, Brewer," the warlord said, clapping him on the back. "This ale is worth more than any battle. Let's call it a truce, on one condition."

"And what's that?" Aldred asked.

"You supply my warriors with this *Siege Ale* whenever we need it!"

The Aftermath

The siege ended without a single weapon being drawn, and Aldred returned to Alesbury a hero. The villagers celebrated with their own barrels of *Siege Ale,* and the warlord kept his promise to maintain peace, as long as Aldred's deliveries arrived on time.

Alesbury became famous for its diplomacy-by-ale strategy, and Aldred's motto, "A full mug ends all wars," was carved above the village gate.

The Legacy

Siege Ale became a symbol of ingenuity and peace. Travelers came from far and wide to try the legendary brew, and Aldred's name was immortalized in both song and tavern tales.

STEM Lesson

Aldred's story shows how creativity and resourcefulness can solve even the most daunting problems. By combining his brewing expertise with a clever plan, he turned a siege into a celebration.

The lesson? Science and innovation can create surprising solutions, and sometimes the best way to win is to share.

800 AD - 850 AD: Brewing in the Early Middle Ages

- **Techniques**: Brewing in Britain continues to centre around traditional herb-flavoured ales. Techniques such as malting, mashing, boiling, and fermenting remain consistent, while experimentation with flavours and fermentation control increases slightly. Hops, still absent from British brewing, are beginning to gain traction in continental Europe.

- **Where Brewing Was Done**: Brewing occurs in rural households, village communal spaces, and monasteries. Monastic brewing expands further, with structured production methods becoming more prominent. Households maintain simple, practical setups for daily brewing needs.

- **How It Would Have Looked**: Household brewing features clay pots, wooden barrels, and drying racks placed near hearths. Village brewing spaces accommodate larger cauldrons and fermentation vessels shared by multiple families. Monastic breweries are increasingly organised, with dedicated brewing rooms and early storage cellars.

- **Involvement of Villagers**: Women lead household brewing, providing ale for daily sustenance. Monks manage monastic brewing operations, often involving local villagers in the supply of ingredients. Villagers also collaborate during communal brewing sessions for feasts and seasonal celebrations.

- **Equipment Used**:

    1. **Clay and Wooden Vessels**: For mashing, boiling, and fermenting.

    2. **Kilns and Racks**: For drying and malting grains.

    3. **Wooden Sieves**: For straining wort before fermentation.

    4. **Barrels and Jars**: For fermentation and storage.

- **Recipes (Detailed)**:

    - **Ingredients**:

        - 7 kg of malted barley or mixed grains

        - Fresh water from wells or streams

        - Herbs such as mugwort, yarrow, and meadowsweet

        - Optional: Honey or dried fruits for sweetness

- **Method**:

    1. **Malting**: Spread grains on drying racks or in kilns for 2-3 days, turning frequently to ensure even drying.

    2. **Crushing**: Coarsely crush dried malt using wooden mallets or stones.

    3. **Mashing**: Mix the crushed malt with warm water (55-65°C) in wooden or clay vessels. Stir and steep for 1-2 hours.

    4. **Boiling**: Boil the wort in cauldrons for 45-60 minutes. Add herbs during the last 15-20 minutes of boiling.

    5. **Fermentation**: Transfer the wort to barrels or jars. Cover loosely and ferment for 4-6 days in a cool, shaded area.

    6. **Storage**: Store the ale in barrels or clay jars. Consume within 2-3 weeks.

- **SPV (Strength, Preservation, and Variability)**:

    - **Strength**: Alcohol content remains consistent at 4-5%.

    - **Preservation**: Moderate; boiling improves longevity slightly, but ale must still be consumed quickly.

    - **Variability**: High, due to the use of wild yeasts and local ingredients.

- **Social Aspect**: Ale continues to play a vital role in everyday life, serving as both a staple beverage and a unifier during communal events. Monastic ale gains a reputation for its quality, attracting pilgrims and travellers. In villages, brewing remains a shared activity, strengthening community bonds. Seasonal celebrations and feasts revolve around the consumption of fresh ale, reinforcing its cultural significance.

Oswald the Brewer: The Ale That "Confused the Vikings"

Setting the Scene

By 800 AD, Viking raids were a constant threat to coastal villages across Britain. These fierce warriors, known for their love of battle and mead, were terrifying to most, but not to Oswald the Brewer. Living in a small coastal village in Northumbria, Oswald was a man of quirky ideas and an unshakable belief that his ale could solve any problem.

"Why fight the Vikings with swords," he often said, "when you can confuse them with a proper pint?"

The Viking Arrival

One misty morning, the villagers awoke to the sight of longships on the horizon. The Vikings were coming. Panic spread through the village as everyone prepared to flee, everyone except Oswald.

"Run if you must," he told his neighbors, "but I have a plan. These Vikings may have their axes, but I have my *Gobsmacker Ale*!"

"What's *Gobsmacker Ale*?" someone asked.

Oswald grinned. "An ale so strange, it'll leave them questioning reality."

The Brewing of *Gobsmacker Ale*

Oswald quickly got to work brewing his secret weapon. His goal was to create an ale that was both irresistible and utterly bewildering. His ingredients included:

- Barley malt for strength, because Vikings loved a strong drink.
- Honey and spices, to lure them in with sweetness.
- Seaweed, because Oswald thought it would "taste like home" to the seafaring raiders.
- And fermented nettle juice, because "a little sting never hurt anyone."

The brewing process was chaotic. Oswald stirred the cauldron while muttering old riddles, claiming it "infused the brew with mystery." When it was ready, the ale was an unsettling greenish-brown color with a frothy head that bubbled like a witch's potion.

The Encounter

When the Vikings landed, axes in hand, they were met not with resistance but with Oswald standing in the village square, holding a barrel of *Gobsmacker Ale* and several mugs.

"Welcome, mighty warriors!" Oswald called. "Before you burn our village, try the finest ale in Northumbria!"

The Vikings paused, puzzled. They weren't used to such greetings. "What's the catch?" their leader growled.

"No catch," Oswald replied. "Think of it as a gift for your long journey."

Intrigued, the leader agreed to try the ale first. He took a sip, then another, and then stared at the mug in confusion. "It's... it's sweet... but salty... and... is that a sting?"

The other Vikings, curious, began drinking too. Their reactions were equally bewildered.

The Chaos

As the Vikings drank more, the effects of *Gobsmacker Ale* began to show. One warrior started laughing uncontrollably, claiming he could hear the sea whispering secrets to him. Another insisted his axe was singing, while a third began an impromptu dance, which the others joined in, thinking it was a battle ritual.

The leader, still drinking, declared, "This is the strangest drink I've ever had, and I *must* have more!"

Oswald, seeing his chance, offered them another barrel. "Take it!" he said. "In fact, take all the ale you want and tell your Viking friends about it. But you'll have to leave us alone if you want more!"

The leader agreed enthusiastically, ordering his men to load the barrels onto their ships.

The Aftermath

The Vikings sailed away, singing sea shanties and shouting praises for Oswald's ale. The villagers, emerging from their hiding places, cheered their unlikely hero.

"You've saved us!" they cried.

Oswald shrugged modestly. "All in a day's work. Now, who wants the leftover ale?"

The Legacy

Word of *Gobsmacker Ale* spread, and soon other villages were requesting barrels to use as Viking deterrents. Oswald's ale became so famous that even Viking skalds composed songs about the "magic drink that tamed the Northmen."

STEM Lesson

Oswald's story is a testament to creativity and resourcefulness. By using his skills and a bit of unconventional thinking, he turned a dangerous situation into a legendary victory.

The lesson? Science and innovation aren't just about solving problems, they're about looking at challenges from a new perspective. And sometimes, the strangest ideas are the most effective.

850 AD - 900 AD: Brewing in the Early Medieval Period

- **Techniques**: Brewing practices in Britain continue to evolve slowly. Herb-flavoured ales remain the standard, with malting, mashing, boiling, and fermenting as established techniques. The use of wild yeasts dominates fermentation, while experimentation with regional herbs enhances flavour diversity. Hops are still absent from British brewing but are increasingly used on the continent.

- **Where Brewing Was Done**: Brewing is primarily a household activity, supplemented by village communal brewing spaces and monasteries. Monastic breweries expand their production and refine techniques, creating a wider influence on brewing standards.

- **How It Would Have Looked**: Household brewing remains a modest activity, with clay pots, wooden barrels, and drying racks arranged near hearths. Village brewing spaces accommodate larger-scale equipment, such as communal cauldrons and fermentation vessels. Monastic breweries feature more advanced setups, including larger kilns, dedicated storage areas, and early attempts at controlling fermentation environments.

- **Involvement of Villagers**: Women oversee household brewing, producing ale for daily consumption. Monks continue to innovate within monastic breweries, with villagers contributing grains, honey, and herbs for larger-scale brewing projects. Villagers also participate in communal brewing sessions, especially for seasonal festivals.

- **Equipment Used**:

  1. **Clay and Wooden Vessels**: Used for mashing and fermenting.
  2. **Kilns and Racks**: For drying and malting grains.
  3. **Wooden Sieves**: To strain wort before fermentation.
  4. **Barrels and Jars**: For fermentation and short-term storage.

- **Recipes (Detailed)**:

  - **Ingredients**:

    - 6-8 kg of malted barley, oats, or wheat
    - Fresh water from wells or streams

        - Herbs such as mugwort, heather, and yarrow
        - Optional: Honey or dried fruits for sweetness
    - **Method**:
        1. **Malting**: Spread grains on drying racks or in kilns for 2-3 days, turning frequently for even drying.
        2. **Crushing**: Coarsely crush dried malt using wooden mallets or stones.
        3. **Mashing**: Mix the crushed malt with warm water (55-65°C) in wooden or clay vessels. Stir and steep for 1-2 hours.
        4. **Boiling**: Boil the wort in cauldrons for 45-60 minutes. Add herbs during the last 15-20 minutes of boiling.
        5. **Fermentation**: Transfer the wort to barrels or jars. Cover loosely and allow to ferment for 4-6 days in a cool, shaded area.
        6. **Storage**: Store the ale in barrels or clay jars. Consume within 2-3 weeks.
- **SPV (Strength, Preservation, and Variability)**:
    - **Strength**: Alcohol content remains consistent at 4-5%.
    - **Preservation**: Moderate; boiling and improved fermentation techniques slightly enhance longevity.
    - **Variability**: High, due to regional ingredients and reliance on wild yeasts.
- **Social Aspect**: Ale remains a staple beverage, integral to daily sustenance and social gatherings. Monastic breweries grow in reputation, producing ale for pilgrims and local communities. Seasonal festivals and feasts revolve around communal brewing and ale consumption, reinforcing its cultural and social importance. The continued absence of hops means that British ales maintain their distinct herbal flavour profiles, setting them apart from the early hopped beers emerging on the continent.

Eadric the Brewer: The Ale That "Fooled the Danes"

Setting the Scene

By 850 AD, the Viking Age was in full swing, and the Danes were raiding their way across Britain. Villages and towns fortified themselves, and every person did their part to defend their home. In the small settlement of Alehaven, Eadric the Brewer was known for his exceptional ale, and his even more exceptional knack for avoiding hard work.

"If we're going to fight the Danes," Eadric often said, "let's do it with brains, not brawn, and maybe a good brew."

The Danish Threat

One morning, the villagers of Alehaven spotted a fleet of longships approaching. The Danes were coming, and the villagers scrambled to prepare. The blacksmith sharpened weapons, the farmers hid their livestock, and the warriors practiced their battle cries.

Eadric, meanwhile, calmly sipped his latest ale. "Why waste energy fighting," he mused, "when I can outsmart them?"

The village elder glared at him. "Eadric, this is no time for one of your lazy schemes!"

"Lazy? No," Eadric replied with a grin. "Brilliant? Absolutely. Just you wait."

The Brewing of "Dane's Delight"

Eadric got to work creating a brew he called *Dane's Delight*. His goal was to make an ale so irresistible, it would distract the Danes from pillaging the village. His recipe included:

- Extra-malted barley for a rich, hearty flavor.
- Wild honey and apples, to give it a sweetness the Danes would adore.
- A pinch of wild herbs for a "mysterious edge."
- And a touch of fermented nettle juice, because Eadric thought it was funny when people's faces tingled after drinking.

The brewing process was a spectacle. Eadric stirred the bubbling pot with dramatic flourishes, claiming the secret to great ale was "a touch of theater." The resulting brew was golden, frothy, and surprisingly potent.

The Plan

When the Danes landed, Eadric met them at the village gate, holding a barrel of *Dane's Delight* and a stack of mugs.

"Welcome, mighty warriors!" he shouted. "Before you raid, why not enjoy a drink to celebrate your victory in advance?"

The Danish leader, a burly man named Bjorn the Boisterous, raised an eyebrow. "What trickery is this?"

"No trick," Eadric replied. "Think of it as a gift from Alehaven, a taste of the finest ale in Britain. You'll raid happier after a few mugs!"

Intrigued, Bjorn accepted the offer. "Pour me one, then. But if it's bad, we'll take your barrels *and* your head."

The Reactions

The first sip was met with silence. Bjorn frowned, and Eadric held his breath.

Then, the Viking leader's eyes widened. "This... this is *incredible*!" he bellowed, downing the rest of the mug in one gulp.

The other Danes quickly demanded their own mugs, and soon the raiders were laughing, singing, and toasting Eadric. "Another round!" Bjorn shouted, slapping Eadric on the back so hard he nearly fell over.

The Chaos

As the Danes drank more, *Dane's Delight* began to work its magic. One warrior decided to reenact a Viking raid using a chicken as a stand-in for a villager, while another attempted to teach the locals a "battle dance" that looked suspiciously like falling over repeatedly.

Bjorn, now thoroughly drunk, declared, "This village is under my protection! No one raids Alehaven while I'm around!"

Eadric grinned. "I'm glad you like the ale, Bjorn. There's more where that came from, if you promise to leave us in peace."

"Done!" Bjorn roared, raising his mug.

The Aftermath

The next morning, the Danes stumbled back to their ships, groaning about their pounding heads but singing praises for *Dane's Delight*. Bjorn, true to his word, declared Alehaven off-limits to future raids, and the village became a haven of peace in the middle of Viking chaos.

Eadric, hailed as a hero, proudly declared, "Sometimes, a good ale is mightier than the sword."

The Legacy

Dane's Delight became a local legend, with travelers coming from far and wide to try the ale that saved a village. Eadric's barrel, adorned with carvings of drinking Vikings, was displayed in the village square as a reminder that wit and ale can turn enemies into allies.

STEM Lesson

Eadric's story highlights the importance of using creativity and innovation to solve problems. By understanding the power of his craft and the desires of his "enemy," he found a peaceful and humorous solution to a potentially violent situation.

The lesson? Science and ingenuity can be powerful tools for diplomacy, even if they come in the form of a frothy mug.

900 AD - 950 AD: Brewing in Early Medieval Britain

- **Techniques**: Brewing in Britain continues to centre around traditional techniques of malting, mashing, boiling, and fermenting. Herb-flavoured ales remain the norm, with wild yeasts driving fermentation. While hops gain traction in continental Europe, they are not yet part of British brewing practices. Experiments with new herbs and flavourings occur regionally.

- **Where Brewing Was Done**: Brewing is a predominantly domestic activity, supplemented by communal brewing in villages and monasteries. Monastic breweries continue to refine their methods, introducing incremental innovations and influencing local brewing practices. Wealthier households may have more extensive brewing setups for hosting guests and feasts.

- **How It Would Have Looked**: Brewing in rural households features clay pots and wooden barrels near hearths. Village brewing spaces are equipped with larger cauldrons and shared fermentation vessels. Monastic breweries have dedicated brewing areas with organised layouts, including drying kilns, boiling cauldrons, and storage facilities.

- **Involvement of Villagers**: Women maintain their role as primary household brewers, while monks lead larger-scale production in monasteries. Villagers contribute resources such as grains and herbs to communal brewing efforts, particularly during festivals and celebrations. Wealthier estates employ servants or labourers for brewing tasks.

- **Equipment Used**:

    1. **Clay and Wooden Vessels**: For mashing, boiling, and fermenting.

    2. **Drying Racks and Kilns**: For preparing malted grains.

    3. **Wooden Sieves**: To strain wort before fermentation.

    4. **Barrels and Jars**: For fermentation and storage.

- **Recipes (Detailed)**:

    - **Ingredients**:

        - 7-8 kg of malted barley, oats, or wheat

        - Fresh water from wells or streams
        - Herbs such as mugwort, heather, yarrow, and meadowsweet
        - Optional: Honey or dried fruits for added sweetness
    - **Method**:
        1. **Malting**: Dry grains on racks or in kilns for 2-3 days, turning frequently to ensure even drying.
        2. **Crushing**: Coarsely crush dried malt using wooden mallets or stones.
        3. **Mashing**: Combine the crushed malt with warm water (55-65°C) in wooden or clay vessels. Stir thoroughly and steep for 1-2 hours.
        4. **Boiling**: Boil the wort in large cauldrons for 45-60 minutes. Add herbs during the final 15-20 minutes of boiling.
        5. **Fermentation**: Transfer the cooled wort to barrels or jars. Cover loosely and allow to ferment for 4-6 days in a cool, shaded area.
        6. **Storage**: Store the ale in barrels or clay jars. Consume within 2-3 weeks.
- **SPV (Strength, Preservation, and Variability)**:
    - **Strength**: Maintains a steady alcohol content of 4-5%.
    - **Preservation**: Moderate, with boiling improving shelf life slightly.
    - **Variability**: High, influenced by wild yeasts and regional ingredient variations.
- **Social Aspect**: Ale continues to be a cornerstone of daily life, serving as both nourishment and a communal beverage. Monastic ales gain wider acclaim, attracting pilgrims and local patrons. In villages, brewing remains a collaborative activity, with ale playing a central role in festivals, feasts, and rituals. While hops are absent from British ales, the

rich tradition of herb-flavoured brewing reinforces its cultural identity and distinction from continental beers.

Wynfrith the Brewer: The Ale That "Turned a Battle into a Banquet"

Setting the Scene

By 900 AD, Britain was a land of shifting alliances, Viking raids, and local lords constantly squabbling over territory. In the heart of Mercia, in the small village of Barleyford, Wynfrith the Brewer was known for two things: his knack for crafting powerful ales and his ability to avoid getting involved in politics.

"Wars come and go," Wynfrith often said, "but people always need ale."

However, Wynfrith's peaceful existence was turned upside down when two rival lords, Ealdred and Cynric, brought their armies to Barleyford, each claiming the village as their own.

The Brewing Crisis

As the armies camped on opposite sides of the village, the villagers begged Wynfrith for help. "If they fight, they'll destroy everything!"

"What do you expect me to do?" Wynfrith asked. "I'm a brewer, not a warrior!"

"Use your ale!" the village elder pleaded.

Wynfrith stroked his chin. "An ale that could stop a battle... Hmm. This might be my finest brew yet."

The Brewing of "Battle Brew"

Determined to save the village, Wynfrith set out to craft an ale so irresistible it would distract the warring lords from their feud. He called it *Battle Brew*. His recipe included:

- Barley malt soaked in honey to create a sweet, rich base.
- A handful of juniper berries for a bold, earthy flavor.
- A touch of ginger root for a fiery kick, because "no battle is complete without a little spice."

- And a pinch of valerian root, known for its calming properties, just in case things got out of hand.

The brew was prepared in a massive cauldron, and Wynfrith stirred it with a boat oar for dramatic effect. "This isn't just ale," he declared to the watching villagers. "This is liquid diplomacy!"

The Plan

Once the *Battle Brew* was ready, Wynfrith filled two barrels and rolled them to the battlefield. Standing boldly between the two armies, he shouted, "Before you spill blood, why not share a drink? This is Barleyford's finest ale, brewed for warriors like you!"

The lords hesitated. "What's your game, brewer?" Ealdred demanded.

"No game," Wynfrith replied. "Just ale. After all, wouldn't it be better to toast your victory than to fall on the battlefield?"

Intrigued (and slightly thirsty), the lords agreed to taste the ale before fighting.

The Reactions

The first sips were met with wide eyes and murmurs of approval.

"This is... extraordinary!" Cynric exclaimed, wiping foam from his beard.
"Ale worthy of a king," Ealdred agreed, raising his mug high.

Encouraged, Wynfrith poured more for the armies. Soon, both sides were laughing, toasting, and sharing exaggerated tales of their exploits.

The Chaos

As the ale flowed, the rivalry between the two lords turned into a drinking contest. Ealdred claimed he could drink a barrel faster than Cynric, while Cynric declared himself the "King of the Mug."

The soldiers, not wanting to be outdone, joined in, creating a lively festival in the middle of the battlefield. Someone started a game of tug-of-war using a discarded rope, while another group attempted to wrestle a pig that had wandered into the chaos.

Wynfrith, watching from the sidelines, grinned. "Who needs swords when you have ale?"

The Aftermath

By morning, the two lords were too hungover to remember why they had been fighting in the first place. Over breakfast (and a great deal of water), they agreed to a truce.

"This village is too valuable to destroy," Ealdred said.
"Agreed," Cynric replied. "Especially with a brewer like Wynfrith."

The lords declared Barleyford a neutral zone, promising to protect it rather than fight over it.

The Legacy

Battle Brew became legendary, known as the ale that turned a battle into a banquet. Wynfrith's fame spread far and wide, and travelers came to Barleyford to taste the brew that stopped a war. Wynfrith's motto, "Peace through pints," was etched onto the village tavern door, and his massive brewing cauldron was turned into a fountain.

STEM Lesson

Wynfrith's story is a testament to the power of creativity and resourcefulness. By using his brewing skills and understanding the psychology of his audience, he found a peaceful solution to a violent problem.

The lesson? Innovation doesn't just solve problems, it brings people together, even in the most unlikely of circumstances. And sometimes, the right mix of ingredients can change history.

950 AD - 1000 AD: Brewing on the Cusp of Change

- **Techniques**: Brewing in Britain remains rooted in traditional methods of malting, mashing, boiling, and fermenting. Herb-flavoured ales continue to dominate, with local ingredients dictating flavour profiles. Wild yeasts remain the primary fermenting agent, though some monastic breweries begin experimenting with yeast cultivation. Hops are still absent from British brewing, but their use is becoming more established on the continent.

- **Where Brewing Was Done**: Brewing takes place in rural homes, communal village spaces, and monasteries. Monastic breweries lead the way in improving brewing consistency and production scale. Wealthier estates often have dedicated brewing areas to supply ale for feasts and hospitality.

- **How It Would Have Looked**: Household brewing setups are simple, with clay pots, wooden barrels, and drying racks positioned near hearths. Village communal brewing sites feature larger cauldrons and shared fermentation vessels, fostering collaboration among families. Monastic breweries exhibit increasingly organised layouts, with dedicated malting areas, boiling rooms, and fermentation cellars.

- **Involvement of Villagers**: Women continue to dominate household brewing, ensuring a steady supply of ale for daily consumption. Monks oversee monastic brewing operations, producing ale for their communities and travellers. Villagers contribute ingredients and labour to communal brewing efforts, particularly during festivals and harvest seasons.

- **Equipment Used**:

    1. **Clay and Wooden Vessels**: For mashing, boiling, and fermenting.

    2. **Kilns and Drying Racks**: For malting grains.

    3. **Wooden Sieves**: To strain wort before fermentation.

    4. **Barrels and Jars**: For fermentation and short-term storage.

- **Recipes (Detailed)**:

    - **Ingredients**:

        - 7-8 kg of malted barley, oats, or wheat

        - Fresh water from wells or streams
        - Herbs such as mugwort, heather, and yarrow
        - Optional: Honey or dried berries for sweetness

    - **Method**:

        1. **Malting**: Spread grains on drying racks or in kilns for 2-3 days, turning frequently to ensure even drying.
        2. **Crushing**: Coarsely crush dried malt using wooden mallets or stones.
        3. **Mashing**: Combine the crushed malt with warm water (55-65°C) in wooden or clay vessels. Stir thoroughly and steep for 1-2 hours.
        4. **Boiling**: Boil the wort in large cauldrons for 45-60 minutes. Add herbs during the final 15-20 minutes of boiling.
        5. **Fermentation**: Transfer the cooled wort to barrels or jars. Cover loosely and allow to ferment for 4-6 days in a cool, shaded area.
        6. **Storage**: Store the ale in barrels or clay jars. Consume within 2-3 weeks.

- **SPV (Strength, Preservation, and Variability)**:
    - **Strength**: Maintains a steady alcohol content of 4-5%.
    - **Preservation**: Moderate, with boiling and careful fermentation improving shelf life slightly.
    - **Variability**: High, influenced by regional herbs and wild yeast fermentation.

- **Social Aspect**: Ale remains central to daily life, providing nourishment and hydration. Monastic breweries gain recognition for their improved ales, serving both local communities and pilgrims. Villages rely on communal brewing to meet the demand for festivals, feasts, and seasonal gatherings. The absence of hops ensures British ales retain their unique herbal flavours, differentiating them from the early hopped beers of continental Europe. Brewing continues to be a shared cultural activity, fostering collaboration and community ties.

Cynhelm the Brewer: The Ale That "Bewitched the Earl"

Setting the Scene

By 950 AD, Anglo-Saxon England was a land of earls, monks, and growing towns. Brewing ale was a vital craft, and every village had its resident brewer. In the town of Brewburh, Cynhelm the Brewer was famed for two things: his exceptional ales and his ability to talk his way out of trouble.

"Life is like a good ale," Cynhelm often said. "You stir it well, add a touch of magic, and hope it doesn't explode."

Cynhelm's talent for brewing was about to face its greatest test when Earl Wulfric, a notoriously grumpy noble, announced he was visiting Brewburh.

The Earl's Demands

Earl Wulfric was known for his bad temper and his love of feasts. "If Brewburh wants my protection," Wulfric declared, "you must serve me an ale worthy of an earl. Fail, and I'll find a village that can!"

The townsfolk panicked. "What if he doesn't like it?" they fretted.

Cynhelm, however, saw an opportunity. "Fear not, friends," he said. "I'll brew an ale so enchanting, it will make Wulfric smile, or at least stop scowling long enough to finish his mug."

The Brewing of "Earl's Enchantment"

Cynhelm decided to craft a brew that was as bold and complex as the earl himself. His ingredients included:

- Barley malt for richness, because "an earl deserves the finest base."
- Clover honey, to add a touch of sweetness and "soften his sourness."
- Juniper berries, for a regal, earthy flavor.

- And a pinch of sage, because Cynhelm believed it would "clear the earl's grumpy mind."

As Cynhelm stirred the brew, he added an extra flourish: a whispered rhyme he claimed would "bewitch" the ale. "A touch of charm for the grumpiest soul," he said, winking.

The Feast

When Earl Wulfric arrived, he looked around the town square with a scowl. "Where's this famous ale?" he barked.

Cynhelm stepped forward, carrying a barrel of *Earl's Enchantment* and a polished wooden mug. "Your lordship," he said with a bow, "allow me to present Brewburh's finest creation, brewed in your honor."

Wulfric sniffed the ale suspiciously, then took a sip. The crowd held its breath.

The Transformation

To everyone's astonishment, the earl's face softened. He took another sip, then another, and finally let out a hearty laugh. "By the gods, this is magnificent!" he exclaimed.

The villagers cheered, but Cynhelm wasn't done. "Your lordship," he said, "this ale is only the beginning. It's best enjoyed with a story."

The earl, intrigued, gestured for him to continue.

The Tale of the Bewitched Ale

Cynhelm launched into an exaggerated tale about how he had to battle a flock of enchanted geese to gather the honey and outwit a mischievous sprite to harvest the sage.

The earl, now thoroughly amused and on his second mug, roared with laughter. "You're as clever as this ale, Cynhelm!"

Encouraged by the earl's mood, the villagers joined in, inventing even wilder parts of the story. By the end of the night, the earl was laughing so hard he nearly fell off his chair.

The Aftermath

The next morning, Wulfric declared Brewburh under his personal protection. "Any village that brews an ale like this deserves my favor," he said.

Cynhelm became a local legend, and *Earl's Enchantment* became the pride of Brewburh. The recipe was passed down through generations, always with a whispered rhyme added for "a touch of magic."

The Legacy

Years later, travelers would come to Brewburh to taste the ale that made a grumpy earl laugh. Cynhelm's motto, "Charm your ale, charm the world," was etched above the town's tavern door, and his tale became a favorite in feasts and fairs across the land.

STEM Lesson

Cynhelm's story highlights the power of combining skill, creativity, and a touch of storytelling to solve challenges. His understanding of flavors, paired with his flair for presentation, turned a potentially disastrous visit into a triumph.

The lesson? Science and craftsmanship are about more than just formulas, they're about creating experiences that connect people, even the grumpiest of earls.

1000 AD - 1050 AD: Brewing in the High Medieval Transition

- **Techniques**: Brewing techniques in Britain remain focused on traditional methods, including malting, mashing, boiling, and fermenting. Herb-flavoured ales dominate, with local ingredients dictating flavour profiles. Monastic breweries begin to refine yeast cultivation, improving fermentation consistency. Hops are still largely absent, though some exposure to continental brewing practices introduces the concept.

- **Where Brewing Was Done**: Brewing occurs in rural households, village communal spaces, and monasteries. Monastic breweries expand their production capacity and influence, supplying ale for both local consumption and pilgrim hospitality. Wealthier estates maintain dedicated brewing facilities to cater to feasts and guests.

- **How It Would Have Looked**: Household brewing setups remain practical, with clay pots, wooden barrels, and drying racks arranged near hearths. Village communal brewing spaces are equipped with larger cauldrons and shared fermentation vessels. Monastic breweries grow in complexity, featuring structured layouts with malting areas, boiling rooms, and fermentation cellars.

- **Involvement of Villagers**: Women lead household brewing efforts, ensuring a steady supply of ale for daily needs. Monks oversee large-scale monastic brewing, producing ale for their communities and travellers. Villagers contribute ingredients and labour to communal brewing projects, particularly for seasonal festivals and celebrations.

- **Equipment Used**:

    1. **Clay and Wooden Vessels**: For mashing, boiling, and fermenting.

    2. **Kilns and Drying Racks**: For malting grains.

    3. **Wooden Sieves**: To strain wort before fermentation.

    4. **Barrels and Jars**: For fermentation and storage.

- **Recipes (Detailed)**:

    - **Ingredients**:

        - 7-8 kg of malted barley, oats, or wheat

        - Fresh water from wells or streams
        - Herbs such as mugwort, heather, and yarrow
        - Optional: Honey or dried berries for sweetness
    - **Method**:
        1. **Malting**: Spread grains on drying racks or in kilns for 2-3 days, turning frequently to ensure even drying.
        2. **Crushing**: Coarsely crush dried malt using wooden mallets or stones.
        3. **Mashing**: Combine the crushed malt with warm water (55-65°C) in wooden or clay vessels. Stir thoroughly and steep for 1-2 hours.
        4. **Boiling**: Boil the wort in large cauldrons for 45-60 minutes. Add herbs during the final 15-20 minutes of boiling.
        5. **Fermentation**: Transfer the cooled wort to barrels or jars. Cover loosely and allow to ferment for 4-6 days in a cool, shaded area.
        6. **Storage**: Store the ale in barrels or clay jars. Consume within 2-3 weeks.
- **SPV (Strength, Preservation, and Variability)**:
    - **Strength**: Consistent alcohol content of 4-5%.
    - **Preservation**: Moderate, with boiling and careful fermentation improving longevity slightly.
    - **Variability**: High, influenced by regional herbs and wild yeast fermentation.
- **Social Aspect**: Ale remains a central part of daily life, serving as nourishment and a social unifier. Monastic breweries gain prestige for their high-quality ales, catering to local communities and pilgrims alike. Villages depend on communal brewing to meet demand for festivals, feasts, and seasonal gatherings. Exposure to continental brewing practices begins to influence British brewing subtly, setting the stage for future developments.

Godric the Brewer: The Ale That "Crowned the Fool"

Setting the Scene

By 1000 AD, Anglo-Saxon England was a land of feasting, festivities, and fiercely competitive brewers. In the bustling town of Mugwort-on-Thames, Godric the Brewer was known for his unorthodox methods and his ability to turn any event into an excuse to showcase his latest ale.

"Brewing," Godric liked to say, "is both an art and a weapon, depending on how strong you make it."

Godric's fame reached its peak when he was tasked with brewing ale for the town's annual Feast of Fools, a chaotic celebration where a "Fool King" was crowned, and mischief ruled the day.

The Foolish Challenge

The Feast of Fools was the highlight of the year, a day when the roles of lords and peasants were reversed, and everyone competed to outdo each other in absurdity. This year, the townsfolk begged Godric to brew an ale that would capture the spirit of the festival.

"Make it strong!" the blacksmith shouted.
"Make it sweet!" demanded the miller's wife.
"Make it... funny!" added the jester.

Godric grinned. "Funny, you say? Then brace yourselves, for I shall brew the most ridiculous ale ever created."

The Brewing of "Fool's Froth"

Determined to live up to the challenge, Godric devised a brew that was as unpredictable as the Feast of Fools itself. His recipe included:

- Barley malt for strength, because "a proper fool needs courage."
- Apples, for a fruity sweetness, to "tickle the tongue."
- Wild herbs from the nearby meadow, to add a touch of whimsy.
- And a secret ingredient: a splash of fermented turnip juice, because Godric thought it would "surprise the palate."

The brewing process was, in true Godric fashion, chaotic. He danced around the cauldron, humming nonsense songs and occasionally tossing in a pinch of this or that "for luck." The resulting ale was golden, fizzy, and surprisingly fragrant, though its taste left even Godric scratching his head.

The Feast Begins

On the day of the Feast, Godric unveiled his creation: *Fool's Froth*. He arrived at the town square with a cart loaded with barrels, each decorated with painted faces and jester hats.

"Behold!" he declared. "An ale fit for fools and kings alike!"

The townsfolk cheered and eagerly filled their mugs.

The Reactions

The first sips were met with laughter and confusion.

"It's sweet... no, it's sour... wait, is that turnip?" one villager exclaimed.
"My tongue feels like it's dancing!" another shouted.

But the strangest effect of *Fool's Froth* was its apparent ability to embolden even the shyest of drinkers. The baker, normally quiet and reserved, climbed onto a table and proclaimed himself the "Turnip King." The blacksmith challenged a chicken to a staring contest, and the chicken seemed to win.

The crowd, now thoroughly entertained, began chanting for the crowning of the Fool King.

The Fool King Debacle

As tradition dictated, the Fool King was chosen by a contest. This year's challenge, inspired by Godric's ale, was to balance a mug of *Fool's Froth* on one's head while reciting a limerick.

One by one, contestants failed hilariously, spilling ale everywhere. But then Godric, emboldened by his own brew, decided to enter the contest himself. Balancing a mug on his head, he recited:

"There once was a brewer so wise,
Who made ale with a turnip surprise.
The fools drank it down,
And in laughter they drowned,
Till the chickens were crowned in disguise!"

The crowd roared with laughter and crowned Godric the Fool King on the spot.

The Aftermath

The Feast of Fools was declared the most successful in living memory, thanks to Godric and his absurd ale. *Fool's Froth* became a festival staple, and Godric's tale of being crowned Fool King was retold at every feast.

The Legacy

Fool's Froth became a symbol of joy, creativity, and the power of not taking life too seriously. Godric's motto, "Every brew should have a bit of fun," was etched above the town's tavern door, and his painted barrels became a popular decoration for future festivals.

STEM Lesson

Godric's story highlights the importance of experimentation and embracing the unexpected. His willingness to take risks and infuse humor into his craft turned a simple brew into a legendary experience.

The lesson? Innovation often requires a playful spirit. Don't be afraid to experiment, and remember, sometimes the quirkiest ideas lead to the most memorable outcomes.

1050 AD - 1100 AD: Brewing in the Norman Transition

- **Techniques**: Brewing during this period remains rooted in traditional methods such as malting, mashing, boiling, and fermenting. While herbs continue to dominate as flavouring agents, exposure to Norman and continental practices begins to introduce hops to British brewing in small quantities. Monastic breweries lead in refining techniques, including better yeast management and more consistent malting processes.

- **Where Brewing Was Done**: Brewing takes place in rural homes, village communal spaces, and monasteries. The Norman influence sees some wealthier households and estates adopting more structured brewing facilities. Monasteries continue to expand their brewing capabilities, producing ale for communities and the increasing number of pilgrims.

- **How It Would Have Looked**: Household brewing setups are simple, with clay pots, wooden barrels, and drying racks near hearths. Village communal spaces feature larger cauldrons and fermentation vessels shared by families. Monastic breweries grow increasingly sophisticated, with designated malting, boiling, and storage areas. Early experiments with hops are seen in select monasteries and estates influenced by continental methods.

- **Involvement of Villagers**: Women oversee household brewing for daily needs, while monks refine monastic brewing techniques for larger-scale production. Villagers contribute grains, honey, and herbs to communal brewing projects and work collaboratively during festivals and harvest seasons. Wealthier estates employ workers to manage brewing operations.

- **Equipment Used**:

    1. **Clay and Wooden Vessels**: For mashing, boiling, and fermenting.

    2. **Kilns and Drying Racks**: For malting grains.

    3. **Wooden Sieves**: To strain wort before fermentation.

    4. **Barrels and Jars**: For fermentation and short-term storage.

- **Recipes (Detailed)**:

    - **Ingredients**:

        - 7-8 kg of malted barley, oats, or wheat
        - Fresh water from wells or streams
        - Herbs such as mugwort, heather, yarrow, and occasional hops
        - Optional: Honey or dried berries for sweetness
    - **Method**:
        1. **Malting**: Spread grains on drying racks or in kilns for 2-3 days, turning frequently for even drying.
        2. **Crushing**: Coarsely crush dried malt using wooden mallets or stones.
        3. **Mashing**: Combine the crushed malt with warm water (55-65°C) in wooden or clay vessels. Stir thoroughly and steep for 1-2 hours.
        4. **Boiling**: Boil the wort in large cauldrons for 45-60 minutes. Add herbs or hops during the final 15-20 minutes of boiling.
        5. **Fermentation**: Transfer the cooled wort to barrels or jars. Cover loosely and allow to ferment for 4-6 days in a cool, shaded area.
        6. **Storage**: Store the ale in barrels or clay jars. Consume within 2-3 weeks.
- **SPV (Strength, Preservation, and Variability)**:
    - **Strength**: Consistent alcohol content of 4-5%.
    - **Preservation**: Slightly improved by early use of hops in select brews and refined fermentation practices.
    - **Variability**: Moderate, influenced by the integration of hops and evolving malting processes.
- **Social Aspect**: Ale remains central to daily life, providing sustenance and a sense of community. Monastic breweries gain prominence as centres of innovation and quality production, while villagers depend on communal brewing to meet demand for festivals and gatherings. The Norman influence introduces subtle changes to British brewing, laying

the groundwork for the future integration of hops and other continental practices.

Ealdric the Brewer: The Ale That "Fooled the Normans"

Setting the Scene

By 1050 AD, England was a land of bustling towns, growing trade, and brewing excellence. The Normans were making their presence known, and Anglo-Saxon England was on the verge of monumental change. In the lively market town of Hopford, Ealdric the Brewer was a local hero, known for his ability to brew ales that could lift the spirits of even the grumpiest villager.

One day, however, Ealdric's brewing skills would face their greatest test when a group of Norman knights marched into town, demanding food, drink, and respect.

The Norman Arrival

The Normans arrived in Hopford, led by a haughty knight named Sir Godefroi. "We are here to assess your town," Sir Godefroi announced, "and we expect a proper feast. Do not disappoint us!"

The townsfolk were nervous. The Normans were known for their stern demeanor, and nobody wanted to anger them.

"Ealdric," the mayor whispered, "you must brew an ale that will impress them. Something grand, something... Norman."

Ealdric stroked his chin. "A Norman ale, you say? I have just the idea."

The Brewing of "Conqueror's Brew"

Ealdric decided to craft an ale that would both flatter and confuse the Normans. His ingredients included:

- Barley malt, soaked overnight in cider to give it a sharp, fruity edge.
- Local honey, to add sweetness and "charm."
- Wild thyme, for an earthy, sophisticated aroma.
- And a splash of apple vinegar, to create an unexpected tang.

As Ealdric stirred the brew, he chuckled. "This ale will make them think they're drinking something Norman, but it's pure Hopford ingenuity!"

The Feast

When the feast began, Sir Godefroi and his knights were seated at the head of the long table, flanked by nervous villagers. Ealdric entered dramatically, carrying a barrel of his *Conqueror's Brew* adorned with a hastily painted Norman crest.

"Sir Godefroi," Ealdric said with a bow, "allow me to present a special ale brewed in honor of your arrival. It is inspired by Norman sophistication and the finest traditions of Hopford."

Sir Godefroi raised an eyebrow but agreed to taste it.

The Reactions

The Normans took their first sips cautiously. Sir Godefroi's face remained unreadable for a moment, and then he nodded. "It's... unusual," he said.

"It has a boldness," added another knight.
"Quite... sharp," said a third, wincing slightly but not wanting to admit it.

Ealdric smiled. "It's a blend of strength and refinement, much like Norman culture itself!"

The knights, flattered, drank more, their initial reservations fading with each sip. Soon, they were toasting to "Norman greatness" and demanding more of *Conqueror's Brew.*

The Chaos

As the evening progressed, the ale's hidden power revealed itself. The cider-soaked barley and apple vinegar created a unique mix of tangy strength that the Normans weren't prepared for.

One knight attempted to give a speech about Norman superiority but slurred so much that the villagers burst into laughter. Another insisted on teaching the local blacksmith a "Norman dance," which mostly involved tripping over barrels.

Sir Godefroi, now thoroughly tipsy, declared, "This ale! It must be sent to Duke William himself! He'll know we've found the finest drink in England!"

The Aftermath

The next morning, the Normans woke with sore heads but fond memories. Sir Godefroi, embarrassed by his drunken antics but impressed by the ale, declared Hopford under his protection.

"You have the spirit of a true brewer," he told Ealdric, "and your ale will surely inspire Duke William's court!"

Ealdric, hiding a grin, replied, "We are honored, Sir Godefroi. We shall brew more of this... Norman ale for your next visit."

The Legacy

Conqueror's Brew became famous across Hopford, celebrated as the ale that fooled the Normans. The villagers toasted Ealdric's ingenuity for years, and his motto, "Brew boldly, fool wisely," was carved into the town's tavern sign.

STEM Lesson

Ealdric's story is a lesson in creativity, adaptability, and using local resources to solve problems. By blending familiar ingredients in unexpected ways, he created something that impressed even his toughest critics.

The lesson? Science and innovation are about more than just invention, they're about understanding your audience and crafting solutions that work (and sometimes make them laugh).

1100 AD - 1150 AD: Brewing in the Age of Monastic Expansion

- **Techniques**: Brewing during this period sees further refinement, with monks at the forefront of innovation. Traditional techniques of malting, mashing, boiling, and fermenting remain consistent, but the integration of hops begins to take hold in select regions influenced by continental Europe. Monasteries develop more advanced yeast cultivation methods, enhancing fermentation control and consistency.

- **Where Brewing Was Done**: Brewing takes place in rural households, communal village spaces, and increasingly sophisticated monastic breweries. Wealthy estates and manors also establish dedicated brewing facilities to supply ale for feasts and retainers.

- **How It Would Have Looked**: Household brewing remains modest, centred around hearths with clay pots and wooden barrels. Village brewing spaces feature shared equipment, such as large cauldrons and fermentation vessels. Monastic breweries expand significantly, with dedicated malting areas, boiling rooms, and fermentation cellars, reflecting their growing influence on brewing practices. Early hopped ales begin to emerge in areas with strong Norman influence.

- **Involvement of Villagers**: Women continue to lead household brewing, while monks manage large-scale monastic operations. Villagers contribute ingredients and labour to communal brewing projects, particularly for festivals and harvests. Wealthier estates employ dedicated brewers to maintain production for their households and workers.

- **Equipment Used**:

    1. **Clay and Wooden Vessels**: For mashing, boiling, and fermenting.

    2. **Kilns and Drying Racks**: For malting grains.

    3. **Wooden Sieves**: To strain wort before fermentation.

    4. **Barrels and Jars**: For fermentation and storage.

- **Recipes (Detailed)**:

    - **Ingredients**:

        - 7-8 kg of malted barley, oats, or wheat

        - Fresh water from wells or streams
        - Herbs such as mugwort, heather, yarrow, and increasing use of hops
        - Optional: Honey or dried fruit for sweetness
    - **Method**:
        1. **Malting**: Spread grains on drying racks or in kilns for 2-3 days, turning frequently for even drying.
        2. **Crushing**: Coarsely crush dried malt using wooden mallets or stones.
        3. **Mashing**: Combine the crushed malt with warm water (55-65°C) in wooden or clay vessels. Stir thoroughly and steep for 1-2 hours.
        4. **Boiling**: Boil the wort in large cauldrons for 45-60 minutes. Add herbs or hops during the final 15-20 minutes of boiling.
        5. **Fermentation**: Transfer the cooled wort to barrels or jars. Cover loosely and allow to ferment for 4-6 days in a cool, shaded area.
        6. **Storage**: Store the ale in barrels or clay jars. Consume within 2-3 weeks.
- **SPV (Strength, Preservation, and Variability)**:
    - **Strength**: Maintains a steady alcohol content of 4-5%.
    - **Preservation**: Improved slightly by the early use of hops and better fermentation control.
    - **Variability**: Moderate, with regional differences influenced by the adoption of hops and local ingredient availability.
- **Social Aspect**: Ale remains integral to daily life, serving as nourishment and a social unifier. Monastic ales gain renown for their quality and are distributed to both local communities and travelling pilgrims. Communal brewing in villages ensures a steady supply for feasts and festivals, reinforcing communal bonds. The introduction of hops marks

a subtle but significant shift, laying the foundation for the transformation of British brewing in the coming centuries.

Alfric the Brewer: The Ale That "Saved the Taxman"

Setting the Scene

By 1100 AD, Norman rule was firmly established in England. Taxes were high, feasts were extravagant, and every villager dreaded the arrival of the king's tax collectors. In the bustling village of Maltwick, Alfric the Brewer was known for his wit, charm, and his ability to brew ales that could make even the sourest monk smile.

One day, however, Alfric's brewing skills were put to the ultimate test when the king's taxman, Sir Reginald, arrived with a particularly bad mood and a bottomless appetite for gold.

The Taxman's Arrival

Sir Reginald, a portly and pompous man, stomped into Maltwick with a ledger in one hand and a quill in the other. "By order of King Henry, you owe three barrels of grain, ten pounds of silver, and an extra tithe for... my efforts," he announced, smirking.

The villagers groaned. They had barely enough to eat, let alone pay extra taxes. Desperate, they turned to Alfric for help.

"Alfric," the baker pleaded, "you're the cleverest man in Maltwick. Do something!"

Alfric rubbed his chin thoughtfully. "If the taxman wants extra, we'll give him something... unexpected."

The Brewing of "Taxman's Ale"

Alfric retreated to his brewery and began crafting a brew that would distract, charm, and hopefully confound Sir Reginald. His recipe included:

- Barley malt for richness, because "taxmen like things heavy."
- A splash of honey, to sweeten his temper.

- Wild elderberries, for a fruity tang that would "tickle his ledger-loving tongue."
- And a secret ingredient: dandelion root, because Alfric believed it would "keep him preoccupied."

He stirred the pot with a wooden spoon, muttering, "This isn't just ale; it's diplomacy in a mug."

The Grand Presentation

The next morning, Alfric approached Sir Reginald, carrying a large barrel of *Taxman's Ale* and wearing his finest tunic.

"Your lordship," Alfric said with a bow, "Maltwick humbly offers you this ale, brewed specially in your honor. A token of our gratitude for your... tireless work."

Sir Reginald sniffed suspiciously but couldn't resist the rich aroma wafting from the barrel. "Very well," he said, "pour me a mug."

The First Sip

Sir Reginald took a cautious sip, then paused. The villagers held their breath.

"It's... quite good," Reginald said, taking another sip. "Sweet, yet bold. And is that... elderberry?"

Alfric beamed. "Indeed, your lordship. A flavor as complex and noble as your duties."

Flattered, Sir Reginald drank more, his mood improving with each gulp.

The Chaos

As Sir Reginald worked his way through the barrel, the ale's effects began to show. He attempted to calculate the village's taxes but kept forgetting his sums, distracted by the "extraordinary" tang of the elderberries.

"Such a remarkable brew," he slurred, "deserves a toast!" He raised his mug, spilling half of it on his ledger.

The villagers, emboldened by the sight of the muddled taxman, joined in, laughing and toasting Alfric's cleverness.

Eventually, Sir Reginald declared, "No taxes today! This village has... provided ample tribute with this ale!"

The Aftermath

The next morning, Sir Reginald left Maltwick with a pounding headache and no memory of waiving the taxes. The villagers, overjoyed, hailed Alfric as a hero.

"We'll never forget your *Taxman's Ale*!" they cheered.

Alfric, ever modest, replied, "It wasn't just the ale, it was knowing when to pour it."

The Legacy

Taxman's Ale became legendary, known as the brew that saved a village. Travelers came from far and wide to taste it, and Alfric's motto, "Brew bold, think bolder," was etched onto the village tavern door.

STEM Lesson

Alfric's story is a testament to creative problem-solving and the power of innovation. By combining his brewing skills with his understanding of human nature, he turned a difficult situation into a triumph.

The lesson? Science, creativity, and timing can be powerful tools for turning challenges into opportunities, and maybe even saving a few silver coins along the way.

1150 AD - 1200 AD: Brewing in the Age of Early Hopped Ales

- **Techniques**: Brewing practices continue to evolve, with monks leading advancements in brewing methods. The use of hops becomes more prevalent, particularly in areas influenced by continental Europe. Malting, mashing, boiling, and fermenting techniques are refined, and yeast management further improves in monastic settings, leading to more consistent ales.

- **Where Brewing Was Done**: Brewing takes place in households, village communal spaces, monasteries, and manorial estates. Monastic breweries grow more sophisticated, and wealthier estates begin to establish larger brewing facilities to cater to their needs. Villages maintain communal brewing traditions, ensuring the local population has access to ale.

- **How It Would Have Looked**: Household brewing remains simple, with clay pots, wooden barrels, and drying racks arranged near hearths. Village brewing spaces feature larger shared equipment, including cauldrons and fermentation vessels. Monastic breweries expand to include separate areas for malting, boiling, and fermentation, with storage cellars for aging ales. Hops are introduced in small quantities in some regions, changing the look and taste of certain ales.

- **Involvement of Villagers**: Women continue to lead household brewing for daily sustenance. Monks manage monastic brewing operations, producing high-quality ales for local communities and pilgrims. Villagers contribute to communal brewing projects, providing ingredients and labour for seasonal and festival brews. Wealthier estates employ professional brewers to oversee larger-scale production.

- **Equipment Used**:

    1. **Clay and Wooden Vessels**: For mashing, boiling, and fermenting.

    2. **Kilns and Drying Racks**: For malting grains.

    3. **Wooden Sieves**: To strain wort before fermentation.

    4. **Barrels and Jars**: For fermentation and storage.

    5. **Large Cauldrons**: For boiling wort in monastic and communal setups.

- **Recipes (Detailed)**:

- **Ingredients**:
    - 8 kg of malted barley, oats, or wheat
    - Fresh water from wells or streams
    - Herbs such as yarrow, heather, and mugwort, with increasing use of hops
    - Optional: Honey or dried fruits for added sweetness
- **Method**:
    1. **Malting**: Dry grains on racks or in kilns for 2-3 days, turning frequently to ensure even drying.
    2. **Crushing**: Coarsely crush malted grains using wooden mallets or stones.
    3. **Mashing**: Combine the crushed malt with warm water (55-65°C) in wooden or clay vessels. Stir thoroughly and steep for 1-2 hours.
    4. **Boiling**: Boil the wort in large cauldrons for 45-60 minutes. Add herbs or hops during the last 15-20 minutes of boiling.
    5. **Fermentation**: Transfer the cooled wort to barrels or jars. Cover loosely and allow to ferment for 4-6 days in a cool, shaded area.
    6. **Storage**: Store the ale in barrels or clay jars. Consume within 2-3 weeks.

- **SPV (Strength, Preservation, and Variability)**:
    - **Strength**: Maintains a steady alcohol content of 4-6%.
    - **Preservation**: Improved with the increased use of hops, which act as a natural preservative.
    - **Variability**: Moderate, with regional differences based on local herbs and hops adoption.
- **Social Aspect**: Ale continues to be a central part of daily life, offering both nutrition and a social focus. Monastic ales gain a reputation for quality and are sought after by locals and travellers alike. Villages rely

on communal brewing to meet the demand for feasts and festivals, strengthening community ties. The growing use of hops represents a turning point in British brewing, setting the stage for future innovations in flavour and preservation.

Osric the Brewer: The Ale That "Stole the Tournament"

Setting the Scene

By 1150 AD, England was a land of knights, tournaments, and feasts fit for kings. Brewing was an essential craft, as no feast or celebration was complete without barrels of ale. In the bustling town of Meadford, Osric the Brewer was the talk of the tavern, known for his audacious experiments and his belief that "ale can solve anything."

One day, Osric's boldness would be tested when a local knight's tournament brought lords, squires, and plenty of trouble to town.

The Tournament Trouble

The Earl of Meadford hosted an annual tournament, drawing knights from far and wide. The event was meant to showcase bravery, skill, and chivalry, but it was also notorious for feasting, brawling, and egos running wild.

This year, the Earl made a special request to Osric: "Brew an ale worthy of this grand event. Strong enough to inspire courage, but not so strong that it causes chaos."

Osric grinned. "A challenge fit for a brewer! Leave it to me, my lord."

The Brewing of "Knight's Draught"

Osric decided to brew an ale that would embody the spirit of the tournament. His recipe included:

- Barley malt for a hearty, robust flavor, "to strengthen a knight's resolve."
- A touch of honey, "to sweeten their victories."
- A handful of wild mint for a refreshing finish, "to cool their tempers."
- And a dash of ginger, "to give them a little fire in their hearts."

The brewing process was as dramatic as the tournament itself. Osric stirred the pot with a jousting lance (because why not?) and declared, "This ale shall be as bold as a charging knight and as smooth as a troubadour's song!"

The Big Reveal

On the day of the tournament, Osric unveiled his creation: *Knight's Draught*. He arrived at the tournament grounds with a cart laden with barrels, each one decorated with shields and painted knights.

"Lords and ladies," Osric proclaimed, "behold Meadford's finest ale, brewed to honor your valor and thirst!"

The crowd cheered as the first mugs were poured.

The Reactions

The knights, squires, and spectators took their first sips cautiously. Then came the smiles.

"It's hearty, yet refreshing!" one knight exclaimed.
"Ale fit for a champion!" shouted another.

Even the Earl himself raised his mug in approval. "Osric, you've outdone yourself!"

The Chaos

But as the ale flowed, the true spirit of the tournament began to shine, complete with unexpected hilarity.

- One knight, emboldened by the ginger, challenged a squire to a "duel of rhymes" and lost spectacularly.

- Another claimed *Knight's Draught* made him "see the future" and insisted his opponent would drop their lance on the next tilt, which, coincidentally, happened.

- The minstrel, inspired by the ale's minty finish, composed an impromptu song titled *The Ale That Conquered the Lance.*

The real highlight came when a group of knights, after a few too many mugs, decided to joust on foot using brooms instead of lances. The crowd, roaring with laughter, declared it the most entertaining match of the day.

The Aftermath

By evening, the tournament grounds had transformed into a massive feast, with knights toasting their victories, and their defeats, with *Knight's Draught*.

The Earl, thoroughly pleased, announced that Osric's ale would be the official drink of Meadford tournaments.

"My good Osric," the Earl said, raising his mug, "your ale has brought more joy to this tournament than any lance or sword!"

Osric, ever humble, replied, "Well, my lord, it's easier to brew harmony than to fight for it."

The Legacy

Knight's Draught became legendary, known as the ale that made tournaments more fun than fierce. Osric's jousting-lance stirring technique became a local tradition, and Meadford's tournaments grew famous not just for their knights, but for their ale-fueled antics.

STEM Lesson

Osric's story is a lighthearted reminder of how science and creativity can bring people together. By experimenting with flavors and understanding his audience, Osric turned a simple drink into a unifying experience.

The lesson? Craftsmanship is about more than just skill, it's about connecting with people and creating something memorable. And sometimes, the best inventions come with a touch of humor.

1200 AD - 1250 AD: Brewing in the Age of Expansion

- **Techniques**: Brewing practices in Britain continue to improve during this period, with the use of hops becoming more widespread. Monastic brewers lead the way in refining malting, mashing, boiling, and fermentation processes, resulting in ales with better consistency and longer preservation. Yeast management techniques improve, enhancing the predictability of fermentation outcomes.

- **Where Brewing Was Done**: Brewing occurs in households, village communal spaces, monasteries, and manorial estates. Monastic breweries expand their influence, producing high-quality ales for both local consumption and trade. Wealthy estates establish more sophisticated brewing facilities to cater to their retainers and guests.

- **How It Would Have Looked**: Household brewing remains centred around hearths, with clay pots and wooden barrels used for small-scale production. Village communal spaces are equipped with shared cauldrons and fermentation vessels, fostering collaboration among families. Monastic breweries become increasingly organised, featuring separate areas for malting, boiling, fermentation, and storage. The introduction of hops changes the appearance and taste of ales, with dried hop cones stored in monastic facilities.

- **Involvement of Villagers**: Women manage household brewing, while monks oversee large-scale monastic operations. Villagers contribute ingredients and labour to communal brewing efforts, especially during festivals and seasonal celebrations. Wealthier estates employ professional brewers to manage production for their households and workers.

- **Equipment Used**:

    1. **Clay and Wooden Vessels**: For mashing, boiling, and fermenting.

    2. **Kilns and Drying Racks**: For malting grains.

    3. **Wooden Sieves**: To strain wort before fermentation.

    4. **Barrels and Jars**: For fermentation and storage.

    5. **Large Cauldrons**: For boiling wort in monastic and communal setups.

    6. **Hop Drying Racks**: Used to prepare hops for brewing.

- **Recipes (Detailed)**:
  - **Ingredients**:
    - 8-10 kg of malted barley, oats, or wheat
    - Fresh water from wells or streams
    - Hops (increasingly common)
    - Optional: Honey or dried fruit for added sweetness
  - **Method**:
    1. **Malting**: Dry grains on racks or in kilns for 2-3 days, turning frequently to ensure even drying.
    2. **Crushing**: Coarsely crush malted grains using wooden mallets or stones.
    3. **Mashing**: Combine the crushed malt with warm water (55-65°C) in wooden or clay vessels. Stir thoroughly and steep for 1-2 hours.
    4. **Boiling**: Boil the wort in large cauldrons for 45-60 minutes. Add hops during the last 20 minutes of boiling.
    5. **Fermentation**: Transfer the cooled wort to barrels or jars. Cover loosely and allow to ferment for 4-6 days in a cool, shaded area.
    6. **Storage**: Store the ale in barrels or clay jars. Consume within 3-4 weeks.
- **SPV (Strength, Preservation, and Variability)**:
  - **Strength**: Alcohol content stabilises at 4-6%.
  - **Preservation**: Improved due to the increasing use of hops, which extend shelf life.
  - **Variability**: Moderate, influenced by regional adoption of hops and brewing conditions.
- **Social Aspect**: Ale remains a staple of daily life, with its role expanding in trade and cultural exchanges. Monastic ales become sought after for

their quality, serving both local communities and travellers. Communal brewing in villages continues to strengthen community ties, while hops introduce a new dimension to British brewing. Seasonal festivals and feasts are marked by the sharing of freshly brewed ale, reinforcing its place as a cornerstone of medieval society.

Wilfred the Brewer: The Ale That "Won the Feast"

Setting the Scene

By 1200 AD, brewing was a vital craft in England, with ale flowing freely at every feast, market, and celebration. In the bustling town of Kettleshire, Wilfred the Brewer was known for his bold experiments and even bolder claims. "There's no problem so big," he liked to say, "that a bigger ale can't solve."

One day, Wilfred's brewing skills were put to the test when the town was chosen to host the Baron's annual Harvest Feast, a grand event where local brewers competed for the title of "Ale of the Year."

The Baron's Challenge

The Baron of Kettleshire was a man of extravagant tastes, and he expected nothing less than perfection at his feast. "Brewers!" he announced, "I demand an ale that embodies the spirit of the harvest, bold, rich, and unforgettable! Impress me, and your ale will be served in my hall for a year. Disappoint me, and you'll be remembered... poorly."

The stakes were high, and the brewers of Kettleshire were nervous, except for Wilfred. "This is my chance," he declared. "I'll brew an ale so extraordinary, it'll knock the Baron's silk stockings off!"

The Brewing of "Baron's Bounty"

Wilfred decided to create an ale that captured the essence of the harvest season. His recipe included:

- Barley malt, roasted to perfection, for a hearty, nutty flavor.
- Honey from the village hives, to add a golden sweetness.
- A blend of spices, cinnamon, cloves, and nutmeg, because Wilfred believed "no feast is complete without a little spice."

- And a splash of cider, to give the brew a fruity tang and a touch of mischief.

As he stirred the pot, Wilfred added a pinch of dried elderflowers, declaring, "For luck and a touch of magic!" The brew bubbled and hissed like a cauldron, filling the air with a warm, spicy aroma.

The Feast Begins

On the day of the Harvest Feast, the town square was alive with music, laughter, and the clinking of mugs. The brewers lined up their barrels, each one eager to impress the Baron. Wilfred, ever the showman, arrived last, pulling a cart adorned with garlands and a sign that read *Baron's Bounty: The Taste of Victory.*

The Baron, seated at a grand table, began sampling the ales one by one. Some were too bitter, others too sweet, and one, to everyone's horror, had turned sour.

Finally, it was Wilfred's turn. With a flourish, he poured a mug of *Baron's Bounty* and presented it to the Baron.

The First Sip

The Baron took a sip, then paused. The crowd held its breath.

"This..." the Baron began, "is extraordinary!" He took another sip, then another, and finally let out a hearty laugh. "It's like drinking the harvest itself!"

The crowd erupted in cheers, but Wilfred wasn't done. "Your lordship," he said, "*Baron's Bounty* isn't just an ale, it's an experience."

The Baron, intrigued, raised an eyebrow. "Go on."

The "Experience"

Wilfred invited the Baron to close his eyes and imagine the golden fields of barley, the buzzing of bees, and the scent of autumn spices. The Baron, thoroughly enchanted (and already on his second mug), declared the ale "a work of art."

Inspired by the moment, the villagers began acting out scenes from the harvest, miming bee-keeping, threshing wheat, and even pretending to be apples falling from trees. The Baron laughed so hard he nearly spilled his ale.

The Aftermath

By the end of the feast, there was no question: *Baron's Bounty* was the winner. The Baron, still chuckling over the "harvest performance," decreed that Wilfred's ale would be served at every banquet in his hall.

Wilfred, ever humble, declared, "It's not just about the ale, it's about the story it tells."

The Legacy

Baron's Bounty became a legend in Kettleshire, and Wilfred's theatrical presentation inspired other brewers to pair their ales with stories, songs, and even puppet shows. The phrase "Drink the harvest" became a local toast, and Wilfred's elderflower-luck charm was said to ensure every brew's success.

STEM Lesson

Wilfred's story demonstrates the importance of combining creativity, science, and storytelling to create something truly memorable. His understanding of flavor profiles and his ability to connect with his audience turned a simple ale into an unforgettable experience.

The lesson? Great innovation isn't just about the product, it's about how you share it with the world. And a touch of showmanship never hurts.

1250 AD - 1300 AD: Brewing in a Time of Trade and Innovation

- **Techniques**: Brewing practices in Britain become increasingly sophisticated. The use of hops is now widely adopted, significantly improving the preservation and flavour of ales. Monastic brewers refine yeast cultivation and fermentation techniques, creating more consistent and higher-quality products. Improved malting methods ensure greater control over flavour profiles.

- **Where Brewing Was Done**: Brewing takes place in households, village communal spaces, monasteries, and manorial estates. Monasteries remain centres of brewing innovation, while wealthy estates expand their brewing operations to supply their households and retainers. Brewing for trade begins to emerge as surplus production grows.

- **How It Would Have Looked**: Household brewing is still a practical activity centred around hearths, with small clay pots and wooden barrels. Village communal brewing spaces are equipped with larger cauldrons, fermentation vessels, and shared tools. Monastic breweries are highly organised, featuring dedicated malting areas, boiling rooms, fermentation cellars, and storage facilities for hops and ale. The rise in trade introduces new opportunities for transporting ales in barrels.

- **Involvement of Villagers**: Women continue to manage household brewing, while monks oversee large-scale monastic operations. Villagers contribute labour and ingredients to communal brewing efforts, particularly during festivals and harvest seasons. Professional brewers begin to emerge, employed by wealthier estates and towns to produce ale for trade and local markets.

- **Equipment Used**:

    1. **Clay and Wooden Vessels**: For mashing, boiling, and fermenting.

    2. **Kilns and Drying Racks**: For malting grains.

    3. **Wooden Sieves**: To strain wort before fermentation.

    4. **Barrels**: For fermentation, storage, and transport.

    5. **Large Cauldrons**: For boiling wort in monastic and communal setups.

    6. **Hop Drying Racks**: Used to prepare hops for brewing.

- **Recipes (Detailed)**:
    - **Ingredients**:
        - 8-10 kg of malted barley, oats, or wheat
        - Fresh water from wells or streams
        - Hops (widely used)
        - Optional: Honey or dried fruit for additional sweetness
    - **Method**:
        1. **Malting**: Dry grains on racks or in kilns for 2-3 days, turning frequently to ensure even drying.
        2. **Crushing**: Coarsely crush malted grains using wooden mallets or stones.
        3. **Mashing**: Combine the crushed malt with warm water (55-65°C) in wooden or clay vessels. Stir thoroughly and steep for 1-2 hours.
        4. **Boiling**: Boil the wort in large cauldrons for 60-90 minutes. Add hops during the last 30 minutes of boiling.
        5. **Fermentation**: Transfer the cooled wort to barrels. Cover loosely and allow to ferment for 5-7 days in a cool, shaded area.
        6. **Storage**: Store the ale in barrels. Consume within 4-6 weeks or transport for trade.
- **SPV (Strength, Preservation, and Variability)**:
    - **Strength**: Alcohol content stabilises at 5-6%.
    - **Preservation**: Significantly improved due to the widespread use of hops.
    - **Variability**: Reduced, as brewing techniques and equipment become more standardised.
- **Social Aspect**: Ale continues to play a central role in daily life, serving as both a staple beverage and a key social unifier. Monastic ales remain

highly prized, while village and estate brewing supports local consumption and trade. The rise of professional brewers signals a shift toward commercial brewing, with surplus ale transported to nearby towns and markets. Seasonal festivals and community gatherings are defined by the sharing of ale, reinforcing its importance in medieval British culture.

Geoffrey the Brewer: The Ale That "Foiled the Knightly Duel"

Setting the Scene

By 1250 AD, England was a land of knights, lords, and elaborate feasts. Brewing was an honored craft, and every castle and village relied on their local brewer to keep spirits high and tankards full. In the bustling market town of Alethorpe, Geoffrey the Brewer was known for his quick wit, clever experiments, and his knack for brewing ales that could either start or stop an argument.

Geoffrey's talent for turning chaos into comedy was about to be tested when two feuding knights brought their quarrel to town.

The Knightly Feud

Sir Baldwin of Westfield and Sir Eustace of Greenholm were rival knights with a longstanding grudge. No one remembered what started it, something about a misplaced falcon or an insult over stew, but their rivalry was legendary.

One day, both knights arrived in Alethorpe, claiming the local manor as part of their lands. Heated arguments broke out in the market square, and soon the knights were challenging each other to a duel.

The townsfolk were terrified. "If they fight, they'll destroy the square!" cried the blacksmith.

Geoffrey, polishing a mug in his tavern, grinned. "Let them come. I've got just the thing to settle their quarrel."

The Brewing of "Knight's Resolve"

Geoffrey set out to brew an ale that would disarm even the fiercest knights. His recipe was bold and cheeky:

- Barley malt for strength, "to match their egos."
- Wild honey, for sweetness, "to soften their tempers."

- A touch of hops, "to keep them grounded."
- And a splash of fermented gooseberry juice, "for a zing they won't forget."

As he brewed, Geoffrey muttered, "If this doesn't stop their duel, at least it'll give them something to think about mid-swing."

The Duel's Eve
The next day, Sir Baldwin and Sir Eustace stood in the square, swords drawn and tempers high. The villagers gathered nervously, expecting the worst.

Before the knights could charge, Geoffrey marched into the square carrying two mugs of his *Knight's Resolve*.

"Before you fight," he announced, "you must drink. It's tradition here in Alethorpe, no duel begins without a toast!"

The knights, intrigued and perhaps a little thirsty, lowered their swords. "Very well," Sir Baldwin said. "Pour us this 'toast-worthy' ale."

The First Sip
Geoffrey handed each knight a mug, and they took cautious sips. Then came the reactions:

"This... this is magnificent!" exclaimed Sir Baldwin, wiping foam from his mustache.
"It's sweet, but sharp!" Sir Eustace added. "Like a well-honed blade!"

Encouraged by the knights' approval, Geoffrey poured another round.

The Chaos
As the knights drank more of *Knight's Resolve*, their rivalry took a humorous turn.

- Sir Baldwin declared himself the "King of Alethorpe" and began ordering imaginary armies to fetch more ale.
- Sir Eustace insisted on reciting (bad) poetry about his "victory," though he forgot most of the words halfway through.
- A crowd favorite was when the knights decided to reenact their duel using loaves of bread as swords.

The villagers, once terrified, now roared with laughter. Geoffrey leaned against a barrel, grinning. "Better breadsticks than broadswords," he muttered.

The Aftermath

By nightfall, the knights were too drunk to fight. They slumped onto benches, laughing and toasting each other as "worthy opponents."

In the morning, with pounding heads and vague memories of bread duels, Sir Baldwin and Sir Eustace declared a truce. "The real victory," Sir Baldwin said, raising a mug of water, "is friendship... and Geoffrey's ale."

The knights left Alethorpe with a newfound respect for each other, and a barrel of *Knight's Resolve* for the road.

The Legacy

Geoffrey's *Knight's Resolve* became a local legend, known as the ale that could stop wars before they started. Knights from across the land began visiting Alethorpe, not to duel, but to toast to peace (and taste the infamous gooseberry zing).

The town's motto, "Resolve, not rivalry," was etched above the tavern door, and Geoffrey's barrel-stirring antics were celebrated in songs and plays for generations.

STEM Lesson

Geoffrey's story highlights the power of creativity and understanding human nature. By using his brewing skills and a touch of humor, he turned a potentially violent situation into a celebration.

The lesson? Science and craft aren't just about solving technical problems, they're about creating connections, diffusing tension, and making people laugh. And sometimes, a little zing goes a long way.

1300 AD - 1350 AD: Brewing in the Age of Expansion and Resilience

- **Techniques**: Brewing in Britain continues to develop, with hops firmly established as a key ingredient. Improved malting, mashing, and fermentation techniques result in more consistent ales. Yeast management advances, particularly in monastic breweries, leading to greater control over fermentation. Trade and commerce further standardise brewing methods.

- **Where Brewing Was Done**: Brewing occurs in households, village communal spaces, monasteries, and urban breweries. Monasteries remain central to brewing innovation, while urban breweries begin to emerge in response to growing trade and population centres. Wealthy estates maintain their brewing operations to supply retainers and guests.

- **How It Would Have Looked**: Household brewing setups remain practical and small-scale, with clay pots, wooden barrels, and simple tools near hearths. Communal village brewing areas are equipped with large cauldrons and fermentation barrels, shared by families. Monastic breweries and urban breweries are highly organised, featuring dedicated malting areas, boiling rooms, fermentation cellars, and storage facilities for hops and ale. The rise of trade sees barrels of ale transported to towns and markets.

- **Involvement of Villagers**: Women continue to oversee household brewing for family needs. Monks manage monastic brewing operations, producing high-quality ales for local consumption and trade. Villagers contribute labour and resources to communal brewing projects, while urban breweries employ professional brewers to meet growing demand.

- **Equipment Used**:

    1. **Clay and Wooden Vessels**: For mashing, boiling, and fermenting.
    2. **Kilns and Drying Racks**: For malting grains.
    3. **Wooden Sieves**: To strain wort before fermentation.
    4. **Barrels**: For fermentation, storage, and transport.
    5. **Large Cauldrons**: For boiling wort in monastic, communal, and urban setups.
    6. **Hop Drying Racks**: Used to prepare hops for brewing.

- **Recipes (Detailed)**:
    - **Ingredients**:
        - 8-12 kg of malted barley, oats, or wheat
        - Fresh water from wells or streams
        - Hops (standardised and widely used)
        - Optional: Honey or dried fruit for additional sweetness
    - **Method**:
        1. **Malting**: Dry grains on racks or in kilns for 2-3 days, turning frequently for even drying.
        2. **Crushing**: Coarsely crush malted grains using wooden mallets or stones.
        3. **Mashing**: Combine the crushed malt with warm water (55-65°C) in wooden or clay vessels. Stir thoroughly and steep for 1-2 hours.
        4. **Boiling**: Boil the wort in large cauldrons for 60-90 minutes. Add hops during the last 30 minutes of boiling.
        5. **Fermentation**: Transfer the cooled wort to barrels. Cover loosely and allow to ferment for 5-7 days in a cool, shaded area.
        6. **Storage**: Store the ale in barrels. Consume within 4-6 weeks or transport for trade.
- **SPV (Strength, Preservation, and Variability)**:
    - **Strength**: Alcohol content stabilises at 5-6%.
    - **Preservation**: Improved due to the widespread and consistent use of hops.
    - **Variability**: Reduced, as brewing methods and equipment are increasingly standardised.
- **Social Aspect**: Ale continues to be a central element of daily life, providing both nourishment and social connection. Monastic ales

maintain their reputation for quality, while urban breweries begin catering to growing towns and markets. The professionalisation of brewing sees the rise of guilds and regulated trade, marking a shift toward commercial brewing practices. Seasonal festivals, community gatherings, and market days feature ale prominently, reinforcing its importance in British society.

Randolf the Brewer: The Ale That "Outwitted the Monks"

Setting the Scene

By 1300 AD, monasteries were not just places of prayer but also hubs of innovation, particularly in brewing. Monks were famed for their skill in crafting ales, which they brewed to fund their abbeys. In the small town of Hopsbury, however, Randolf the Brewer was a proud challenger to monastic brewing dominance.

Randolf, a cheeky and resourceful brewer, loved to boast, "A monk's ale may save your soul, but mine will make you laugh!" His rivalry with the nearby Abbey of St. Frothias had been a friendly one, until the monks decided to host an ale competition.

The Monkly Challenge

One day, a delegation from St. Frothias arrived in Hopsbury, led by the stern-faced Abbot Bernard. "We, the brewers of St. Frothias, invite you to an ale competition," the abbot announced. "The winner's ale will be declared the finest in the county, and their recipe immortalized in song."

Randolf grinned. "I accept! But be warned, holy men, this competition will be spirited, in every sense of the word."

The abbot frowned. "We'll see if your heathen brews can stand against the purity of ours."

The Brewing of "Sinner's Smile"

Determined to win, Randolf decided to craft an ale that was as bold and unconventional as himself. His recipe included:

- Barley malt for a rich, nutty base.

- A generous helping of honey, because "sweetness wins hearts."
- Juniper berries, for an earthy sharpness.
- And a pinch of cinnamon and cloves, "to remind the monks of their own spiced cider experiments."

Randolf added an extra touch of theatrics by brewing the ale in a massive oak barrel adorned with carvings of grinning devils. "If they want to preach about sin, I'll give them something to smile about," he joked.

The Day of the Competition

The competition was held in the abbey's courtyard, where a long table was set with barrels from both the monks and Randolf. Villagers, nobles, and even the local sheriff had gathered to witness the showdown.

The monks presented their ale first, a golden brew they called *Heaven's Dew*. It was crisp, clean, and, as Randolf muttered under his breath, "about as exciting as holy water."

Then it was Randolf's turn. He rolled his barrel of *Sinner's Smile* into the courtyard, grinning mischievously.

"Ladies and gentlemen," he declared, "my ale doesn't just save your thirst, it brings you joy!"

The Reactions

The first sips of *Sinner's Smile* left the crowd wide-eyed.

"It's sweet, but fiery!" exclaimed the sheriff.
"Earthy, yet spicy!" added a noblewoman.
Even Abbot Bernard, reluctantly taking a sip, paused and muttered, "It's... complex."

But the true hilarity began when the monks, curious about the competition, sampled *Sinner's Smile* themselves. One monk, clearly unused to the strength of Randolf's brew, hiccupped loudly and declared, "The devil's in the details, and this ale is sinful indeed!"

The crowd roared with laughter, and Randolf seized the moment. "See? Even the monks agree, it's heavenly with a touch of mischief!"

The Chaos

As the competition wore on, the villagers, monks, and nobles drank more of *Sinner's Smile*. The usually stoic Abbot Bernard began chuckling uncontrollably, while another monk attempted to juggle apples (and failed spectacularly).

The sheriff, inspired by the brew's fiery kick, challenged a monk to an arm-wrestling contest, which ended with the table collapsing.

Randolf, watching the chaos with a satisfied grin, leaned against his barrel. "I think we know who won," he whispered to a villager.

The Aftermath

The next morning, with sore heads and vague memories of singing bawdy songs with monks, the judges announced their decision.

"The ale of St. Frothias is pure and divine," the sheriff said. "But Randolf's *Sinner's Smile*... well, it made us laugh until we cried. The winner is clear!"

Randolf was crowned the champion brewer of Hopsbury, and *Sinner's Smile* became a local legend. Even the monks, despite their initial grumbles, began ordering barrels for "special occasions."

The Legacy

Sinner's Smile became famous far beyond Hopsbury, celebrated as the ale that outwitted the monks. Randolf's motto, "A little sin never hurt anyone," was etched onto the tavern sign, and his devil-carved barrel became a local tourist attraction.

STEM Lesson

Randolf's story highlights the importance of creativity, humor, and understanding your audience. By combining his brewing skills with a touch of theatrics, he created an ale that didn't just satisfy taste buds but brought people together in laughter.

The lesson? Innovation is about more than just technique, it's about creating an experience people will never forget. And a little spice always helps.

1350 AD - 1400 AD: Brewing Through Times of Change

- **Techniques**: Brewing practices remain steady with hops now firmly established as a key ingredient. Improved malting processes and yeast cultivation techniques continue to enhance consistency and quality. Urban breweries grow in prominence, using increasingly standardised methods to meet rising demand in towns and cities.

- **Where Brewing Was Done**: Brewing is conducted in households, village communal spaces, monasteries, urban breweries, and manorial estates. Monastic brewing operations begin to decline slightly in prominence, with urban breweries stepping in to supply growing urban populations. Professional brewing guilds emerge, standardising practices and setting quality benchmarks.

- **How It Would Have Looked**: Household brewing remains modest, with clay pots, wooden barrels, and hearth-based setups. Communal village brewing spaces feature shared tools and larger cauldrons. Urban breweries are well-organised operations, equipped with large boiling cauldrons, fermentation barrels, and storage areas for hops and ale. Brewing on estates caters to retainers and local markets, reflecting a semi-commercial scale.

- **Involvement of Villagers**: Women maintain their role in household brewing, while professional brewers dominate urban and estate production. Villagers contribute labour and materials for communal brewing projects, especially during harvests and festivals. The emergence of brewing guilds marks a shift toward regulated and professionalised brewing.

- **Equipment Used**:

    1. **Clay and Wooden Vessels**: For mashing, boiling, and fermenting.

    2. **Kilns and Drying Racks**: For malting grains.

    3. **Wooden Sieves**: To strain wort before fermentation.

    4. **Barrels**: For fermentation, storage, and transport.

    5. **Large Cauldrons**: For boiling wort in urban, monastic, and communal setups.

    6. **Hop Drying Racks**: For preparing hops for brewing.

- **Recipes (Detailed)**:
    - **Ingredients**:
        - 8-12 kg of malted barley, oats, or wheat
        - Fresh water from wells or streams
        - Hops (fully standardised and widely used)
        - Optional: Honey or dried fruit for additional sweetness
    - **Method**:
        1. **Malting**: Dry grains on racks or in kilns for 2-3 days, turning frequently for even drying.
        2. **Crushing**: Coarsely crush malted grains using wooden mallets or stones.
        3. **Mashing**: Combine the crushed malt with warm water (55-65°C) in wooden or clay vessels. Stir thoroughly and steep for 1-2 hours.
        4. **Boiling**: Boil the wort in large cauldrons for 60-90 minutes. Add hops during the last 30 minutes of boiling.
        5. **Fermentation**: Transfer the cooled wort to barrels. Cover loosely and allow to ferment for 5-7 days in a cool, shaded area.
        6. **Storage**: Store the ale in barrels. Consume within 4-6 weeks or transport for trade.
- **SPV (Strength, Preservation, and Variability)**:
    - **Strength**: Alcohol content stabilises at 5-6%.
    - **Preservation**: Improved significantly due to the consistent use of hops.
    - **Variability**: Further reduced as brewing methods are standardised through guild practices.
- **Social Aspect**: Ale continues to be an essential part of daily life, providing both sustenance and a focal point for social interaction. Urban

breweries begin catering to a broader market, while brewing guilds ensure quality and regulate competition. Seasonal festivals, communal gatherings, and trade fairs highlight the centrality of ale in medieval society. The professionalisation of brewing sets the stage for its evolution into a more commercial enterprise in the centuries to come.

Hugh the Brewer: The Ale That "Beat the Plague Doctor"

Setting the Scene

By 1350 AD, the Black Death was ravaging Europe, and England was no exception. Villages were desperate for solutions, and strange remedies became commonplace. In the small town of Brewminster, however, Hugh the Brewer was more focused on crafting the perfect ale than worrying about plagues.

Hugh, known for his odd humor and inventive brewing methods, often joked, "Ale is the best medicine, because it makes you forget what's ailing you."

One day, his brewing skills and comedic timing would save the town in the most unexpected way.

The Plague Doctor's Visit

When a wandering plague doctor arrived in Brewminster, the townsfolk were on edge. Dressed in a long cloak and a terrifying beaked mask, the doctor claimed to have cures for the plague, but his remedies were bizarre and expensive.

"I need all your garlic, vinegar, and coins," the doctor announced, "to prepare my miraculous cure."

The villagers, skeptical but desperate, looked to Hugh for guidance. "What do we do?" they asked.

Hugh grinned. "If this doctor wants to cure us, let's cure him first, with my *Plaguebreaker Ale*."

The Brewing of "Plaguebreaker Ale"

Hugh decided to brew an ale that would impress (and confound) the plague doctor. His recipe included:

- Barley malt, "to give it strength."

- Local honey, "for sweetness to balance his sour face."
- Dried herbs, including rosemary and thyme, "because they smell better than his garlic."
- And a splash of cider vinegar, "to outdo his potions."

As he brewed, Hugh added a pinch of nettles for a "zing," muttering, "Let's see if his beak can handle this."

The Grand Presentation

The next morning, Hugh carried a barrel of *Plaguebreaker Ale* to the town square, where the doctor was assembling his remedies. "Good doctor," Hugh called, "before you work your miracles, try the finest ale in Brewminster. It's known to cure all ills, or at least make you forget them."

The doctor, intrigued and perhaps a little thirsty, agreed to sample the ale. "But if this fails to impress," he warned, "you'll owe me double for my cure."

The First Sip

The doctor tilted his mask slightly and took a cautious sip. Then another. His eyes widened.

"This is... remarkable!" he exclaimed. "It's tangy, yet smooth. Sweet, yet sharp. What is your secret?"

Hugh leaned in and whispered, "A brewer never reveals his secrets, but let's just say it's brewed with more care than your garlic vinegar."

The Chaos

As the doctor continued to drink, the villagers, emboldened by his reaction, began sampling the ale themselves. The tension in the square dissolved into laughter as the townsfolk started joking about the doctor's bizarre remedies.

- The blacksmith challenged the doctor to a "garlic duel," holding cloves like swords.
- The baker fashioned a loaf into a beaked mask and waddled around, mimicking the doctor's voice.
- One particularly bold farmer tied herbs to his boots and declared himself "immune by osmosis."

The doctor, flustered but tipsy, tried to regain control of the crowd, but his own laughter betrayed him.

The Aftermath

By evening, the doctor had abandoned his remedies and was merrily singing drinking songs with the villagers. "This *Plaguebreaker Ale* is all the cure I need!" he declared, clinking mugs with Hugh.

The next morning, the doctor departed with a barrel of Hugh's ale and no mention of his cures. The villagers, delighted with their newfound morale, hailed Hugh as a hero.

The Legacy

Plaguebreaker Ale became a symbol of resilience and humor in the face of adversity. Visitors from neighboring towns came to Brewminster to sample the legendary brew, and Hugh's motto, "Laughter and ale are the best medicine," was carved above the tavern door.

STEM Lesson

Hugh's story demonstrates the power of creativity, science, and humor in solving problems. His understanding of flavors and human nature turned a potentially grim situation into a moment of joy and unity.

The lesson? Innovation isn't just about fixing what's broken, it's about lifting spirits, building connections, and bringing a little laughter to tough times.

1400 AD - 1450 AD: Brewing in the Pre-Renaissance Era

- **Techniques**: Brewing in Britain continues to develop with increasingly refined techniques. Hops are firmly entrenched as a key ingredient, enhancing both flavour and preservation. Urban breweries adopt standardised methods to cater to growing urban markets. Brewing guilds enforce quality controls, ensuring consistent production standards. Advances in malting and yeast management lead to more predictable fermentation and higher-quality ales.

- **Where Brewing Was Done**: Brewing takes place in households, village communal spaces, urban breweries, monasteries, and manorial estates. Urban breweries grow in scale and sophistication, becoming central to supply for towns and cities. Monastic brewing continues but loses dominance as professional brewing becomes more commercialised.

- **How It Would Have Looked**: Household brewing remains practical, featuring clay pots, wooden barrels, and hearth-based setups. Village communal brewing spaces utilise shared equipment, including large cauldrons and fermentation vessels. Urban breweries are well-equipped, with dedicated boiling rooms, fermentation areas, and large storage facilities for barrels. Hops are stored in drying sheds or cool storage areas for brewing use throughout the year.

- **Involvement of Villagers**: Women continue to brew ale for household consumption, while professional brewers dominate urban and estate brewing operations. Brewing guilds organise production in towns, setting standards for ale quality and fair trade. Villagers support communal brewing projects and contribute labour during festivals and harvests.

- **Equipment Used**:

    1. **Clay and Wooden Vessels**: For mashing, boiling, and fermenting.
    2. **Kilns and Drying Racks**: For malting grains.
    3. **Wooden Sieves**: To strain wort before fermentation.
    4. **Barrels**: For fermentation, storage, and transport.
    5. **Large Cauldrons**: For boiling wort in communal, urban, and estate setups.

6. **Hop Drying Racks**: For preparing hops for brewing.

- **Recipes (Detailed)**:
    - **Ingredients**:
        - 8-12 kg of malted barley, oats, or wheat
        - Fresh water from wells or streams
        - Hops (widely used and standardised)
        - Optional: Honey or dried fruits for additional sweetness
    - **Method**:
        1. **Malting**: Dry grains on racks or in kilns for 2-3 days, turning frequently to ensure even drying.
        2. **Crushing**: Coarsely crush malted grains using wooden mallets or stones.
        3. **Mashing**: Combine the crushed malt with warm water (55-65°C) in wooden or clay vessels. Stir thoroughly and steep for 1-2 hours.
        4. **Boiling**: Boil the wort in large cauldrons for 60-90 minutes. Add hops during the last 30 minutes of boiling.
        5. **Fermentation**: Transfer the cooled wort to barrels. Cover loosely and allow to ferment for 5-7 days in a cool, shaded area.
        6. **Storage**: Store the ale in barrels. Consume within 4-6 weeks or transport for trade.
- **SPV (Strength, Preservation, and Variability)**:
    - **Strength**: Alcohol content stabilises at 5-6%.
    - **Preservation**: Further improved by the consistent use of hops and advanced storage techniques.
    - **Variability**: Reduced, as brewing methods and equipment are increasingly standardised.

- **Social Aspect**: Ale remains central to daily life, with urban breweries becoming hubs of production and trade. Brewing guilds ensure fair practices and high-quality ales, bolstering the reputation of British brewing. Seasonal festivals, community gatherings, and market days prominently feature ale, reinforcing its cultural and economic significance. The increasing commercialisation of brewing reflects the broader societal changes of the pre-Renaissance era, setting the stage for future industrialisation and global trade.

Thomas the Brewer: The Ale That "Tricked the Tax Collectors"

Setting the Scene

By 1400 AD, brewing was a thriving trade in England, but so were taxes. Brewers were subject to heavy levies on their ales, and tax collectors, dubbed "ale counters", were feared and loathed across the land. In the bustling town of Brewminster, Thomas the Brewer was a local favorite, known for his quick wit, creative ales, and uncanny ability to stay one step ahead of trouble.

When news spread that the king's ale counters were on their way, the townsfolk panicked. But Thomas, as always, had a plan.

The Ale Counter Crisis

The ale counters were notorious for their strict assessments and fines. "Every drop of ale must be accounted for," they declared. "No barrel untaxed!"

When the mayor of Brewminster warned Thomas about their arrival, he grinned. "Let them come," he said. "They may count my barrels, but they won't know what they're counting."

"What do you mean?" the mayor asked nervously.

"Trust me," Thomas replied. "I'll brew something they'll never forget."

The Brewing of "Counterfeit Ale"

Thomas decided to create an ale so baffling that even the most diligent tax collector wouldn't know what to do with it. His recipe included:

- Barley malt, as usual, for a solid base.
- A mix of wild herbs and flowers, "to keep them guessing."

- A touch of molasses, for an unusual sweetness.
- And a generous dose of dandelion root, "to make it taste... strange."

He also added a secret ingredient: a splash of fermented beet juice, which turned the ale a shocking shade of purple.

As he stirred the pot, Thomas chuckled. "This isn't just ale, it's confusion in a barrel."

The Tax Day Ruse

When the ale counters arrived, Thomas greeted them with a large smile and a cart full of barrels marked *Royal Reserve*. "Welcome, fine gentlemen!" he said. "I've prepared something special for your inspection."

The ale counters, suspicious but intrigued, demanded to sample the ale.

Thomas poured them each a mug of the bright purple brew. The first sips were met with furrowed brows.

"It's... unusual," one muttered.
"Is that... lavender? Or beets?" another asked, sniffing the mug.

Thomas nodded solemnly. "Indeed, gentlemen. It's a rare and experimental brew, crafted for its medicinal properties. The villagers call it *Counterfeit Ale* because it's so unlike anything else. Surely such a unique concoction doesn't qualify for the standard ale tax?"

The Chaos

The ale counters, clearly unsure how to classify the brew, began arguing amongst themselves.

- "It's ale, so it must be taxed!" one declared.
- "But it's purple!" another countered. "Ale isn't purple!"
- "What if it's a potion?" the third asked nervously. "Do we tax potions?"

Meanwhile, the townsfolk, emboldened by Thomas's antics, began offering their own (wild) theories about the ale's properties.

- "I hear it cures warts!" shouted the blacksmith.
- "Nonsense," said the baker. "It's for warding off witches!"

- "I drank it last week," added the miller, "and my cow gave more milk than ever!"

The ale counters, thoroughly confused and slightly tipsy, eventually decided that *Counterfeit Ale* was too bizarre to tax. "We'll... consult the king," they mumbled before leaving town with their ledgers and a few barrels of the mysterious brew.

The Aftermath

With the ale counters gone, the townsfolk erupted in cheers. Thomas was hailed as a hero, and *Counterfeit Ale* became the talk of Brewminster.

When word spread that the king himself had sampled the ale and declared it "peculiar, but oddly refreshing," Thomas added a crown symbol to his barrels and began marketing it as a royal favorite.

The Legacy

Counterfeit Ale became a local legend, known as the brew that outwitted the tax collectors. Thomas's ingenuity inspired other brewers to experiment with flavors, colors, and even a bit of harmless mischief.

Above the tavern door, a new motto was etched: "Where there's a barrel, there's a way."

STEM Lesson

Thomas's story highlights the power of creativity and adaptability in problem-solving. By understanding both the rules and human nature, he turned a potentially costly situation into an opportunity for laughter and success.

The lesson? Innovation isn't just about making something new, it's about finding clever ways to navigate challenges. And sometimes, the best solutions are the ones that make people smile (and scratch their heads).

1450 AD - 1500 AD: Brewing in the Dawn of the Renaissance

- **Techniques**: Brewing continues to improve with advancements in technology and standardisation. Hops are universally used, solidifying their role in flavouring and preserving ale. Brewing guilds enforce strict quality controls and standardised methods, ensuring consistency across urban breweries. Improved malting and fermentation techniques result in more predictable and higher-quality ales.

- **Where Brewing Was Done**: Brewing takes place in households, village communal spaces, urban breweries, monasteries, and manorial estates. Urban breweries dominate production, catering to a growing urban population and expanding trade networks. Monastic brewing persists but is overshadowed by professional brewing guilds and larger commercial operations.

- **How It Would Have Looked**: Household brewing remains small-scale and practical, utilising clay pots and wooden barrels near hearths. Communal brewing spaces in villages feature shared cauldrons and fermentation vessels. Urban breweries are large, well-organised facilities with separate areas for malting, boiling, fermentation, and storage. Hops and malted grains are stored in dedicated warehouses, and barrels of ale are prepared for transport to markets.

- **Involvement of Villagers**: Women continue to oversee household brewing for daily consumption, while professional brewers dominate urban and estate production. Villagers contribute to communal brewing efforts during festivals and harvest seasons. Brewing guilds regulate urban production, employing skilled brewers and apprentices.

- **Equipment Used**:

    1. **Clay and Wooden Vessels**: For mashing, boiling, and fermenting.

    2. **Kilns and Drying Racks**: For malting grains.

    3. **Wooden Sieves**: To strain wort before fermentation.

    4. **Barrels**: For fermentation, storage, and transport.

    5. **Large Cauldrons**: For boiling wort in communal, urban, and estate setups.

    6. **Hop Drying Racks**: For preparing hops for brewing.

- **Recipes (Detailed)**:
    - **Ingredients**:
        - 8-12 kg of malted barley, oats, or wheat
        - Fresh water from wells or streams
        - Hops (widely used and fully standardised)
        - Optional: Honey or dried fruits for additional sweetness
    - **Method**:
        1. **Malting**: Dry grains on racks or in kilns for 2-3 days, turning frequently for even drying.
        2. **Crushing**: Coarsely crush malted grains using wooden mallets or stones.
        3. **Mashing**: Combine the crushed malt with warm water (55-65°C) in wooden or clay vessels. Stir thoroughly and steep for 1-2 hours.
        4. **Boiling**: Boil the wort in large cauldrons for 60-90 minutes. Add hops during the last 30 minutes of boiling.
        5. **Fermentation**: Transfer the cooled wort to barrels. Cover loosely and allow to ferment for 5-7 days in a cool, shaded area.
        6. **Storage**: Store the ale in barrels. Consume within 4-6 weeks or transport for trade.
- **SPV (Strength, Preservation, and Variability)**:
    - **Strength**: Alcohol content stabilises at 5-6%.
    - **Preservation**: Improved further by consistent use of hops and better storage practices.
    - **Variability**: Minimised, as brewing techniques are standardised by guild regulations.

- **Social Aspect**: Ale remains essential to both daily sustenance and social life. Urban breweries dominate the production landscape, supplying towns, cities, and trade routes. Brewing guilds ensure high-quality standards, strengthening the reputation of British ales. Seasonal festivals and market days revolve around ale, cementing its role in community bonding and economic activity. This period marks the rise of brewing as a professionalised and highly organised industry, setting the stage for further innovation during the Renaissance.

Edmund the Brewer: The Ale That "Broke the Guild"

Setting the Scene

By 1450 AD, brewing was not just a trade but a highly regulated profession. Brewers' guilds controlled everything from recipes to pricing, and anyone who brewed outside the rules was fined, or worse. In the lively town of Barleydown, Edmund the Brewer was a loveable rogue who followed one rule: "Ale should bring joy, not paperwork."

When the Barleydown Brewers' Guild announced a new set of strict brewing regulations, Edmund decided he'd had enough. "If they want rules, I'll give them something worth writing about!" he declared.

The Guild's New Rules

The Brewers' Guild, led by the pompous Master Gervais, declared that all ales must conform to a "purity code":

1. Only barley, water, and hops could be used.
2. All barrels must be stamped and registered with the guild.
3. No "unorthodox methods or ingredients" were allowed.

"These rules will elevate brewing to an art!" Master Gervais proclaimed.

Edmund rolled his eyes. "Art? Brewing is already an art, an art of fun. Let's see what they think of my next masterpiece."

The Brewing of "Guildbuster Ale"

Edmund decided to brew an ale that would mock the guild's rules while delighting the townsfolk. His recipe included:

- Barley malt, because he wasn't *entirely* reckless.
- Wild honey and a touch of molasses, "for sweetness the guild doesn't deserve."
- Juniper berries, to "give it a rebellious kick."
- And a handful of rose petals, "to make it fancy, because Gervais loves fancy."

He brewed it in his backyard, using an old kettle instead of a guild-approved barrel. To top it off, he painted a mocking seal on the side of the barrel: a donkey wearing a crown.

The Unveiling

On market day, Edmund rolled his barrel of *Guildbuster Ale* into the square, shouting, "Come one, come all! Taste the ale the guild doesn't want you to drink!"

The townsfolk, always eager for something new, gathered around. The first sips were met with laughter and surprise.

"It's sweet, but sharp!" said the baker.
"And is that... rose?" asked the blacksmith.

Even the town's priest, known for his strict ways, took a sip and muttered, "Heavenly, but don't tell the bishop."

The Guild's Fury

When Master Gervais heard about the rogue ale, he stormed into the square, flanked by his guild members. "What is the meaning of this?" he bellowed.

Edmund, holding a mug of his ale, grinned. "Just giving the people what they want, Gervais, an ale with a little imagination."

"You're breaking every rule in the book!" Gervais snapped. "This ale is unregistered, unregulated, and... what is that on the barrel?"

"A donkey in a crown," Edmund replied cheerfully. "A tribute to you, Master Gervais."

The crowd erupted in laughter, and even a few guild members struggled to hide their smiles.

The Tasting Standoff
Determined to assert his authority, Gervais demanded to taste the ale. "If it's as outrageous as you claim, I'll shut you down immediately!"

Edmund poured him a mug with a flourish. Gervais took a sip, then paused. His stern expression wavered.

"It's... quite good," he admitted grudgingly. "Too good for someone outside the guild."

Emboldened by the crowd's cheers, Edmund said, "If it's good enough for you, maybe it's time the guild loosened its reins. Brewing should be about joy, not rules!"

The Chaos
The situation spiraled hilariously out of control when the other guild members began sampling the ale.

- One declared it "the finest thing I've tasted since last harvest!"
- Another suggested adding honey to their own brews, causing a loud argument about tradition.
- Meanwhile, the blacksmith started reenacting the guild seal as a pantomime donkey, much to the crowd's delight.

Even Gervais, after his third mug, loosened his doublet and began waxing poetic about "the freedom of creativity."

The Aftermath
By the end of the day, Gervais declared that Edmund's *Guildbuster Ale* would be registered as a special "festival brew," exempt from the guild's rules. "Let this be a reminder," he slurred, "that ale is about community... and also rose petals."

Edmund, ever gracious, toasted Gervais and offered to help the guild "innovate" its recipes. The townsfolk, thrilled by the day's antics, celebrated long into the night.

The Legacy
Guildbuster Ale became a local favorite, celebrated as the ale that "broke the rules and mended the town." Edmund's cheeky seal became the unofficial emblem of Barleydown, and his motto, "Brew bold, laugh louder," was etched into the town square.

Even Master Gervais, now a regular at Edmund's tavern, admitted that a little rebellion was good for the soul, and the ale.

STEM Lesson

Edmund's story highlights the importance of challenging conventions and embracing creativity. By experimenting with flavors and humor, he created something that not only delighted his audience but also redefined what brewing could be.

The lesson? Innovation thrives when we're willing to question the rules and think outside the barrel. And a bit of fun never hurts.

1500 AD - 1550 AD: Brewing in the Early Modern Era

- **Techniques**: Brewing enters a period of significant innovation with the Renaissance spurring advancements in science and technology. Hops are universally used, and brewing guilds enforce rigorous quality controls. New fermentation techniques and refined malting processes produce ales with greater consistency and flavour complexity. The introduction of thermometers and hydrometers, although rare, begins to influence advanced brewing practices in wealthier operations.

- **Where Brewing Was Done**: Brewing continues in households, communal village spaces, urban breweries, monasteries, and manorial estates. Urban breweries dominate production, while monasteries further decline in their role as commercial brewing hubs. Large-scale brewing for export and trade begins to rise, with ports and cities playing a central role.

- **How It Would Have Looked**: Household brewing remains small-scale, featuring hearth-based setups with clay pots and wooden barrels. Village brewing spaces utilise shared equipment, while urban breweries operate as large, structured facilities with dedicated areas for malting, boiling, fermentation, and storage. Warehouses for storing hops and malted grains become common, and barrels of ale are transported via carts and ships for trade.

- **Involvement of Villagers**: Women manage household brewing, while professional brewers dominate urban and estate operations. Brewing guilds regulate urban production, ensuring fair practices and high standards. Villagers contribute to communal brewing efforts, particularly for festivals and seasonal gatherings. Trade networks begin to involve skilled labourers and merchants in the distribution of ale.

- **Equipment Used**:

    1. **Clay and Wooden Vessels**: For mashing, boiling, and fermenting.

    2. **Kilns and Drying Racks**: For malting grains.

    3. **Wooden Sieves**: To strain wort before fermentation.

    4. **Barrels**: For fermentation, storage, and transport.

5. **Large Cauldrons**: For boiling wort in communal, urban, and estate setups.

6. **Hop Drying Racks**: For preparing hops for brewing.

7. **Early Thermometers and Hydrometers**: Rarely used but emerging in advanced brewing operations.

- **Recipes (Detailed)**:

  - **Ingredients**:

    - 8-14 kg of malted barley, oats, or wheat
    - Fresh water from wells or streams
    - Hops (fully standardised and widely used)
    - Optional: Honey or spices for additional flavour complexity

  - **Method**:

    1. **Malting**: Dry grains on racks or in kilns for 2-3 days, turning frequently for even drying.
    2. **Crushing**: Coarsely crush malted grains using wooden mallets or stones.
    3. **Mashing**: Combine the crushed malt with warm water (55-65°C) in wooden or clay vessels. Stir thoroughly and steep for 1-2 hours.
    4. **Boiling**: Boil the wort in large cauldrons for 60-90 minutes. Add hops during the last 30 minutes of boiling.
    5. **Fermentation**: Transfer the cooled wort to barrels. Cover loosely and allow to ferment for 5-7 days in a cool, shaded area.
    6. **Storage**: Store the ale in barrels. Consume within 4-6 weeks or transport for trade.

- **SPV (Strength, Preservation, and Variability)**:

  - **Strength**: Alcohol content stabilises at 5-6%.

    - **Preservation**: Further improved by the universal use of hops and better storage practices.
    - **Variability**: Minimized in urban breweries due to guild-enforced standardisation.
- **Social Aspect**: Ale remains integral to daily life, providing nourishment and a key element of social gatherings. Urban breweries thrive as centres of production, employing skilled brewers and apprentices. Brewing guilds ensure quality and regulate trade, bolstering the reputation of British ales. Ports and markets become hubs for the export of ale, marking the beginnings of Britain's global brewing influence. Seasonal festivals, feasts, and market days highlight ale's enduring role in community life and economic activity.

Walter the Brewer: The Ale That "Fooled the Royal Inspectors"

Setting the Scene

By 1500 AD, brewing was not only an essential craft but also a lucrative business closely monitored by the crown. King Henry VII had recently imposed new taxes on ale, claiming that the "royal treasury must be filled with every frothy drop." To enforce this, royal inspectors roamed the country, ensuring that no brewer was evading taxes.

In the small town of Hopshire, Walter the Brewer was renowned for his cunning wit and unconventional ales. When word spread that royal inspectors were coming to town, the townsfolk turned to Walter for help.

The Royal Threat

The royal inspectors were notorious for their ruthless methods. "They'll measure every barrel and count every mug," warned the town's mayor. "If we can't pay, they'll fine us into the ground!"

Walter, leaning against a barrel, grinned. "Don't worry, friends. If they want to count barrels, let's give them something worth counting."

"What do you mean?" asked the baker.

Walter winked. "I'll brew an ale so baffling, they'll forget what they're inspecting."

The Brewing of "King's Favour Ale"

Walter set out to create an ale that would distract, confuse, and charm the royal inspectors. His recipe included:

- Barley malt for richness, "because royalty loves luxury."
- Wildflowers, "to make it smell like a royal garden."
- A touch of lemon peel, "for a zesty surprise."
- And a pinch of nettles, "to add a little sting."

He also added an unusual twist: dried marigold petals, which turned the ale a bright golden color. "If it looks like liquid gold," Walter reasoned, "they'll think it's worth more than their taxes."

The Inspectors Arrive

When the royal inspectors arrived, dressed in fine cloaks and with an air of authority, the townsfolk watched nervously. Walter, however, greeted them with a barrel marked *King's Favour Ale* and a smug smile.

"Gentlemen," he said, "before you begin your inspections, may I offer you a taste of Hopshire's finest brew? It's named in honor of His Majesty himself."

The inspectors, curious and a bit thirsty, agreed. "But be quick," one said. "We have much to measure."

The First Sip

Walter poured each inspector a mug of the shimmering golden ale. They sipped cautiously, then paused.

"This... this is extraordinary!" exclaimed the lead inspector.
"It's light, but bold!" added another.
"And is that a hint of lemon?"

Walter nodded proudly. "Only the finest for those who serve the king."

The Distraction

As the inspectors drank more, their focus on taxes quickly faded.

- One inspector began composing a poem about the ale, though it mostly rhymed "gold" with "bold."

- Another insisted on measuring the barrel "for scientific purposes" but ended up spilling half of it in his enthusiasm.
- The lead inspector, now on his third mug, declared, "This ale should be sent to the king immediately! It's a royal treasure!"

The townsfolk, seeing their plan work, stifled their laughter as the inspectors argued about how to transport the "priceless" ale back to London.

The Chaos

The situation reached peak hilarity when one inspector, inspired by the ale's golden hue, tried to polish a coin with it, declaring it a "secret royal recipe." Another, convinced the ale had magical properties, attempted to balance the barrel on his head as a "show of loyalty to the crown."

Walter, ever the showman, encouraged their antics. "Gentlemen," he said, "perhaps you'd like another barrel for your journey? A gift to His Majesty, of course."

The Aftermath

By the end of the day, the inspectors were too enchanted (and tipsy) to complete their work. They left town with two barrels of *King's Favour Ale* and a promise to "sing Hopshire's praises at court."

The townsfolk erupted in cheers as Walter was lifted onto their shoulders. "You've saved us!" they cried.

Walter grinned. "Just another day at the brewery."

The Legacy

King's Favour Ale became a local legend, celebrated as the ale that fooled the crown. Travelers came from far and wide to taste the "royal brew," and Walter's motto, "Brew bold, tax smarter," became the unofficial slogan of Hopshire.

Even King Henry VII, upon tasting the ale, reportedly declared, "If all taxes tasted like this, I'd drink to them daily!"

STEM Lesson

Walter's story demonstrates the power of innovation, creativity, and understanding human psychology. By crafting an ale that appealed to both the senses and the ego, he outwitted the inspectors and saved his town.

The lesson? Science and art can solve problems in unexpected ways, and sometimes, the best solution comes in a golden mug.

1550 AD - 1600 AD: Brewing During the Elizabethan Era

- **Techniques**: Brewing sees further standardisation and innovation during the Elizabethan era. Hops are universally used, and brewing guilds maintain strict quality control. The widespread use of thermometers and hydrometers begins to take root among wealthier brewers, improving fermentation accuracy and efficiency. Experimentation with new ingredients and techniques, including stronger ales and porters, starts to emerge.

- **Where Brewing Was Done**: Brewing occurs in households, communal village spaces, urban breweries, and estates. Urban breweries dominate the production landscape, catering to local demand and expanding trade networks. Ports play a critical role in the export of British ales to Europe and beyond, as the British Empire's influence begins to grow.

- **How It Would Have Looked**: Household brewing remains practical and small-scale, centred around hearths with clay pots and wooden barrels. Communal village brewing spaces utilise shared equipment, while urban breweries operate as large, structured facilities with distinct areas for malting, boiling, fermentation, and storage. Warehouses for hops and malted grains are integral, supporting large-scale production. Estate breweries produce ale for domestic consumption and regional trade.

- **Involvement of Villagers**: Women continue to manage household brewing for family needs. Professional brewers dominate urban production, regulated by guilds to ensure quality. Villagers contribute to communal brewing efforts, particularly during festivals and agricultural cycles. Merchants and traders expand ale's reach through export and regional markets.

- **Equipment Used**:

    1. **Clay and Wooden Vessels**: For mashing, boiling, and fermenting.

    2. **Kilns and Drying Racks**: For malting grains.

    3. **Wooden Sieves**: To strain wort before fermentation.

    4. **Barrels**: For fermentation, storage, and transport.

5. **Large Cauldrons**: For boiling wort in communal, urban, and estate setups.

6. **Hop Drying Racks**: For preparing hops for brewing.

7. **Thermometers and Hydrometers**: Increasingly common among advanced brewing operations.

- **Recipes (Detailed)**:
  - **Ingredients**:
    - 10-14 kg of malted barley, oats, or wheat
    - Fresh water from wells or streams
    - Hops (fully standardised and widely used)
    - Optional: Spices, honey, or fruits for flavour enhancement
  - **Method**:
    1. **Malting**: Dry grains on racks or in kilns for 2-3 days, turning frequently for even drying.
    2. **Crushing**: Coarsely crush malted grains using wooden mallets or stones.
    3. **Mashing**: Combine the crushed malt with warm water (55-65°C) in wooden or clay vessels. Stir thoroughly and steep for 1-2 hours.
    4. **Boiling**: Boil the wort in large cauldrons for 60-90 minutes. Add hops during the last 30 minutes of boiling.
    5. **Fermentation**: Transfer the cooled wort to barrels. Cover loosely and allow to ferment for 5-7 days in a cool, shaded area.
    6. **Storage**: Store the ale in barrels. Consume within 4-6 weeks or transport for trade.
- **SPV (Strength, Preservation, and Variability)**:
  - **Strength**: Alcohol content stabilises at 5-7%.

  - **Preservation**: Significantly improved due to consistent use of hops and advanced storage methods.
  - **Variability**: Further reduced as brewing methods and tools become increasingly standardised.
- **Social Aspect**: Ale remains central to British life, sustaining communities and serving as a symbol of social gatherings and celebrations. Urban breweries flourish, employing skilled workers and apprentices. Brewing guilds enforce standards and expand trade, enhancing the reputation of British ales abroad. Ale becomes a staple of maritime trade, supporting sailors and explorers during the early stages of global expansion. Seasonal festivities and market days revolve around ale, solidifying its place in the cultural and economic fabric of the era.

Margery the Brewer: The Ale That "Stopped the Witch Trial"

Setting the Scene
By 1550 AD, England was a land of superstition and suspicion. Witch trials were becoming increasingly common, and anyone with a knack for unusual crafts could easily find themselves accused of "dark practices." In the village of Wortwood, Margery the Brewer was known for her eccentric ales, which she brewed with strange herbs and a touch of humor.

Margery often joked, "If brewing ale makes me a witch, then I must be the happiest one alive!" But one day, her brewing landed her in unexpected trouble.

The Witchcraft Accusation
One morning, the village gossip, Edwina, pointed a crooked finger at Margery. "Her ales are too strange to be natural!" she declared. "She must be using witchcraft!"

The villagers, already wary of Margery's habit of singing to her barrels and foraging for "odd plants," began to murmur. Soon, Margery found herself dragged before the town bailiff.

"You stand accused of witchcraft," the bailiff declared. "What say you in your defense?"

Margery, unfazed, grinned and said, "I say let's settle this with a pint."

The Brewing of "Witch's Brew"

Determined to clear her name (and poke fun at her accusers), Margery decided to brew an ale that embraced the very accusations against her. Her recipe included:

- Barley malt, as a nod to tradition.
- A pinch of wild thyme, "to calm their foolish nerves."
- Lavender for a soothing aroma, "because even gossips need to relax."
- A splash of blackberry juice, turning the ale a deep, mysterious purple.
- And a handful of marigold petals, which Margery claimed were "for luck, but if they think it's magic, so be it!"

She brewed the ale in her largest cauldron, cackling theatrically as she stirred. "Let them taste the 'witchcraft,'" she muttered, "and see what it really is."

The Trial and the Ale

When the day of her trial arrived, the villagers gathered in the square, eager to see what would happen. Margery appeared carrying a barrel labeled *Witch's Brew* and a stack of mugs.

"Before you judge me," she announced, "taste the evidence of my so-called witchcraft. If it's truly magical, perhaps it will turn you into frogs."

The villagers hesitated, but curiosity won out. The bailiff took the first sip, followed by Edwina and then the rest of the crowd.

The Reactions

The first sips were met with surprise.

"It's sweet and fruity!" exclaimed the blacksmith.
"With a hint of flowers," added the baker's wife.
"Is this lavender?" Edwina muttered, looking embarrassed.

The bailiff, who had been frowning throughout the trial, took a long gulp and sighed. "This is... delightful," he admitted. "If this is witchcraft, then perhaps we need more witches."

The Chaos
As the villagers drank more, the mood shifted from suspicious to celebratory.

- The blacksmith began twirling his hammer and declared, "This ale gives me the strength of ten men!"
- Edwina, now tipsy and giggling, apologized to Margery and admitted, "I only accused you because your ales are better than mine."
- The bailiff, inspired by the ale's color, tried to compose a poem about "the magic of blackberry." It wasn't very good, but everyone clapped anyway.

By the end of the trial, the square had turned into a spontaneous festival.

The Verdict
The bailiff, raising his mug, declared, "Margery, you are hereby acquitted of all charges! If brewing this ale is witchcraft, then may you never stop practicing it."

The villagers cheered, and Margery poured another round, saying, "Let's toast to the real magic, hard work and a good laugh!"

The Aftermath
Witch's Brew became a staple in Wortwood, celebrated as the ale that saved Margery and united the village. Even Edwina became a regular customer, often joking, "I'll have a mug of your finest sorcery!"

Margery's cauldron, once seen as suspicious, became a symbol of her ingenuity and was eventually placed in the village square as a tribute to her triumph.

The Legacy
Margery's story became a local legend, passed down as a tale of wit and resilience. Her motto, "Brewing isn't magic, it's just a little herb and a lot of heart," was etched onto the door of her tavern, and *Witch's Brew* became famous far beyond Wortwood.

STEM Lesson
Margery's story highlights the importance of creativity, resourcefulness, and humor in overcoming challenges. Her ability to turn fear into curiosity and suspicion into celebration demonstrates the transformative power of innovation.

The lesson? Science and creativity can dispel fear and build connections. And sometimes, the best way to prove your point is to serve it in a mug.

1600 AD - 1650 AD: Brewing in the Age of Expansion and Revolution

- **Techniques**: Brewing during this period undergoes significant refinement, influenced by advancements in science and expanding trade. Hops remain a staple ingredient, and brewing guilds enforce rigorous quality standards. Thermometers and hydrometers become more widespread, improving the consistency and efficiency of brewing processes. The development of stronger ales, porters, and stouts begins, catering to changing tastes and export demands.

- **Where Brewing Was Done**: Brewing occurs in households, communal village spaces, urban breweries, and estates. Urban breweries dominate production, catering to growing domestic demand and the increasing export of British ales. Estate breweries support local consumption and regional trade. Brewing becomes a major export commodity, facilitated by expanding maritime trade routes.

- **How It Would Have Looked**: Household brewing remains modest, with clay pots, wooden barrels, and simple tools near hearths. Communal brewing spaces in villages utilise shared equipment, including large cauldrons and fermentation barrels. Urban breweries are large and well-organised, with specialised areas for malting, boiling, fermentation, and storage. Warehouses store hops, malted grains, and barrels of ale ready for transport to ports and markets.

- **Involvement of Villagers**: Women continue to oversee household brewing, while professional brewers dominate urban and estate production. Guilds regulate brewing practices in towns and cities, employing skilled brewers and apprentices. Villagers contribute to communal brewing efforts during festivals and agricultural cycles, while merchants and traders expand the distribution of ale.

- **Equipment Used**:

    1. **Clay and Wooden Vessels**: For mashing, boiling, and fermenting.

    2. **Kilns and Drying Racks**: For malting grains.

    3. **Wooden Sieves**: To strain wort before fermentation.

    4. **Barrels**: For fermentation, storage, and transport.

5. **Large Cauldrons**: For boiling wort in communal, urban, and estate setups.
6. **Hop Drying Racks**: For preparing hops for brewing.
7. **Thermometers and Hydrometers**: Commonly used in advanced brewing operations.

- **Recipes (Detailed)**:
  - **Ingredients**:
    - 10-14 kg of malted barley, oats, or wheat
    - Fresh water from wells or streams
    - Hops (fully standardised and widely used)
    - Optional: Spices, honey, or fruits for flavour enhancement
  - **Method**:
    1. **Malting**: Dry grains on racks or in kilns for 2-3 days, turning frequently for even drying.
    2. **Crushing**: Coarsely crush malted grains using wooden mallets or stones.
    3. **Mashing**: Combine the crushed malt with warm water (55-65°C) in wooden or clay vessels. Stir thoroughly and steep for 1-2 hours.
    4. **Boiling**: Boil the wort in large cauldrons for 60-90 minutes. Add hops during the last 30 minutes of boiling.
    5. **Fermentation**: Transfer the cooled wort to barrels. Cover loosely and allow to ferment for 5-7 days in a cool, shaded area.
    6. **Storage**: Store the ale in barrels. Consume within 4-6 weeks or transport for trade.
- **SPV (Strength, Preservation, and Variability)**:

   - **Strength**: Alcohol content stabilises at 5-8%, with stronger ales emerging for export.
   - **Preservation**: Improved further by consistent use of hops and better storage practices.
   - **Variability**: Minimised in urban breweries due to guild-enforced standardisation.
- **Social Aspect**: Ale continues to be a staple of British life, providing sustenance and serving as a focal point for social gatherings. Urban breweries thrive, supplying growing towns, cities, and export markets. Brewing guilds maintain high standards and support apprenticeships, ensuring the continued evolution of the craft. Ale becomes a key export commodity, supporting Britain's expanding global influence. Seasonal festivals, feasts, and market days revolve around ale, reflecting its enduring cultural and economic importance.

Gideon the Brewer: The Ale That "Fooled the Puritans"

Setting the Scene

By 1600 AD, England was a land of shifting politics and religious reform. The Puritans, with their stern ways and disapproval of "worldly pleasures," were gaining influence. Taverns, the heart of social life, became targets of their scorn. In the lively village of Hopswell, Gideon the Brewer was known for his lively ales and even livelier sense of humor.

When word spread that a group of Puritans planned to inspect Hopswell's tavern for "moral corruption," Gideon saw an opportunity to outwit them, with ale, of course.

The Puritan Inspection

The Puritans were led by the dour-faced Reverend Ezekiel Prynne, who declared, "Ale is the devil's drink, and laughter is his snare! We shall cleanse this village of its sinful indulgences."

The villagers were worried. "They'll shut down the tavern!" the blacksmith fretted. "And what's a village without ale?"

Gideon chuckled. "Don't worry, friends. If they want to sniff out sin, I'll give them something saintly to sniff instead."

The Brewing of "Pious Pint"

Gideon set out to brew an ale that would confuse, charm, and maybe even convert the Puritans. His recipe included:

- Barley malt, as always, "for the foundation of all good things."
- A dash of rosemary, which he claimed symbolized "purity."
- A hint of sage, "to make it smell like a Sunday roast."
- And a touch of lavender, "for a heavenly aroma."

For the finishing touch, Gideon crafted a label for his barrel that read *Pious Pint: Blessed by the Brewers' Guild of St. Maltitude.*

The Day of the Inspection

When Reverend Prynne and his followers arrived, the villagers watched nervously as the Puritans marched into the tavern. Gideon greeted them with exaggerated solemnity, bowing deeply. "Welcome, Reverend. Before you condemn us, may I offer you a taste of our *Pious Pint*? It is brewed with reverence and inspired by the virtues of patience and temperance."

The Reverend narrowed his eyes. "Pious, you say? We shall see."

The First Sip

Gideon poured a mug of the golden ale, the rosemary and lavender giving it a fragrant aroma. Prynne took a cautious sip, then paused.

"This is... surprisingly mild," he said, sipping again. "And the aroma is... soothing."

"It is brewed with ingredients of purity," Gideon said with a straight face. "To inspire calm reflection and gratitude for simple blessings."

The other Puritans, curious, began sampling the ale.

The Turn of Events

The effects of *Pious Pint* were immediate and amusing.

- One Puritan remarked that the rosemary reminded him of his grandmother's herb garden and began reminiscing loudly.
- Another claimed the ale was "a refreshing change" from the "harshness of the world."
- Reverend Prynne, now on his second mug, declared, "This brew... it is almost holy!"

The villagers, stifling their laughter, joined in, toasting to "virtue" and "the wisdom of moderation."

The Chaos

As the ale flowed, the Puritans' stern demeanor began to soften.

- One Puritan challenged the blacksmith to a hymn-singing contest, only to forget the words halfway through.
- Another started sniffing the barrels, declaring, "This tavern smells like the fields of heaven!"
- Reverend Prynne attempted to compose a sermon about the virtues of ale but ended up singing a psalm instead.

By the end of the inspection, the Puritans were laughing, toasting, and thoroughly distracted from their original mission.

The Aftermath

The next morning, Reverend Prynne, nursing a mild headache, declared, "The tavern of Hopswell is not a den of sin, but a place of community and contemplation. Let it remain open, for the good of the village."

The villagers cheered, and Gideon was hailed as a hero.

The Legacy

Pious Pint became the talk of the region, with travelers coming to Hopswell to taste the "heavenly ale that tamed the Puritans." Gideon's motto, "Blessed are the brewers," was carved above the tavern door, and the Reverend's psalm became a drinking song sung for years to come.

STEM Lesson

Gideon's story is a testament to the power of creativity, science, and understanding your audience. By blending flavors and crafting a clever narrative, he turned potential adversaries into allies and saved the heart of his village.

The lesson? Innovation isn't just about making something new—it's about finding clever ways to solve problems and bring people together.

1650 AD - 1700 AD: Brewing in the Age of Empires and Innovation

- **Techniques**: Brewing continues to evolve with scientific advancements and the increasing demand for exported ales. Hops remain a central ingredient, and brewing processes become more efficient with the widespread use of thermometers and hydrometers. Innovations such as the development of pale ales and the refinement of stouts and porters emerge, driven by changing tastes and global trade.

- **Where Brewing Was Done**: Brewing is conducted in households, communal village spaces, urban breweries, and estates. Urban breweries dominate, supplying towns and cities as well as exporting to Europe and the colonies. Estate breweries cater to local needs, while household brewing begins to decline in urban areas due to the availability of commercially produced ale.

- **How It Would Have Looked**: Household brewing remains limited to rural areas, utilising hearth-based setups with clay pots and wooden barrels. Urban breweries operate as large-scale enterprises, featuring malting houses, boiling rooms, fermentation areas, and expansive storage facilities for hops and barrels. Warehouses near ports store ale destined for export, reflecting Britain's growing role in global trade.

- **Involvement of Villagers**: Women continue to manage household brewing in rural areas, while professional brewers dominate urban production. Brewing guilds regulate the industry, ensuring quality and standardisation. Merchants and traders expand ale's reach through maritime networks, and skilled labourers support the growing scale of urban breweries.

- **Equipment Used**:

    1. **Clay and Wooden Vessels**: For mashing, boiling, and fermenting in smaller setups.
    2. **Kilns and Drying Racks**: For malting grains.
    3. **Wooden Sieves**: To strain wort before fermentation.
    4. **Barrels**: For fermentation, storage, and transport.
    5. **Large Cauldrons**: For boiling wort in urban and estate breweries.
    6. **Hop Drying Racks**: For preparing hops for brewing.

7. **Thermometers and Hydrometers**: Widely used in professional brewing setups.

- **Recipes (Detailed)**:
  - **Ingredients**:
    - 10-14 kg of malted barley, oats, or wheat
    - Fresh water from wells or streams
    - Hops (standardised and universally used)
    - Optional: Spices, honey, or fruits for specialised ales
  - **Method**:
    1. **Malting**: Dry grains on racks or in kilns for 2-3 days, turning frequently for even drying.
    2. **Crushing**: Coarsely crush malted grains using wooden mallets or stones.
    3. **Mashing**: Combine the crushed malt with warm water (55-65°C) in wooden or metal vessels. Stir thoroughly and steep for 1-2 hours.
    4. **Boiling**: Boil the wort in large cauldrons for 60-90 minutes. Add hops during the last 30 minutes of boiling.
    5. **Fermentation**: Transfer the cooled wort to barrels. Cover loosely and allow to ferment for 5-7 days in a cool, shaded area.
    6. **Storage**: Store the ale in barrels. Consume within 4-6 weeks or transport for trade.
- **SPV (Strength, Preservation, and Variability)**:
  - **Strength**: Alcohol content stabilises at 5-8%, with stronger ales and porters becoming popular for export.
  - **Preservation**: Enhanced by hops and improved storage techniques, allowing for longer transportation.

  - **Variability**: Reduced as urban breweries and guilds enforce standardised practices.

- **Social Aspect**: Ale remains central to British life, serving as a staple beverage and a key element of social gatherings. Urban breweries thrive as hubs of production and trade, supplying ale to a growing global market. The professionalisation of brewing through guilds and technological advancements ensures high-quality production. Seasonal celebrations, market fairs, and maritime expeditions are all fuelled by ale, highlighting its importance in Britain's cultural and economic landscape.

Tobias the Brewer: The Ale That "Sank the Navy's Pride"

Setting the Scene

By 1650 AD, England was embroiled in naval expansion and trade rivalries. The seas were filled with ships, and sailors relied heavily on ale to sustain them during their long voyages. In the bustling port town of Tankard-on-Sea, Tobias the Brewer was known for his strong ales and even stronger opinions.

Tobias often said, "If you can't sail a ship after drinking my ale, maybe you weren't much of a sailor to begin with."

One day, Tobias found himself at odds with a group of naval officers who claimed they needed a "properly modest ale" for their fleet. What followed became the talk of the town, and the docks.

The Navy's Request

A group of stern naval officers marched into Tobias's tavern, The Foamy Barrel, demanding a meeting. "We need an ale that will keep our sailors steady and disciplined," declared Captain Horace Briggs. "No more of this strong brew that makes them sing and stumble!"

Tobias grinned. "An ale that keeps them steady? That's no ale at all! But fear not, Captain, I'll craft something 'fit for sailors.'"

The Brewing of "Admiral's Folly"

Tobias decided to brew an ale that would teach the officers a lesson about underestimating both brewers and sailors. His recipe included:

- Barley malt for a hearty base.
- A touch of molasses, "to remind them of the colonies."
- A generous dose of ginger, "to add a fiery kick."
- And, for the pièce de résistance, a secret ingredient: fermented seaweed, "to give it the taste of the ocean."

He brewed the ale in a barrel marked *Admiral's Folly,* claiming it was "as steady as the waves."

The Presentation

When the ale was ready, Tobias invited Captain Briggs and his officers to the tavern for a tasting. With a flourish, he poured mugs of the foamy, briny brew and handed them to the officers.

"Gentlemen," Tobias said, "this is *Admiral's Folly,* brewed to keep your sailors steady on their feet and strong in their duties."

The officers sipped cautiously, then nodded. "It's... unusual," said Captain Briggs. "But it has a certain... maritime quality."

The Chaos

Convinced they'd found the perfect brew, the officers ordered several barrels for the fleet's next voyage. Tobias, suppressing a grin, delivered the barrels personally, wishing them "fair winds and smooth sailing."

But *Admiral's Folly* was anything but smooth. As the sailors drank it on their voyage, the ale's fiery ginger kick and briny seaweed flavor had unexpected effects:

- One sailor, convinced he'd become a merman, jumped overboard to "join his people."
- Another started reciting Shakespearean soliloquies to the ship's mast, claiming it was his long-lost love.
- The captain, trying to maintain order, tripped over a barrel and ended up tangled in a fishing net, earning the nickname "Net Admiral."

By the time the fleet returned to port, the officers were too embarrassed to explain why half their crew was singing sea shanties backwards.

The Aftermath
Captain Briggs stormed into The Foamy Barrel, demanding an explanation. "What have you done, Tobias?"

Tobias feigned innocence. "Why, Captain, I brewed exactly what you asked for, an ale that kept them steady. Steadily entertained, that is."

The captain, realizing he'd been outwitted, sighed and muttered, "Next time, we'll stick to water."

The Legacy
Admiral's Folly became an instant legend in Tankard-on-Sea. Sailors from across the coast came to try "the ale that sank the navy's pride," and Tobias's tavern became a hub of laughter and storytelling. The barrel with "Net Admiral" carved into it hung proudly above the bar as a reminder of Tobias's triumph.

The STEM Lesson
Tobias's story demonstrates the importance of understanding your audience and the power of creativity in problem-solving. By cleverly crafting a brew that highlighted the absurdity of the officers' request, he turned a potential conflict into a lasting tale of humor and ingenuity.

The lesson? Science and art are best used with a touch of wit, and a healthy dose of seaweed.

1700 AD - 1750 AD: Brewing in the Age of Industrial Growth

- **Techniques**: Brewing begins to shift towards industrialisation as technological advancements transform production. The development of pale ales continues, driven by innovations in malting techniques, particularly the use of coke-fired kilns that produce lighter malt. Stouts and porters grow in popularity, becoming staples of urban and export markets. Scientific approaches to fermentation further refine consistency and efficiency.

- **Where Brewing Was Done**: Brewing occurs predominantly in urban breweries, estates, and ports. Large-scale urban breweries dominate, supplying cities and export markets with growing efficiency. Estate breweries support local needs and regional trade, while household brewing declines significantly in urban areas due to the accessibility of commercially brewed ale.

- **How It Would Have Looked**: Urban breweries are vast, structured facilities with specialised areas for malting, mashing, boiling, fermentation, and storage. Malting houses and hop warehouses near ports facilitate the storage and preparation of essential ingredients. Barrels of ale are transported by carts and ships to supply expanding domestic and international markets. In rural areas, estate breweries and smaller communal spaces maintain traditional setups for local consumption.

- **Involvement of Villagers**: Professional brewers and skilled labourers dominate the brewing industry, particularly in urban centres. Brewing guilds regulate practices, ensuring quality and fair competition. Merchants and traders handle the distribution of ale, supported by maritime networks. Rural villagers contribute to estate and communal brewing efforts, particularly during harvests and festivals.

- **Equipment Used**:

    1. **Coke-Fired Kilns**: For producing lighter malt used in pale ales.

    2. **Large Copper Cauldrons**: For boiling wort in urban breweries.

    3. **Thermometers and Hydrometers**: Widely used for precision in brewing processes.

    4. **Barrels**: For fermentation, storage, and transport.

    5. **Hop Drying Ovens**: For preparing hops for brewing.

6. **Fermentation Vats**: For large-scale production in urban setups.

- **Recipes (Detailed)**:
    - **Ingredients**:
        - 10-14 kg of pale malt or roasted barley (depending on ale type)
        - Fresh water from wells or streams
        - Hops (universally used and carefully dried)
        - Optional: Spices, molasses, or honey for export ales
    - **Method**:
        1. **Malting**: Dry grains using coke-fired kilns for 2-3 days, turning frequently to achieve the desired colour and flavour.
        2. **Crushing**: Crush malted grains to a coarse consistency.
        3. **Mashing**: Combine the crushed malt with warm water (60-70°C) in large wooden or metal vessels. Stir thoroughly and steep for 1-2 hours.
        4. **Boiling**: Boil the wort in copper cauldrons for 60-90 minutes, adding hops during the last 30 minutes.
        5. **Fermentation**: Transfer the cooled wort to fermentation vats. Cover loosely and allow to ferment for 5-7 days in a controlled environment.
        6. **Storage**: Store the ale in barrels. Consume within 4-6 weeks or prepare for export.
- **SPV (Strength, Preservation, and Variability)**:
    - **Strength**: Alcohol content stabilises at 5-9%, with stronger porters and export ales gaining popularity.
    - **Preservation**: Improved by the use of hops and controlled storage methods.
    - **Variability**: Further reduced in urban breweries due to industrialisation and standardised processes.

- **Social Aspect**: Ale remains central to British culture, thriving in both urban and rural settings. Urban breweries cater to a burgeoning population and expanding trade routes, solidifying British ale as a key export product. The professionalisation of brewing through guilds and industrial techniques enhances quality and scale, marking the beginning of a more globalised brewing industry. Festivals, public houses, and market days are centred around ale, reflecting its continued importance in social and economic life.

Samuel the Brewer: The Ale That "Outwitted the Smugglers"

Setting the Scene

By 1700 AD, smuggling was rampant along the coasts of England. Taxes on imported goods like tea, rum, and luxury items were high, and smugglers thrived by sneaking contraband past the authorities. In the seaside village of Mugshire, Samuel the Brewer was famous for his innovative ales, and his knack for staying out of trouble.

Samuel loved to say, "Why smuggle when you can brew your own treasures?" But when a band of smugglers threatened to use his brewery as a front for their operation, Samuel decided to teach them a lesson they wouldn't forget.

The Smugglers' Plan

One stormy evening, a group of smugglers led by the brash and burly Jasper "Blackbeard" Muggins barged into Samuel's tavern, The Tipsy Tankard.

"Listen here, brewer," growled Jasper. "We've got a shipment coming in, and we need a place to hide it. Your barrels will do nicely."

Samuel, ever calm, raised an eyebrow. "And what's in this 'shipment' of yours?"

"None of your business," Jasper snapped. "Just do as you're told, or we'll find another way to 'use' your barrels, and your head."

Samuel nodded thoughtfully. "Very well. I'll prepare my barrels for you."

The Brewing of "Smuggler's Folly"
Determined to outwit the smugglers, Samuel concocted a plan. He brewed an ale that would expose the smugglers' scheme while giving the villagers a good laugh. His recipe included:

- Barley malt, for a strong base.
- Black treacle, "to match the smugglers' dark hearts."
- An extra dose of hops, for bitterness.
- And a hefty scoop of chili peppers, "to give it a fiery kick they won't forget."

He labeled the barrels *Smuggler's Folly* and added a cheeky seal: a pirate ship sinking in a sea of foam.

The Delivery
When the smugglers returned, Samuel greeted them with a sly grin. "Your barrels are ready," he said, gesturing to the row of freshly sealed casks.

The smugglers, not bothering to inspect the contents, hauled the barrels onto their cart and disappeared into the night. Samuel watched them go, whistling a cheerful tune.

The Grand Reveal
The smugglers' plan was to sell the barrels of *Smuggler's Folly* as exotic rum to unsuspecting buyers. However, the first buyers quickly discovered the truth.

One sip of the fiery ale sent them coughing and spluttering.

"What is this?" shouted a merchant. "It burns like the devil's tea kettle!"

"It's some kind of prank!" another yelled, shaking a fist.

Word spread quickly, and soon the smugglers found themselves the laughingstock of the coast. Jasper, red-faced and furious, returned to Mugshire, determined to confront Samuel.

The Showdown
Jasper stormed into The Tipsy Tankard, a barrel of *Smuggler's Folly* under his arm. "You tricked us!" he bellowed.

Samuel, polishing a mug, looked up innocently. "Tricked you? Why, I simply brewed an ale fit for smugglers, bold, fiery, and full of surprises."

The villagers, gathered around, burst into laughter. "He's got you there, Jasper!" shouted the blacksmith.

Even Jasper couldn't help but chuckle. "Well, brewer, you've made a fool of me. But I'll admit, it's a fine ale, if you like your drink to bite back."

The Aftermath

Smuggler's Folly became a local sensation, with villagers lining up to taste the infamous brew. The smugglers, too embarrassed to continue their scheme, left town in search of easier marks. Samuel, ever the entrepreneur, began exporting the ale under the slogan, "For those who dare!"

The barrel with the sinking pirate ship became a centerpiece in The Tipsy Tankard, a reminder of the day the brewer outsmarted the smugglers.

The Legacy

Samuel's tale spread far and wide, earning him a reputation as both a master brewer and a cunning trickster. His motto, "Brew bold, think bolder," was etched onto the tavern door, and *Smuggler's Folly* became a symbol of wit and resilience.

STEM Lesson

Samuel's story highlights the power of creativity and resourcefulness in overcoming challenges. By using his brewing skills and a touch of humor, he turned a dangerous situation into an opportunity for success and laughter.

The lesson? Science and ingenuity are powerful tools for problem-solving, especially when paired with a dash of cleverness.

1750 AD - 1800 AD: Brewing in the Industrial Revolution

- **Techniques**: Brewing undergoes significant transformation during the Industrial Revolution. Innovations such as steam power and the use of more precise thermometers and hydrometers enhance brewing efficiency and consistency. Pale ales, stouts, and porters dominate the market, with porters gaining immense popularity in urban areas. Improved malting techniques and the continued use of coke-fired kilns produce high-quality, lighter malt for pale ales.

- **Where Brewing Was Done**: Brewing is concentrated in large urban breweries, estates, and ports. Urban breweries expand significantly, adopting industrial-scale production methods to meet the growing demand in domestic and international markets. Estate breweries support local needs and contribute to regional trade, while household brewing becomes rare due to the availability of affordable commercial ale.

- **How It Would Have Looked**: Urban breweries are vast industrial complexes, featuring malting houses, copper boiling vats, fermentation halls, and expansive storage facilities for barrels. Ports become critical hubs for exporting ale, with warehouses storing ale destined for the colonies and Europe. Estate breweries maintain a more traditional appearance but incorporate some industrial innovations, such as improved kilns and fermentation vats.

- **Involvement of Villagers**: Professional brewers and skilled labourers dominate the industry, particularly in urban breweries. Merchants and traders handle the distribution of ale, supported by increasingly efficient transportation networks. In rural areas, estate workers contribute to brewing operations, while villagers participate in festivals and local markets where ale is a central feature.

- **Equipment Used**:

    1. **Steam Engines**: Beginning to power equipment in larger breweries.

    2. **Coke-Fired Kilns**: For producing high-quality malt.

    3. **Large Copper Cauldrons**: For boiling wort in industrial breweries.

    4. **Fermentation Vats**: Designed for large-scale production.

5. **Thermometers and Hydrometers**: Essential for precision brewing.

6. **Barrels and Casks**: For storage and transport.

7. **Hop Drying Ovens**: Standard in larger operations.

- **Recipes (Detailed)**:

    - **Ingredients**:

        - 12-16 kg of pale malt or roasted barley (depending on ale type)

        - Fresh water from wells or reservoirs

        - Hops (carefully dried and standardised)

        - Optional: Molasses or spices for export ales

    - **Method**:

        1. **Malting**: Use coke-fired kilns to dry grains for 2-3 days, achieving the desired flavour and colour.

        2. **Crushing**: Crush malted grains to a coarse consistency using industrial rollers.

        3. **Mashing**: Combine crushed malt with warm water (60-70°C) in large metal vessels. Stir thoroughly and steep for 1-2 hours.

        4. **Boiling**: Boil the wort in copper cauldrons for 60-90 minutes, adding hops during the last 30 minutes.

        5. **Fermentation**: Transfer the cooled wort to large fermentation vats. Cover loosely and ferment for 5-7 days in a controlled environment.

        6. **Storage**: Store the ale in barrels or casks. Consume within 4-6 weeks or prepare for export.

- **SPV (Strength, Preservation, and Variability)**:

    - **Strength**: Alcohol content stabilises at 5-9%, with stronger porters and export ales reaching higher levels.

- **Preservation**: Enhanced by the use of hops and improved storage techniques, allowing for longer transport.
- **Variability**: Minimal in urban breweries due to industrialisation and standardised processes.

- **Social Aspect**: Ale continues to be a cornerstone of British life, providing sustenance and serving as a central feature of social gatherings. Public houses flourish, becoming hubs for community interaction and leisure. Urban breweries thrive, supplying a growing domestic population and exporting to the colonies, Europe, and beyond. Festivals, markets, and celebrations are marked by the consumption of ale, reflecting its enduring cultural and economic significance. The Industrial Revolution positions Britain as a global leader in brewing, setting the stage for further advancements in the 19th century.

Agatha the Brewer: The Ale That "Won the Debate"

Setting the Scene

By 1750 AD, England was in the midst of the Enlightenment. Taverns were not just places to drink but hubs of intellectual debate, where philosophers, inventors, and everyday folks gathered to discuss the latest ideas. In the town of Pintshire, Agatha the Brewer was known for her sharp wit and even sharper ales.

Agatha's motto was, "Why argue when you can toast?" But one day, a fierce debate about the "nature of happiness" threatened to divide her tavern's regulars. Agatha decided it was time to intervene, with a brew, of course.

The Great Debate

The argument began innocently enough. Professor Wigglesworth, a pompous scholar, declared that true happiness came from knowledge. "Ignorance is misery!" he proclaimed, slamming his tankard down.

But Thomas "Big Tom" Butterworth, a farmer with a booming laugh, disagreed. "Happiness is a full belly and a good ale!" he countered, raising his mug.

The tavern soon erupted into chaos, with patrons taking sides. Agatha, watching from behind the bar, shook her head. "If they want to argue about happiness," she muttered, "I'll give them something to be happy about."

The Brewing of "Philosopher's Pint"
Agatha set out to craft an ale that would settle the debate, or at least make everyone too distracted to argue. Her recipe included:

- Barley malt for a robust flavor, "to satisfy Big Tom."
- A touch of nutmeg and cinnamon, "to remind them of warm, happy memories."
- Honey, "to sweeten even the sourest philosopher."
- And a splash of lemon juice, "because happiness needs a little zest."

She brewed the ale with care, stirring it while humming a tune about "frothy harmony." For the finishing touch, she labeled the barrel *Philosopher's Pint: Happiness in Every Sip.*

The Grand Unveiling
When the ale was ready, Agatha rolled the barrel into the middle of the tavern. "Ladies and gentlemen," she called, "I present to you *Philosopher's Pint*, the answer to your debate!"

The debaters paused, intrigued. "What's so philosophical about it?" Professor Wigglesworth asked skeptically.

"Why, it's a blend of intellect and indulgence," Agatha replied with a grin. "Knowledge in the honey, wisdom in the zest, and joy in every drop."

Big Tom chuckled. "Well, I'll drink to that."

The Reactions
The first sips of *Philosopher's Pint* were met with wide eyes and nods of approval.

"It's smooth, but with a kick!" said the blacksmith.
"It's sweet, but also... profound," murmured the schoolteacher.

Even Professor Wigglesworth seemed impressed. "This ale," he declared, "is a metaphor for happiness itself, complex, layered, and deeply satisfying."

Big Tom, now on his second mug, raised his tankard. "I don't know about metaphors, but it tastes like joy to me!"

The Chaos

As the night wore on, the ale worked its magic:

- The professor, emboldened by the honey, challenged Big Tom to a contest to see who could drink the most without spilling a drop. He lost spectacularly.
- Big Tom attempted to give a "philosophical" speech about the importance of pies, drawing cheers and laughter.
- The schoolteacher, inspired by the cinnamon, wrote a poem titled *Ode to the Pint,* which was recited (badly) by the blacksmith.

Agatha, watching the chaos with a satisfied grin, raised her own mug. "Happiness," she declared, "is a tavern full of laughter."

The Aftermath

By the end of the night, the debate was forgotten. Professor Wigglesworth, arm in arm with Big Tom, admitted, "Perhaps happiness isn't about knowledge or ale, it's about sharing both with good company."

Big Tom laughed. "Now that's something we can all toast to!"

The Legacy

Philosopher's Pint became the talk of Pintshire, celebrated as the ale that united scholars and farmers alike. Agatha's tavern, *The Merry Tankard,* became a symbol of harmony and wit, with a new motto carved above the door: "Debate Less, Drink More."

STEM Lesson

Agatha's story demonstrates the power of creativity, craftsmanship, and understanding human nature. By blending flavors and humor, she created not just an ale but an experience that brought people together.

The lesson? Innovation doesn't just solve problems, it builds connections, fosters joy, and sometimes, ends a debate.

1800 AD - 1850 AD: Brewing in the Age of Industrial Expansion

- **Techniques**: Brewing experiences a golden age of industrial innovation during this period. The widespread adoption of steam power transforms production efficiency, while advances in refrigeration and scientific fermentation techniques revolutionise quality control. The development of pale ales, porters, and stouts continues to dominate the market, with the first lagers being introduced through European influences.

- **Where Brewing Was Done**: Brewing is concentrated in urban breweries, estate breweries, and export hubs. Urban breweries become industrial powerhouses, using advanced machinery and large-scale facilities to meet the increasing domestic and global demand for British ale. Estate breweries cater to local needs and regional trade, while smaller rural setups decline further in importance.

- **How It Would Have Looked**: Urban breweries are enormous complexes, featuring steam-powered malting machines, copper vats, fermentation tanks, and extensive barrel storage facilities. Ports are bustling with warehouses storing barrels of ale ready for export. Estate breweries maintain a blend of traditional and industrial practices, reflecting their dual role in serving local and regional markets.

- **Involvement of Villagers**: Professional brewers, engineers, and skilled labourers dominate the industry in urban centres. Merchants and traders manage distribution networks, expanding the reach of British ale globally. Estate workers and villagers contribute to smaller-scale brewing operations and participate in the vibrant pub culture that defines rural and urban life alike.

- **Equipment Used**:

    1. **Steam Engines**: Powering malting, milling, and other brewing equipment.

    2. **Refrigeration Systems**: Emerging technology used in advanced breweries.

    3. **Large Copper Vats**: For boiling wort at an industrial scale.

    4. **Thermometers and Hydrometers**: Standard tools for precise brewing.

    5. **Barrels and Casks**: For storage, aging, and transport.

6. **Hop Drying Ovens**: Integrated into larger brewing setups.
7. **Fermentation Tanks**: Designed for high-capacity production.

- **Recipes (Detailed)**:
  - **Ingredients**:
    - 12-18 kg of pale malt, roasted barley, or mixed grains (depending on ale type)
    - Fresh water from reservoirs
    - Hops (universally used and meticulously prepared)
    - Optional: Sugars or spices for export ales
  - **Method**:
    1. **Malting**: Dry grains using steam-powered kilns for precise control of flavour and colour.
    2. **Crushing**: Use mechanical rollers to crush malted grains to a uniform consistency.
    3. **Mashing**: Combine crushed malt with warm water (60-70°C) in large metal vessels. Stir thoroughly and steep for 1-2 hours.
    4. **Boiling**: Boil the wort in copper vats for 60-90 minutes, adding hops during the last 30 minutes.
    5. **Fermentation**: Transfer the cooled wort to large fermentation tanks. Cover loosely and ferment for 5-7 days in controlled conditions.
    6. **Storage**: Store the ale in barrels or casks. Consume within 4-6 weeks or prepare for long-distance export.
- **SPV (Strength, Preservation, and Variability)**:
  - **Strength**: Alcohol content ranges from 5-10%, with strong export ales and porters becoming increasingly popular.
  - **Preservation**: Enhanced by hops, refrigeration, and airtight storage methods.

  - **Variability**: Minimised through standardised processes and scientific advancements.

- **Social Aspect**: Ale remains a cornerstone of British life, with the rise of public houses and taverns as key social hubs. Urban breweries flourish, employing large workforces and exporting ale to markets across Europe, the Americas, and the colonies. Technological advancements position Britain as the global leader in brewing, while ale plays a central role in celebrations, community events, and everyday social interactions. The industrialisation of brewing sets the stage for further innovation and global competition in the second half of the 19th century.

Harold the Brewer: The Ale That "Ran the Steam Engine"

Setting the Scene

By 1800 AD, the Industrial Revolution was transforming England. Steam engines powered factories, trains, and mills, but in the bustling town of Caskbury, the true engine of life was Harold the Brewer's ale. Harold, a jolly man with a thick beard and an even thicker accent, was known for his eccentric brewing methods and even more eccentric ideas.

"Steam might move trains," Harold often joked, "but it's ale that moves the people!"

One day, Harold's brewing skills were put to the ultimate test when a broken-down steam engine threatened to ruin the town's annual fair.

The Broken Engine

The Caskbury Fair was the highlight of the year, complete with games, food stalls, and a brand-new attraction: a steam-powered carousel. But disaster struck when the engine running the carousel broke down just as the fair was about to open.

"Without the carousel, the fair's ruined!" wailed the mayor.

The town's engineer, Mr. Thistledown, examined the engine and frowned. "We're out of coal, and there's no time to fetch more. We need a miracle to get this thing running."

Harold, sitting nearby with a pint in hand, grinned. "A miracle, you say? What about ale-powered ingenuity?"

The Brewing of "Steam Stout"

Harold rushed back to his brewery and got to work crafting a special ale that could do more than quench thirst. His recipe included:

- Barley malt for strength, "because this is serious business."
- Molasses, "for extra kick and stickiness."
- Ginger, "to add a fiery boost."
- And a generous pinch of salt, "to make it steam like a proper engine."

As the brew bubbled and hissed, Harold chuckled to himself. "If this doesn't power the carousel, at least it'll power the crowd!"

The Big Experiment

Harold returned to the fairgrounds with a keg of *Steam Stout* and a plan. "We'll pour this into the engine's boiler," he declared, "and let the ale do the rest!"

The townsfolk looked skeptical. "You can't run an engine on ale," muttered Mr. Thistledown.

"Why not?" Harold countered. "It runs on steam, and ale makes plenty of that!"

With no better options, the engineer reluctantly agreed. The keg was hoisted up, and Harold himself poured the frothy brew into the boiler.

The Moment of Truth

The crowd held its breath as Mr. Thistledown lit the firebox. For a moment, nothing happened. Then, with a loud hiss and a puff of golden steam, the engine roared to life.

The carousel began to turn, its pipes emitting a faint smell of gingerbread and molasses. The crowd erupted in cheers.

"It's working!" shouted the mayor.
"And it smells delicious!" added a child.

The Chaos
As the carousel spun faster and faster, the *Steam Stout* began to show its true power:

- The horses on the carousel galloped so energetically that riders clung on for dear life.
- The engine's whistle emitted a merry tune, which the townsfolk started singing along to.
- One particularly excited spectator shouted, "I think I can taste the ale in the air!"

Harold, watching proudly, declared, "This is the most fun Caskbury's had in years!"

The Aftermath
By the end of the day, the *Steam Stout*-powered carousel was the star of the fair. Harold was hailed as a hero, and even Mr. Thistledown admitted, "Maybe there's something to this ale-powered nonsense after all."

The mayor, eager to capitalize on the success, commissioned Harold to create more *Steam Stout* "just in case the trains ever run out of coal."

The Legacy
Steam Stout became a Caskbury sensation, celebrated as the ale that powered the fair. Visitors came from far and wide to ride the carousel and taste the brew, which was marketed with the slogan: "The Ale That Moves More Than Mugs."

Harold's motto, "Think outside the barrel," was etched onto a plaque at the fairgrounds, and the town's engineer developed a secret fondness for ginger-flavored ale.

The STEM Lesson
Harold's story highlights the importance of innovation, creativity, and a willingness to experiment. By thinking outside the box (or barrel), he turned a potential disaster into a roaring success and brought joy to his community.

The lesson? Science, ingenuity, and a bit of humor can solve even the strangest problems. And sometimes, the best fuel is the one you can drink afterward.

1850 AD - 1900 AD: Brewing in the Height of the Industrial Revolution

- **Techniques**: The latter half of the 19th century is marked by significant advancements in brewing technology. The widespread use of steam engines and refrigeration systems transforms production capabilities. The adoption of pasteurisation techniques and advancements in microbiology (inspired by Louis Pasteur's discoveries) improve fermentation control and ale preservation. Lager brewing, influenced by European techniques, begins to emerge alongside traditional British ales.

- **Where Brewing Was Done**: Brewing is dominated by urban industrial breweries, with rural estate breweries continuing to serve local markets. Large-scale urban breweries cater to both domestic and export demands, supported by extensive rail and maritime networks. Household brewing all but disappears due to the affordability and availability of commercial ale.

- **How It Would Have Looked**: Urban breweries are large-scale industrial operations, featuring steam-powered malting machines, mechanical bottling lines, copper vats, fermentation tanks, and massive storage warehouses. Ports serve as hubs for exporting ale globally, with dockside warehouses packed with barrels and bottled beer. Estate breweries blend traditional techniques with industrial innovations, serving their local communities and regional trade networks.

- **Involvement of Villagers**: Professional brewers and engineers dominate the workforce in urban breweries. Merchants and traders facilitate the global distribution of British ale. Estate workers and villagers support smaller-scale brewing operations in rural areas, while public houses become the focal points of social life for both urban and rural communities.

- **Equipment Used**:

    1. **Steam Engines**: Driving brewing equipment and bottling lines.
    2. **Refrigeration Systems**: Essential for lager production and storage.
    3. **Pasteurisation Tanks**: For extending shelf life and ensuring quality.
    4. **Mechanical Bottling Lines**: Revolutionising packaging for local and export markets.

5. **Large Copper Vats**: For boiling wort on an industrial scale.
6. **Fermentation Tanks**: Designed for high-volume production.
7. **Barrels and Bottles**: For storage, aging, and transport.

- **Recipes (Detailed)**:
  - **Ingredients**:
    - 12-20 kg of pale malt, roasted barley, or lager malt
    - Fresh water from reservoirs or wells
    - Hops (standardised and meticulously prepared)
    - Optional: Sugars or adjuncts for export ales or lagers
  - **Method**:
    1. **Malting**: Use steam-powered kilns for precise drying, creating pale or roasted malt.
    2. **Crushing**: Use mechanical rollers to achieve a consistent grain crush.
    3. **Mashing**: Combine crushed malt with water (60-70°C) in metal vessels. Stir and steep for 1-2 hours.
    4. **Boiling**: Boil the wort in copper vats for 60-90 minutes, adding hops in stages for bitterness and aroma.
    5. **Fermentation**: Transfer the cooled wort to fermentation tanks. Ferment ales for 5-7 days or lagers for longer at cooler temperatures.
    6. **Pasteurisation and Storage**: Pasteurise the ale for extended shelf life. Store in barrels or bottles for transport and sale.
- **SPV (Strength, Preservation, and Variability)**:
  - **Strength**: Alcohol content ranges from 4-10%, with lighter lagers and strong export ales both in demand.
  - **Preservation**: Improved significantly by pasteurisation, refrigeration, and airtight packaging.

- **Variability**: Minimized through industrial standardisation and microbiological advancements.

- **Social Aspect**: Ale remains central to British culture, with public houses serving as the heart of social interaction. Urban breweries dominate production, employing thousands and supporting the economy through export revenues. The introduction of lagers caters to changing tastes, while traditional ales continue to thrive. Technological advancements, global trade networks, and the rise of branded beers position Britain as a brewing powerhouse on the global stage, setting the standard for the modern beer industry.

Beatrice the Brewer: The Ale That "Invented Happy Hour"

Setting the Scene

By 1850 AD, England was a land of industrial progress and bustling cities. Workers toiled long hours in factories, and the local pub was their sanctuary. In the smoky town of Barrelford, Beatrice the Brewer was famous for her knack for crafting ales that could turn even the gloomiest worker into a laughing optimist.

Beatrice, a sharp-witted woman with a love of tinkering, often joked, "If machinery runs on steam, people run on ale." One day, her brewing genius collided with industrial demands, giving birth to a concept that changed pub culture forever.

The Factory's Problem

The owner of the Barrelford Foundry, Mr. Percival Grumble, barged into Beatrice's pub, *The Jolly Jug,* in a foul mood. "My workers are sluggish!" he growled. "By the end of the day, they're too tired to meet quotas. I need them motivated, but not drunk. What can you do about it?"

Beatrice raised an eyebrow. "So, you want ale that cheers them up without slowing them down? A tall order, but I do love a challenge."

"Do it," Grumble demanded, "and I'll make you the richest brewer in Barrelford."

The Brewing of "Midday Cheer"

Beatrice decided to brew an ale that was light, refreshing, and invigorating, perfect for a quick break during a grueling workday. Her recipe included:

- Barley malt for a mild, smooth base.
- A touch of citrus peel, "to wake up their senses."
- A pinch of mint, "to cool their tempers."
- And a touch of ginger, "for a spark of energy."

To ensure the ale wasn't too strong, she carefully measured the fermentation process, declaring, "This isn't about getting tipsy, it's about keeping spirits high."

The First Trial

Beatrice delivered her new brew, *Midday Cheer,* to the foundry and convinced Mr. Grumble to allow a short ale break for his workers. At exactly noon, she rolled a barrel into the factory courtyard and poured mugs for the tired workers.

The first sips were met with surprised smiles.

"It's light, but it's got a kick!" said a blacksmith.
"Tastes like sunshine in a mug," added a machinist.

Even Mr. Grumble, reluctantly taking a sip, admitted, "It's... tolerable."

The Happy Hour Revolution

Word of *Midday Cheer* spread quickly, and soon workers were flocking to *The Jolly Jug* to enjoy the brew during their breaks. Beatrice cleverly marketed it as "the perfect pint for hardworking hands" and offered discounted prices between noon and 1 p.m., calling it "Happy Hour."

The result was transformative:

- Workers returned to their shifts with renewed energy, whistling as they worked.
- Factory supervisors noticed fewer arguments and more productivity.
- Mr. Grumble, astonished by the results, declared Beatrice "the best investment I've ever made."

The Chaos
Of course, not everything went smoothly.

- One overenthusiastic worker drank three mugs in a row and tried to race a conveyor belt, only to fall into a pile of coal (unharmed but very dirty).
- Another, inspired by the citrusy zing, attempted to invent "lemon-flavored steam" and ended up covering the break room in soot.
- Mr. Grumble himself became so fond of *Midday Cheer* that he insisted on holding staff meetings at the pub, much to Beatrice's amusement.

The Aftermath
Happy Hour became a Barrelford institution, with workers from other factories flocking to Beatrice's pub. Her *Midday Cheer* was so popular that even non-laborers began drinking it, claiming it was "the perfect cure for afternoon yawns."

Mr. Grumble, thrilled by the increased productivity, paid Beatrice handsomely and even offered her a permanent contract to supply the foundry. Beatrice, ever entrepreneurial, used the profits to expand her brewing operation and hired several of her regulars to help.

The Legacy
Beatrice's *Midday Cheer* became the cornerstone of modern pub culture, and the concept of Happy Hour spread across the country. The phrase "a cheerful break for the busiest days" was painted above the door of *The Jolly Jug*, and a statue of Beatrice holding a mug was erected in the town square.

Even Mr. Grumble, once known for his scowls, became famous for his favorite toast: "To work, to ale, and to the genius of Beatrice!"

STEM Lesson
Beatrice's story highlights the power of creativity, experimentation, and understanding human behavior. By tailoring her brewing process to meet a specific need, she not only solved a problem but also transformed workplace culture.

The lesson? Science and innovation can create solutions that are both practical and joyful. And sometimes, the best way to boost productivity is to pour a little happiness into the mix.

1900 AD - 1950 AD: Brewing Through War and Innovation

- **Techniques**: The first half of the 20th century is marked by resilience and adaptation in brewing. World Wars I and II bring material shortages and rationing, leading to lighter, lower-alcohol ales becoming the norm. Advances in microbiology refine fermentation processes, and innovations such as nitrogenation and mechanical filtration improve consistency and quality. Lager production gains popularity, competing with traditional British ales.

- **Where Brewing Was Done**: Brewing remains concentrated in industrial urban breweries, with estate breweries continuing to serve local markets. The decline of smaller rural operations accelerates as mass production becomes the standard. Ports and railways facilitate the widespread distribution of ale domestically and internationally.

- **How It Would Have Looked**: Urban breweries expand their use of industrial technologies, featuring automated bottling lines, refrigeration systems, and large fermentation tanks. Wartime breweries adapt to material shortages by producing lighter beers with reduced alcohol content. Ports and rail hubs are key for transporting barrels and bottles, ensuring a steady supply to both domestic and export markets.

- **Involvement of Villagers**: Professional brewers, factory workers, and engineers form the core workforce in urban breweries. Merchants and distributors manage the expanding global trade networks. Public houses thrive as social hubs, offering affordable ales despite wartime restrictions. In rural areas, estate breweries maintain local traditions but struggle to compete with industrial-scale operations.

- **Equipment Used**:

    1. **Steam and Electric Engines**: Powering automated brewing equipment.

    2. **Refrigeration Systems**: Essential for lager production and large-scale storage.

    3. **Pasteurisation Tanks**: Widely used to extend shelf life and maintain quality.

    4. **Mechanical Bottling Lines**: Revolutionising packaging for mass distribution.

    5. **Fermentation Tanks**: Designed for high-capacity production.

6. **Barrels and Bottles**: For transport and sale.
7. **Filtration Systems**: For producing clearer and more consistent ales.

- **Recipes (Detailed)**:
  - **Ingredients**:
    - 10-18 kg of pale malt, roasted barley, or lager malt
    - Fresh water from reservoirs or municipal supplies
    - Hops (standardised and carefully prepared)
    - Optional: Sugars or adjuncts to compensate for wartime shortages
  - **Method**:
    1. **Malting**: Use industrial kilns for precise drying, producing pale or roasted malt.
    2. **Crushing**: Crush malted grains with mechanical rollers for uniform consistency.
    3. **Mashing**: Combine crushed malt with water (60-70°C) in metal vessels. Stir thoroughly and steep for 1-2 hours.
    4. **Boiling**: Boil the wort in copper vats for 60-90 minutes, adding hops in stages for bitterness and aroma.
    5. **Fermentation**: Transfer the cooled wort to fermentation tanks. Ferment ales for 5-7 days or lagers for 10-14 days at cooler temperatures.
    6. **Pasteurisation and Storage**: Pasteurise the beer for extended shelf life. Store in barrels or bottles for transport and sale.
- **SPV (Strength, Preservation, and Variability)**:
  - **Strength**: Alcohol content averages 3-5% during wartime, with stronger beers resuming popularity post-war.
  - **Preservation**: Improved through pasteurisation, refrigeration, and sealed packaging.

- **Variability**: Minimised through industrial standardisation and scientific advancements.

- **Social Aspect**: Ale continues to be a staple of British culture, providing comfort during challenging times. Public houses remain vital community centres, adapting to wartime restrictions by offering affordable light ales. Urban breweries thrive despite wartime challenges, employing thousands and supporting the war effort through efficiency and innovation. The growing popularity of lagers reflects changing consumer tastes, setting the stage for further diversification in the brewing industry after 1950.

Albert the Brewer: The Ale That "Won the Cricket Match"

Setting the Scene

By 1900 AD, England was enjoying the height of its industrial revolution and empire. Cricket was the national pastime, and village matches were serious business. In the picturesque village of Pintleton, Albert the Brewer was not just known for his ales but also for his relentless enthusiasm for the local cricket team, the Pintleton Pints.

Albert, who loved to say, "A good ale is like a good innings, steady, refreshing, and full of surprises," found himself in a sticky wicket when the Pints faced their long-time rivals, the Mugford Mugs, in the annual cricket match.

The Cricket Conundrum

The Pintleton Pints were on a losing streak, and morale was low. The Mugford Mugs, smug as ever, arrived boasting about their star bowler, "Terrible Ted," who had a knack for knocking out batsmen with terrifying speed.

"What we need," the Pints' captain lamented to Albert at the pub, "is something to lift our spirits and steady our nerves before the match."

Albert grinned. "You need an ale, my friend, not just any ale, but one that'll turn this game around."

The Brewing of "Cricket's Courage"

Albert got to work crafting a brew designed to inspire confidence and camaraderie. His recipe included:

- Barley malt for a sturdy base, "like a good cricket pitch."
- A touch of honey, "to sweeten their spirits."
- A pinch of mint, "to keep them cool under pressure."
- And a dash of ginger, "to give them a fiery edge."

He brewed it in small, portable barrels, declaring, "This isn't just ale; it's liquid strategy!"

The Match Begins

On match day, Albert arrived at the pitch with his barrels of *Cricket's Courage* in tow. Before the game started, he poured mugs for the Pintleton players.

"Drink this," he said, "and you'll feel invincible."

The team sipped cautiously, then nodded in approval. "It's refreshing, but it's got a kick!" said the captain.

The Turnaround

Fueled by *Cricket's Courage*, the Pints took to the field with newfound energy. Even Albert joined in as the team's substitute fielder, equipped with a mug in hand (which he assured everyone was for "hydration purposes").

- The bowler, inspired by the ginger kick, bowled faster than ever, taking three wickets in a single over.
- The batsmen, emboldened by the minty freshness, scored boundary after boundary.
- Albert, stationed at mid-on, caught a high ball with one hand while holding his mug in the other, earning cheers from the crowd.

The Mugford Mugs, meanwhile, were flustered. "What's gotten into them?" grumbled Terrible Ted.

The Chaos

The game reached peak hilarity when Albert decided to replace the drinks trolley with a barrel of *Cricket's Courage*. The Pints, sipping between overs, began inventing celebratory dances for every boundary and wicket.

- One player mimicked a bowler's wind-up, then pirouetted.

- Another performed an elaborate victory jig after catching a ball.
- Even the umpire couldn't keep a straight face, calling, "Not out!" with a chuckle.

The Mugford Mugs, trying to regain focus, ended up arguing among themselves, and Terrible Ted accidentally threw his bowling hat into the stands.

The Victory

Against all odds, the Pintleton Pints triumphed, scoring the winning run in the final over. The crowd erupted in cheers, and the team hoisted Albert onto their shoulders.

"It wasn't just the ale," Albert said, grinning, "but it certainly didn't hurt!"

The Aftermath

Cricket's Courage became the official ale of the Pintleton Pints, and Albert was made an honorary team captain. The Mugford Mugs, thoroughly humbled, requested a rematch, but only if Albert promised to share his brew next time.

The Legacy

Cricket's Courage became a local sensation, with the slogan, "For boundaries, wickets, and courage in a mug." Albert's one-handed catch became the stuff of legend, and his ale was credited with "the best sporting turnaround in Pintleton history."

The barrels used during the match were displayed in the village pub, and Albert's motto, "Brew for victory," was painted above the cricket pavilion door.

STEM Lesson

Albert's story highlights the importance of creativity and resourcefulness. By using his brewing skills to inspire and energize his team, he turned a sporting challenge into a legendary triumph.

The lesson? Science, innovation, and teamwork can create winning moments, and sometimes, a little ale is all it takes to bring people together.

1950 AD - 2000 AD: Brewing in the Modern Era

- **Techniques**: The second half of the 20th century sees brewing evolve into a highly industrialised and globalised industry. Advances in refrigeration, automation, and microbiology allow for unprecedented consistency and efficiency. Innovations such as kegging systems, continuous fermentation, and the widespread adoption of nitrogenation for stouts reshape production and consumption. The craft beer movement emerges in the 1980s and 1990s, reviving traditional brewing methods alongside experimental styles.

- **Where Brewing Was Done**: Brewing is dominated by large-scale commercial breweries, with a resurgence of smaller, independent craft breweries in the latter decades. Urban breweries expand to meet mass-market demands, while microbreweries and brewpubs emerge as a reaction to homogenisation. Exports grow significantly, making British ales and stouts global staples.

- **How It Would Have Looked**: Large commercial breweries operate as industrial giants, with automated systems handling everything from malting to bottling. Smaller craft breweries embrace a blend of traditional and modern methods, focusing on unique flavour profiles and local ingredients. Public houses adapt to serve a growing variety of kegged and bottled beers, reflecting changing consumer tastes.

- **Involvement of Villagers**: Professional brewers, engineers, and scientists lead innovation in industrial breweries, while craft breweries foster a return to community-focused brewing. Public houses remain central to social life, with beer festivals and tasting events gaining popularity. Villagers participate in the craft beer revival through local breweries and community-supported brewing initiatives.

- **Equipment Used**:

    1. **Automated Brewing Systems**: Managing large-scale production efficiently.

    2. **Refrigeration Units**: Ensuring precise temperature control for lagers and ales.

    3. **Kegging Systems**: Revolutionising beer storage and dispensing in pubs.

    4. **Nitrogenation Systems**: Creating smoother textures in stouts and ales.

5. **Microbrewery Equipment**: Small-scale setups for experimental and traditional brewing.
6. **Filtration and Pasteurisation Units**: Ensuring clarity and shelf stability.
7. **Packaging Lines**: For cans, bottles, and kegs.

- **Recipes (Detailed)**:
  - **Ingredients**:
    - 12-20 kg of malted barley, wheat, or adjunct grains
    - Fresh water from municipal or purified sources
    - Hops (ranging from traditional to experimental varieties)
    - Optional: Fruits, spices, or unconventional additives for craft beers
  - **Method**:
    1. **Malting**: Use industrial kilns or small-scale traditional methods to create malt with specific flavour profiles.
    2. **Crushing**: Crush malted grains with automated rollers for uniform consistency.
    3. **Mashing**: Combine crushed malt with water (60-70°C) in large or small vessels. Stir thoroughly and steep for 1-2 hours.
    4. **Boiling**: Boil the wort for 60-90 minutes, adding hops in stages for bitterness, aroma, and flavour.
    5. **Fermentation**: Use controlled environments to ferment ales (5-7 days) or lagers (10-14 days) at precise temperatures.
    6. **Packaging**: Keg, can, or bottle the beer for distribution or local consumption.
- **SPV (Strength, Preservation, and Variability)**:

    - **Strength**: Alcohol content ranges widely from 3-12%, reflecting diverse consumer preferences.
    - **Preservation**: Maximised through pasteurisation, refrigeration, and advanced packaging.
    - **Variability**: Expanded by the craft beer movement, introducing a plethora of styles and experimental brews.
- **Social Aspect**: Beer remains a cornerstone of British culture, with public houses evolving to accommodate diverse offerings. The rise of multinational brewing corporations standardises global beer styles, while the craft beer revolution champions innovation and tradition. Beer festivals, home brewing, and microbreweries become hallmarks of the era, rekindling a sense of community and creativity in brewing. By 2000, British brewing stands as a dynamic mix of industrial efficiency and artisanal passion, setting the stage for continued evolution in the 21st century.

Edith the Brewer: The Ale That "Fooled the Spies"

Setting the Scene

By 1950 AD, England was recovering from World War II, and the Cold War was heating up. Spies and secrets were everywhere, and even small towns weren't immune to the paranoia. In the village of Maltwick, Edith the Brewer was a local legend for her hearty ales and no-nonsense attitude.

Edith, a stout woman with a quick wit and a sharper tongue, often said, "Secrets are like weak ales, they don't last long around here." But when rumors of spies infiltrating her village reached her ears, Edith decided it was time to brew up some mischief of her own.

The Suspicious Strangers

One day, two strangers appeared in Maltwick. They wore dark coats, asked too many questions, and spent hours in Edith's pub, *The Frothy Pint*, scribbling in notebooks.

"They're spies!" whispered Mrs. Crumble, the town gossip.
"Nonsense," said the blacksmith. "They're probably just tax inspectors."

Edith watched the strangers with narrowed eyes. "Whatever they are," she muttered, "they're drinking my ale and not saying a word. That's suspicious enough for me."

The Brewing of "Spycatcher Stout"

Determined to uncover the truth, Edith concocted a plan. She brewed a special batch of ale designed to loosen tongues and reveal secrets. Her recipe included:

- Barley malt for a rich, hearty flavor.
- A dash of honey, "to make it go down easy."
- A touch of licorice root, "to make them talk."
- And a splash of dandelion wine, "for a bit of zing to rattle their nerves."

She labeled the barrels *Spycatcher Stout* and added a cheeky tagline: "For those with secrets to spill."

The Setup

That evening, Edith placed a fresh barrel of *Spycatcher Stout* on the bar and announced, "This one's on the house, for anyone brave enough to try it!"

The villagers, always up for free ale, crowded around. The strangers hesitated, but under the watchful eyes of the locals, they reluctantly accepted mugs of the dark, frothy brew.

The Reactions

The first sips were met with raised eyebrows and murmurs of approval.

"It's strong, but smooth," said the blacksmith.
"And it has a curious... kick," added the baker.

The strangers, sipping cautiously, nodded in agreement. "Delicious," one muttered.

The Spy Unmasking

As the evening wore on, the effects of *Spycatcher Stout* began to show. The villagers grew chatty and jovial, while the strangers started slipping up.

- One, clearly flustered, asked, "So, where's the nearest military base?"

- The other scribbled frantically in his notebook before accidentally dropping it, revealing a page labeled "Operation Maltwick."
- When Edith loudly declared, "This stout could knock secrets out of the KGB!" one of the strangers choked on his drink.

The villagers, now thoroughly suspicious, began peppering the strangers with questions. "What brings you to Maltwick?" "Why are you writing so much?" "Do you like scones?"

The strangers, overwhelmed and slightly tipsy, stammered excuses before hastily leaving the pub.

The Aftermath

The next day, the strangers were gone, leaving behind their half-finished notebooks. Edith, triumphant, declared, "No one can outwit a brewer, especially not in Maltwick!"

The villagers, convinced they had thwarted an international spy ring, toasted Edith and her *Spycatcher Stout*.

The Legacy

Spycatcher Stout became a Maltwick sensation, marketed as "The Ale That Defends the Nation." Travelers came from far and wide to try the brew, and Edith's motto, "Truth in every pint," was etched above the pub's door.

The empty barrel from that fateful night became a centerpiece in the pub, with a plaque reading, "The Night Maltwick Outsmarted the Spies."

STEM Lesson

Edith's story highlights the power of observation, creativity, and community in problem-solving. By combining her brewing expertise with a clever plan, she turned a potentially dangerous situation into a tale of triumph and humor.

The lesson? Science, ingenuity, and a little bit of boldness can go a long way, even against spies.

2000 AD - 2050 AD: Brewing in the Era of Innovation and Sustainability

- **Techniques**: Brewing in the 21st century becomes a fusion of tradition and technology. Advances in artificial intelligence, sustainable practices, and molecular biology redefine brewing methods. Automated systems powered by AI streamline production, while eco-friendly brewing techniques reduce the environmental footprint. Craft beer continues to thrive, with a focus on experimental styles and local ingredients. Innovations like alcohol-free and low-calorie beers meet changing consumer demands.

- **Where Brewing Was Done**: Brewing spans industrial-scale facilities, urban microbreweries, and home-brewing setups. Large corporations dominate global markets, while craft breweries and nano-breweries provide unique, localised offerings. Brewpubs grow in popularity, combining brewing with hospitality. Remote and community-supported breweries emerge, supported by crowdfunding and cooperative ownership.

- **How It Would Have Looked**: Industrial breweries use AI-driven machinery and renewable energy sources, featuring vertical farming systems for hop and grain production. Craft breweries embrace creativity with mixed fermentation, barrel aging, and spontaneous fermentation techniques. Public houses adapt to offer a diverse range of beers, including craft, mainstream, and non-alcoholic options.

- **Involvement of Villagers**: Home brewers and craft beer enthusiasts play a significant role in shaping trends. Community breweries foster local engagement, with villagers contributing ingredients and labour. Brewpubs act as modern-day communal hubs, while festivals and events celebrate the diversity of beer styles and brewing methods.

- **Equipment Used**:

    1. **AI-Driven Systems**: For precision brewing and resource management.
    2. **Renewable Energy Solutions**: Powering brewing operations sustainably.
    3. **Advanced Fermentation Tanks**: With precise temperature and pressure controls.

4. **Vertical Farming Units**: For localised grain and hop production.

5. **Barrel Aging Facilities**: For creating complex, layered beer profiles.

6. **Automated Packaging Lines**: Handling bottles, cans, and kegs efficiently.

7. **Nitrogenation and Carbonation Systems**: Enhancing beer textures.

- **Recipes (Detailed)**:
    - **Ingredients**:
        - 10-25 kg of malted barley, wheat, or alternative grains (e.g., quinoa, millet)
        - Fresh water from sustainable sources
        - Hops (traditional, experimental, or genetically modified varieties)
        - Optional: Fruits, herbs, spices, or unconventional additives like coffee and tea
    - **Method**:
        1. **Malting**: Use solar-powered kilns or local malting houses for grain preparation.
        2. **Crushing**: Use precision rollers to ensure consistent grain crush.
        3. **Mashing**: Combine crushed malt with water (60-70°C) in automated vessels. AI optimises mash efficiency.
        4. **Boiling**: Boil the wort for 60-90 minutes, adding hops in stages for bitterness, aroma, and flavour.
        5. **Fermentation**: Use advanced fermentation tanks for precise temperature and pressure control. Experiment with yeast strains for unique profiles.
        6. **Packaging**: Keg, can, or bottle the beer using automated lines. Sustainable packaging materials are preferred.

- **SPV (Strength, Preservation, and Variability)**:
  - **Strength**: Alcohol content ranges from 0% (non-alcoholic beers) to 15% or more (imperial styles).
  - **Preservation**: Maximised through pasteurisation, advanced packaging, and refrigeration.
  - **Variability**: Expanded dramatically with hybrid styles, unique ingredients, and regional experimentation.
- **Social Aspect**: Beer remains a cultural and social staple, with brewpubs, festivals, and tasting events serving as communal gathering points. Sustainability and inclusivity become key themes, with breweries prioritising eco-friendly practices and diverse offerings. The rise of digital platforms fosters global connections, enabling breweries to reach broader audiences. By 2050, brewing embodies a blend of heritage and innovation, shaping the industry for future generations while celebrating its rich past.

Dave the Brewer: The Ale That "Broke the Internet"

Setting the Scene

By 2000 AD, England was embracing the digital age. The internet was booming, and everyone was discovering the joys (and frustrations) of dial-up modems and email chains. In the village of Hopton-on-Webb, Dave the Brewer was a local legend for his experimental ales and his ambitious attempts to embrace new technology.

Dave often joked, "Brewing may be an ancient craft, but even beer needs a website these days." What started as a light-hearted attempt to modernize his brewery turned into a hilarious tale of technological chaos.

The Website Debacle

One day, Dave decided it was time for *Dave's Mighty Brews* to go digital. With the help of his tech-savvy niece, Lisa, he launched a website to promote his ales.

"Just think," Dave said, "people will be able to order beer online and talk about it in... forums, or whatever those are!"

Lisa, typing furiously, replied, "Sure, Uncle Dave. But maybe keep it simple. No weird ideas."

Dave grinned. "Simple? Where's the fun in that?"

The Brewing of "Cyber Ale"

To celebrate his foray into the digital world, Dave decided to brew a special ale. His recipe included:

- Barley malt, "for tradition."
- A splash of elderflower cordial, "for a modern twist."
- A touch of caffeine, "because the internet never sleeps."
- And a sprinkle of edible glitter, "to make it sparkle like a screen saver."

He called it *Cyber Ale: The Future in a Pint* and designed a futuristic label featuring a pixelated beer mug and the slogan, "Click. Sip. Refresh."

The Internet Goes Wild

To promote *Cyber Ale*, Dave ran a "special offer" on his website: free ale for the first 100 people to sign up. What Dave didn't realize was that Lisa had accidentally left the offer open-ended, with no limit on the number of signups.

Within hours, the website crashed under the weight of thousands of requests.

"Uncle Dave!" Lisa shouted. "Your ale is going viral!"

"Viral?" Dave asked, confused. "Is that good or bad?"

"Both!" Lisa groaned.

The Chaos

As word spread, the chaos escalated:

- Local villagers started lining up outside the brewery, demanding their free pints.
- A group of tech enthusiasts turned up with laptops, insisting they'd "hacked the ale."
- A journalist from *The Hop Times* showed up, calling Dave "a digital pioneer of brewing."

Dave, overwhelmed but secretly thrilled, declared, "We'll give them their ale, if they can tell me how to fix my email!"

The Unexpected Success

Despite the hiccups, *Cyber Ale* became a nationwide sensation. Social media was flooded with glittery beer selfies, and hashtags like #CyberAle and #DrinkTheFuture started trending.

Dave's favorite moment came when a tech CEO ordered a keg for a company party and described it as "the best thing to come out of the internet since cat videos."

The Aftermath

With Lisa's help, Dave eventually got his website back under control. He added a disclaimer: "No more free ale, but plenty of great deals!" The brewery expanded, and Dave became a minor celebrity, known as "the brewer who broke the internet."

The empty keg from the first batch of *Cyber Ale* was displayed in the brewery with a plaque reading, "Proof that tradition and technology can mix, with a little caffeine."

The Legacy

Cyber Ale remained a bestseller, and Dave's brewery became a hub for quirky, tech-inspired beers. He even launched a follow-up ale called *404 Not Found,* marketed as "perfect for when your plans go awry."

Above the brewery door, Dave added a new motto: "Click. Brew. Laugh."

STEM Lesson

Dave's story shows the importance of embracing new ideas while learning from unexpected challenges. By combining traditional brewing techniques with modern technology, he created something truly memorable, even if it didn't go exactly as planned.

The lesson? Innovation is about trying, failing, and finding joy in the chaos. And sometimes, a bit of glitter goes a long way.

The Hidden Tap: The Ale That "Hacked the AI"

Setting the Scene

By 2024, craft brewing was thriving, and technology was shaping nearly every industry. In the heart of a quaint UK village, *The Hidden Tap* was a small but beloved brewery run by Rob, a passionate brewer with a knack for experimenting and an endless curiosity for all things modern.

Rob often joked, "Brewing is half art, half science, and the rest is just pretending you know what you're doing." But when he decided to embrace AI to perfect his latest ale, he had no idea it would lead to a hilarious chain of events.

The AI Experiment

Rob had heard about AI tools that could optimize brewing recipes by analyzing flavors and market trends. Intrigued, he purchased a system called *BrewBot* and set it up in the brewery.

"Right," Rob said, rolling up his sleeves. "Let's see if this AI is smarter than a bloke with a pint and a notebook."

He tasked BrewBot with creating a recipe for *Future Pint*, an ale he wanted to showcase at an upcoming festival.

The Brewing of "Future Pint"

The AI-generated recipe was... unconventional:

- Barley malt, as expected.
- Mango and chili, for "a bold, modern twist."
- Lavender, "to soothe the soul."
- And, most surprisingly, a splash of black coffee, for "a hint of depth and rebellion."

Rob scratched his head. "Mango, chili, and coffee? This is either genius or madness."

Despite his doubts, he followed the recipe, brewing the ale with care. The result was a golden pint that smelled like a tropical coffee shop.

The Festival Chaos

At the Craft Ale Festival, Rob unveiled *Future Pint* with great fanfare, complete with a sign reading: "Crafted by Rob and BrewBot, Technology Never Tasted So Good!"

The first tasters approached cautiously.

"It's... spicy, but smooth," said one.
"And that coffee kick, unexpected, but brilliant!" said another.

Word spread quickly, and soon *Future Pint* had a long line of curious drinkers.

The AI Goes Rogue

Emboldened by the festival's success, Rob decided to let BrewBot design another recipe live, showcasing the AI's capabilities. He connected it to the festival's Wi-Fi, allowing attendees to vote on ingredients through their phones.

But there was a glitch. BrewBot, overwhelmed by the votes and connected to an overly enthusiastic crowd, began generating increasingly bizarre recipes in real-time.

- One ale included marshmallows, seaweed, and turmeric.
- Another suggested jalapeños, mint, and strawberry jam.
- The pièce de résistance was an ale called *Chaos Brew,* which featured pickle brine, chocolate chips, and garlic.

Rob, laughing but panicking, shouted, "Shut it down before someone brews this monstrosity!"

The Crowd's Reaction

The festival-goers, delighted by the chaos, began demanding to taste *Chaos Brew.* "It's the future of beer!" someone shouted.

Not one to back down from a challenge, Rob improvised, mixing small samples of ingredients and letting people try the concoction. Surprisingly, the crowd loved it, if only for the novelty.

"It's so bad, it's good!" declared one brave taster.
"Tastes like a dare," added another, raising their glass.

The Aftermath
Back at *The Hidden Tap*, Rob reflected on the day with a pint of *Future Pint* in hand. Despite the AI mishap, the festival had been a massive success.

He renamed *Chaos Brew* to *AI Madness* and made it a limited-edition ale, marketing it as "The Pint That Broke the System."

BrewBot, meanwhile, was reprogrammed to "think smaller," though Rob secretly kept its original version to spice up slow evenings at the pub.

The Legacy
The Hidden Tap became famous for its blend of tradition and technology, attracting visitors eager to try Rob's inventive brews. The pub's motto, "Where Creativity Pours Freely," was etched above the bar, and a plaque commemorating *Chaos Brew* read: "Proof that humans and AI can both make mistakes, and great beer."

The STEM Lesson
Rob's story highlights the balance between human ingenuity and technology. By embracing AI (and a bit of chaos), he showed how innovation can lead to unexpected success and plenty of laughs.

The lesson? Science and creativity go hand in hand, and sometimes, the best results come from embracing the unexpected.

Printed in Great Britain
by Amazon

63183031R00137